Praise for the *New York Times* bestselling
Paws & Claws Mysteries

"Davis has penned a doggone great new mystery series featuring witty, spirited Holly Miller and her endearing canine sidekick, Trixie . . . The intriguing plot twists will keep you guessing to the very last page."
—Kate Carlisle, *New York Times* bestselling author of
the Bibliophile Mysteries

"Davis has created a town that any pet would love—as much as their owners do. And they won't let a little thing like murder spoil their enjoyment."
—Sheila Connolly, *New York Times* bestselling author of
the County Cork, Museum, and Orchard Mysteries

"Davis has created another charming series with a unique setting, an engaging heroine in Holly Miller and her furry sidekick, Trixie, and a wonderfully quirky supporting cast of characters—two- and four-legged."
—Sofie Kelly, *New York Times* bestselling author of
the Magical Cats Mysteries

"Well-written dialogue, fun characters, and romantic complications that never go as the characters—or the readers—expect . . . Readers will enjoy this skillfully plotted mystery and its biting humor." —Kings River Life Magazine

"A charming blend of small-town eccentrics and big-city greed, *Murder, She Barked* touches all the bases of the cozy mystery—including a bit of romance—and does so with style." —*Richmond Times-Dispatch*

WITHDRAWN

Not a Creature Was Purring

Krista Davis

BERKLEY PRIME CRIME
New York

BERKLEY PRIME CRIME
Published by Berkley
An imprint of Penguin Random House LLC
375 Hudson Street, New York, New York 10014

ISBN: 9781101988589

First Edition: November 2017

Printed in the United States of America
1 3 5 7 9 10 8 6 4 2

Cover art by Mary Ann Lasher
Book design by Kelly Lipovich

To Bill and Karen,
who love animals as much as I do

Acknowledgments

Each Wagtail book inspires readers to send me wonderful stories about their dogs and cats. Reader Bob Giddings suggested the scene on the porch where Mr. Huckle talks with Maggie. Thank you so much, Bob! I hope I did it justice.

In this book, I have included two dogs with ailments. Fear not dear readers, read on. Both of these things happened to my dog Buttercup, on whom the character of Trixie is based. I am not a veterinarian, so any mistakes in describing the medical aspects are my own.

I have included a Christmas recipe that is a family favorite. Readers with a German heritage will recognize the traditional Christmas stollen. But my version is a modern, updated stollen, which we actually like better. It's always the first thing I bake for Christmas.

Thanks as always to my mom, and to my good friends Betsy Strickland, Amy Wheeler, and Susan Erba for being so wonderfully supportive. And thanks also to my dear writing friends, you know who you are, who understand this crazy business.

My lovely agent, Jessica Faust, has been my champion,

and for that I am eternally grateful. I don't know what I would have done without her.

So many editors had a hand in this book: Michelle Vega, Tom Colgan, Jennifer Monroe, and Julie Mianecki. My thanks to you all for making it happen.

One of the most striking differences between a cat and a lie is that a cat has only nine lives.

—Mark Twain

THE THACKLEBERRY FAMILY TREE

Doris Kabilichec Thackleberry—Dale's mother
   Muffy, her Pomeranian

Dale Thackleberry

EmmyLou Thackleberry Blume—Dale's
   daughter
   Maggie, her German shepherd

Barry Blume—EmmyLou's husband

Norma Jeanne Blume—EmmyLou and Barry's
   daughter, Holmes's fiancée

Vivienne Thackleberry—Dale's third wife

Tim Kedrowski—Vivienne's son

Linda Kedrowski—Tim's wife

Tiffany and Blake Kedrowski—Tim and Linda's
   children

Austin Conroy—Tiffany's boyfriend

THE RICHARDSONS

Rose Richardson—Oma's best friend

Holmes Richardson—engaged to Norma Jeanne
   Blume

**MEMBERS OF THE SUGAR MAPLE INN
FAMILY**

Liesel Miller (Oma)—co-owner of the inn
   Gingersnap, golden retriever, the canine
   ambassador of the inn

Holly Miller—Liesel's granddaughter and co-owner of the inn

    Twinkletoes, calico, the feline ambassador of the inn

    Trixie, Jack Russell terrier

Shelley Dixon—waitress at the inn

Zelda York—front desk

Mr. Huckle

WAGTAIL RESIDENTS

Rupert Grimpley

Aunt Birdie Dupuy—Holly's aunt

Marie Carr—foster mother to Ethan and Ava Schroeder

Buck Bradon

One

"Ouch, ouch, ouch!" Zelda whispered.

"I told you to wear gloves," muttered Shelley.

I could barely make them out on the dark porch. It was one in the morning, and Wagtail was slumbering. If it hadn't been for the moon, I wouldn't have been able to see them at all.

"Gloves are too cumbersome," Zelda groused. "I don't know how you can place the lights precisely with woolly fabric on your fingers."

I shivered as a cold wind swept through. My elf tights with one red leg and one green leg weren't thick enough to keep out the chill. We stood on Marie Carr's front porch, hastily wrapping colorful lights on the Christmas tree we were delivering. Shelley passed me the cord of lights. I wrapped them around my section of the tree and handed them to Zelda. "Hush, you guys," I hissed. "Two kids live here. You'll wake them!"

Wagtail, a small town in the mountains of Virginia, had

experienced a boom year by catering to visitors who brought their dogs and cats for a vacation where they could be part of the fun. This year, instead of exchanging gifts with our neighbors or having secret Santas, the town had decided to make the holidays merry for our less-fortunate residents. My grandmother, whom I called Oma, German for grandma, had installed a suggestion box in the lobby of the Sugar Maple Inn, which we ran together. Anyone could stop by and drop off a suggestion for a deserving neighbor or a resident in need. And then the semisecret Elf Squad was dispatched.

An observant person might have noticed that Shelley Dixon, a waitress at the inn, and Zelda York, who worked at the registration desk, had altered their schedules and could have suspected them of being elves. But we were also taking turns at the Sugar Maple Inn booth at the Christkindl Market, so our schedules were all twisted around. As far as I could tell, no one had identified us yet. We weren't worried about the adults but were trying to keep a low profile so we wouldn't spoil Christmas magic for the children of Wagtail.

Shadow Hobbs, the Sugar Maple Inn handyman, had cut the perfectly shaped balsam fir earlier in the day, and we elves had transported it to the Carr house on a golf cart that we had decorated as Santa's sleigh. Our previous forays had caused rumors that Santa's elves had been spotted in Wagtail to spread through the elementary school like wildfire. We had been careful to dress in cute elf attire in case we were seen. Even Trixie, my Jack Russell terrier, wore a red and green dog dress with a hat that curled at the top, just like ours. At the moment, she was sniffing boxes of ornaments we had stacked by the front door.

The Schroeder children were local favorites and had received many notes in the suggestion box. At ages eight and four, Ethan and Ava Schroeder had been orphaned when their parents and only living grandparents were lost in a plane crash. Marie Carr had taken them in as foster children until someone adopted them. Everyone was determined to brighten their holiday.

"I still say we should just leave the lights with the ornaments," said Zelda in a low voice.

"Where's your Christmas spirit? The lights are the worst part of decorating," Shelley hissed back. "This way they can plug it right in, make hot chocolate, and hang ornaments."

Heaven only knew what the tree would look like when the lights were plugged in. Another frigid breeze blew in the night, and I was fairly sure my nose had gone numb.

"I read that the best way to put on the lights is in three triangular sections," whispered Zelda. "Maybe we should try that."

"That's crazy," said Shelley. "You have to zigzag them along the branches so you'll get depth in the lights."

They bickered like sisters, but Shelley and Zelda were part of the Sugar Maple Inn family. When I moved to Wagtail, I hadn't expected to find a family among the employees, but I was delighted that it had worked out that way.

My parents had divorced when I was young, and for the first time in decades, I was where I wanted to be for Christmas—in Wagtail. No planes, no trains, no hasty visits, and best of all, no arguments about where I should be and when. My parents had both started new families, and while I loved them dearly, the truth was that I always felt like an outsider at their new homes.

I had such happy childhood memories of Christmas in Wagtail, and while I knew things would be different seen through my adult eyes, I couldn't help being excited about spending the holiday in Wagtail. I looked forward to the ringing of the church bells and the possibility of Fluffy Cake, which I remembered fondly. Not to mention that my childhood friend and heartthrob, Holmes Richardson, would be home for the holidays.

"There. We're done," whispered Shelley.

At that moment, I spied a flutter in the curtain on the window that overlooked the porch.

"Dash away now!" I whispered, jumping off the porch.

Thank goodness our rush to the sleigh–golf cart caught Trixie's interest and she leaped on board with us. The electric golf cart couldn't go too terribly fast, but I gunned it as Zelda shook sleigh bells attached to a leather horse harness. The merry tinkle made me grin every time. What could be more fun?

"Did you really say *dash away*?" Shelley laughed.

"It just came out. I guess I'm in the spirit of the season."

At that moment, a light blazed upon us, so bright that it briefly blinded me, and I slammed the brakes.

Trixie yelped in surprise.

"It's a sign from heaven," breathed Zelda with wonder in her tone.

I blinked and gazed around.

"Not unless the Grinch has a heavenly connection," muttered Shelley.

She pointed to our right. I squinted against the glare. A gigantic Grinch with huge devious eyes loomed over the roofs of the houses. He must have just been turned on because we would surely have noticed him before. There were no high-rises, billboards, or garish lighting in Wagtail. The moon was usually the only light in the night sky. The Grinch's head had a green cast and glowed as though a strong light must be inside. I guessed it was a blow-up figure.

Even though we were a couple of blocks away, we could hear the notes of "Grandma Got Run Over by a Reindeer" coming from the ghastly fellow.

"I'm all for holiday fun," said Zelda, "but if I thought that guy was going to come down my chimney, I would brick it up. Not to mention that I don't think anyone in the neighborhood, including me, will get much sleep tonight."

I dropped off Zelda first. The repeating song was growing annoying, and lights were flicking on inside houses all over the neighborhood.

Shelley lived on the other side of town, where it was blissfully quiet and only twinkling Christmas lights on trees and rooflines glowed in the night. I drove the electric golf cart back in the direction of the giant Grinch to Rose Richardson's detached garage, where I parked and closed the door. Holmes's grandmother, Rose, was like a grandmother to me too, and happened to be my Oma's best friend. We were hiding the sleigh–golf cart in her garage so children wouldn't see it around town during the day.

Trixie and I walked back to the inn on the path that meandered through the green, the park in the center of Wagtail, which wasn't so green now that snow lay on it. We passed the giant Christmas tree that remained lighted all through the night. Dark Christkindl market stalls lined the perimeter of the green. Bright lights twinkled in the trees that lined the path, and a few snowflakes floated in the air. It was like our own private wonderland, except for the tinkling notes of "Grandma Got Run Over by a Reindeer."

The Sugar Maple Inn loomed at the end of the green, nothing short of splendid. White lights on pine swags graced the railings of the front porch, wound up the columns, and followed the arch of the ceiling between them. By day, white and red ornaments added a touch of color to the greenery. Battery-operated lanterns lined the stairs. Bold black and red buffalo plaid pillows adorned the white rocking chairs, adding a hint of country style. Lights glowed on the lush wreaths that hung in the windows. And on the third floor, on the balcony outside of my bedroom, stood a tree with sparkling lights that seemed to be suspended high in the air.

The windows of the inn were largely dark, save for those on the first floor in the common areas, but at this hour, even those were somewhat muted.

On the second floor, in a guest room window, I thought I spied a face looking out at us. But in the dark, and with the large wreath that hung in the window, I wasn't quite sure.

As I approached, a group of people gathered on the porch. Most of them wore pajamas with winter coats over them.

Trixie and I trotted up the stairs.

Casey Collins, our young night manager, stood in the doorway, looking terrified. "Holly! Holly's here. She can help you." He grabbed me by the arm and tugged me toward him like a shield.

I stumbled inside. "Won't you all come in?"

When everyone had piled into the lobby and the door was closed, Aunt Birdie demanded, "Wake up your grandmother this instant!"

Two

I did my best to stay calm as I faced the surly crowd. Oma was the mayor of Wagtail, but I hated to disturb her sleep for something like this. After all, I was dressed and awake. "I'm guessing you're here about the Grinch?"

"It's forty-five feet tall," said a man whose red plaid pajama pants jutted from under his coat. "No one can sleep."

"Where is it exactly?" I asked.

"At that awful Rupert Grimpley's house," declared Aunt Birdie.

That was enough to make them all start grumbling again. We had a few guests staying at the inn, and I didn't want them awakened by angry townspeople. I didn't know Rupert well. He was a slightly gruff sort.

"Where is Liesel?" Aunt Birdie pressed. Oma and Aunt Birdie had never gotten along very well. My mother lived in California, about as far away as she could get from her older half-sister, Birdie. My father and his sister had high-tailed it out of Wagtail as well, leaving their mother, Oma, to run the family inn. Now that Oma was older, she had brought me on board as her partner. Maybe because they saw themselves as the family matriarchs, Oma and Aunt Birdie were prone to butting heads.

Thin and gaunt, clothes hung beautifully on Aunt Birdie. But her skin sank in under prominent cheekbones and her eyes blazed with fury. In another time, she would have been called a handsome woman. She took great pains with her wardrobe, and even now she was the best dressed person in the room. I felt certain she didn't sleep in those gray wool trousers.

"Yeah!" called someone else. "She's the mayor. She should handle this."

I held up my palm. "I have this under control." A blatant lie, of course. "Now, everyone go home, and I will take care of the Grinch."

They still grumbled as they filed out.

Only Aunt Birdie remained, one eyebrow lifted critically. "You should change clothes before you go. I don't think Rupert will be cowed by an elf."

She was probably right, but I had a secret weapon. "You too, Aunt Birdie, go on home."

Pulling out my cell phone and dialing, I walked up the grand staircase.

Officer Dave Quinlan answered the phone immediately. "If you're calling about the Grinch, I'm on my way. I've already had twenty complaints."

"I'll meet you there," I said.

As fast as I could, I swapped my tights and elf coat for jeans, a sweater, and a puffy jacket. Trixie had taken off her elf hat by herself. I quickly exchanged her elf coat for a red fleece dog coat.

We ran back downstairs.

Casey was still in the lobby. "Your aunt scares me."

Aunt Birdie intimidated a lot of people, and Casey was

still young enough to be easily rattled. He attended community college on nearby Snowball Mountain, and even though he wasn't a kid, he reminded me of the young Harry Potter, with round wire-rimmed glasses and a shock of dark hair that fell over his forehead.

"You're not the only one who feels that way."

"What do I tell people who call and want to speak to your grandmother?" asked Casey.

"Tell them we're already on it." I walked out the door, jogged down the steps and hurried along the sidewalk that bordered the green. Trixie raced ahead of me, sniffing scents as she went. The stores and restaurants to my left were closed, but lights shone in their windows. The Christkindl booths to my right, just inside the green, were shut down for the night as well. I barely noticed them as I drew closer to the Grinch.

He loomed over everything, his sinister eyes angled ominously. The music grew in volume as I approached. No wonder people were complaining. What was Rupert thinking?

Officer Dave and I arrived at the same time. Formerly a sailor in the Navy, he now worked for the police department headquartered on Snowball Mountain, but he lived in Wagtail and knew the residents well.

A crowd of people on the street parted as we walked up. The base of the Grinch took up the entire front yard of Rupert's home. The music blasted, drowning out conversation. We had to walk around the Grinch to get to the porch of his bungalow.

Dave rapped on the front door. "Rupert?" he shouted. "It's Dave Quinlan. Open your door. This is police business."

It wasn't easy to hear Rupert over the music, but from behind the door he yelled, "Ain't done nothin' wrong!"

"Rupert, you're disturbing the peace. Now open up!"

The door swung open just a crack. Rupert peered out at us. "I'm celebratin' the season just like everybody else."

"Come on, Rupert," said Dave. "Nobody can sleep with this racket and the lights beaming into their homes."

"I have a right to decorate. Look over there at the neighbor's house. They have lights all over their house. I don't see you makin' a fuss over that."

Dave crossed his arms over his chest. "They're not shining in bedroom windows, Rupert, nor are they blasting music. Now close down your Grinch for the night."

The door slammed shut.

"You leave me no choice, Rupert!" yelled Dave.

He leaned over to me. "Look around for the electric line. He's probably got it plugged in somewhere out here."

Dave called it right. In less than two minutes we located the cord. Dave moved a chair out of the way on the porch, and I yanked the plug.

The sudden stillness came as a shock. But after a moment of silence, the crowd in the street cheered.

Dave whispered, "Let's stand on the other side of the porch. Unless I miss my guess, Rupert will be out here any second to plug it back in."

Sure enough, the door opened wide and Rupert ran outside, so intent on the electrical connection that he didn't notice us.

Rupert bent to pick up the electric cord but Dave stopped him.

I hurried to stand in the doorway so Rupert wouldn't be able to retreat into his house and slam the door. But I stopped cold at the sight of his living room.

A large live pine tree stood near the fireplace. Ornaments, bows, and garlands of beads covered every inch of the tree. A lighted star beamed on the top.

Four more decorated trees between two and four feet tall stood around the room. Five knit stockings, each a different color, hung from the mantel, which was covered with fresh greens and a hand-carved reindeer collection.

But the most enchanting part of all was the ceiling. Rupert had draped white fairy lights all the way across the room in rows. It was like looking up at stars.

I could hear the two men talking behind me and turned around.

"Rupert, I'm glad you're in the Christmas spirit," said Dave. "But you have to be reasonable. Folks need their sleep, and they're pretty crabby if they don't get it."

"I know who reported me. It's that Aunt Birdie of hers." Rupert pointed at me. "She's the orneriest woman I ever met."

I could imagine that he would think that. I did, too. Aunt Birdie was never satisfied with anything. And Rupert, in his grubby jeans held up by old suspenders, and a baseball cap on his head that had seen better days, probably didn't appeal to her much. He wasn't unattractive. His dark hair had gone prematurely gray, but his eyebrows remained black. When he smiled, his fleshy face lit up and his belly jiggled, not unlike a bowl full of jelly. I guessed him to be in his early forties.

He frowned at Dave. "I ain't in trouble with the law, am I?"

Dave shot him a look that would have put the most hardened criminal in his place.

"What are you gonna tell your granma?" he asked me.

I wasn't sure. I wanted to give him a chance to be reasonable. "What would you like me to tell her?"

"That I done paid some man in Houston, Texas, four hunnert dollars for this here Grinch, and I aim to use it."

Not exactly what I had hoped for. "Do you think you could decrease the volume when it's on and turn the Grinch off around ten or eleven?"

"Whoa! Ever'body in the house!" Rupert yelled.

The Grinch must have been deflating, because it suddenly sagged around the porch, blocking us in.

"Trixie! Trixie! I don't see her." Panicked, I searched the porch.

"She's right here," Dave said calmly.

I entered the house and spotted my little darling with her back paws on a kitchen chair and her front paws on the kitchen table. She was chewing a cookie she had stolen from the table. "Trixie!"

She didn't have the decency to hide or act ashamed. In fact, she snarfed it down in a hurry before I could take it away from her.

"Won't hurt her none. That's an oatmeal cookie. No raisins. Never have cottoned to raisins."

"I'm sorry. I'll buy you more."

"Buy 'em?" Rupert chuckled. "I bake my own cookies."

We followed him into a kitchen dressed for Christmas, from the poinsettia rugs on the floor to the dish towels, Grinch cookie jar, Santa and Mrs. Claus mugs on the table, and lighted Christmas village all around the tops of the cabinets. I counted four different kinds of cookies cooling on racks in the kitchen.

"What's wrong?" he asked. "Ain't you never seen Christmas cookies?"

"They're beautiful," I said.

"My granny taught me to bake." He held out the tray of oatmeal cookies to Dave and me.

I took one and bit into it. No wonder Trixie couldn't resist! It was chewy cinnamon heaven.

Dave mumbled, "These are really good," through a mouthful of cookie. He swallowed and said, "But that doesn't mean you can inconvenience your neighbors. Understood?"

Rupert leaned back against the kitchen counter, narrowed his eyes, and peered at Dave. "Your skin gettin' a little green there? I didn't need to pay for a Grinch. Looks like Wagtail has a Grinch of its own. What you got against Christmas, Officer Dave?"

Dave was not amused.

But I was still laughing when we left by the back door. The big green Grinch that had collapsed over Rupert's house looked like it was hugging it. Everyone had gone home, and peace had returned to the street.

"Tell your grandmother that I'll be over in the morning to discuss this," said Dave. "There's probably some kind of ordinance on the books about noise and lights."

I promised I would tell her and headed back to the inn.

There was no sign of Casey in the lobby. He was probably grabbing a snack in the kitchen. The only one waiting for our return was my beloved Twinkletoes. My long-haired calico cat stretched on the grand staircase before sauntering down to greet us.

She turned her face up as I ran my hand over her head. As cats often do, Twinkletoes had chosen me as her person. Symmetrical rectangles of butterscotch and dark chocolate fur adorned the top of her head as though they were sunglasses and she had pushed them up on her head. She was mostly white, with the characteristic calico pattern, but her fluffy tail was dark chocolate through and through, especially beautiful and eye-catching when she wrapped it around her white front paws. Exotic large green eyes fairly glowed in her white face.

The three of us tiptoed up to our apartment on the third floor of the inn and went straight to bed. I lay in the semi-dark, feeling like a safe child who didn't want to take her eyes off the bright, lighted tree on the balcony. But it had been a long day, and sleep overcame me in spite of myself.

I was comfortably snuggled under one of the Sugar Maple Inn's fluffy down comforters with Trixie at my side and Twinkletoes sleeping near my pillow when the phone rang.

Casey, who stayed up to keep an eye on things while the rest of us slept, whispered, "There's a lady crying down here. I don't know what to do."

Three

I promised to come right down. It was still dark outside. I rubbed my eyes and peered at the time. It was six in the morning, but I felt like it was the middle of the night.

I pulled on jeans and a big sweater and ran down the stairs.

Halfway down, I heard her quiet sobs. A few early birds were already drinking coffee in the dining area while the woman with a dark brown bob wept in front of the fireplace in the Dogwood Room. She stood alone with her back to me, sniffling. I watched her for a few seconds, debating whether I should interfere or let her have her moment.

Trixie had no such qualms. She ran straight to the woman, looked up at her, and wagged her little tail as hard as she could.

The woman saw me when she turned and knelt to the floor. Her bangs and hair bent at angles, as though she'd slept on them oddly during the night. She wore no makeup, not that it could have concealed those red-rimmed eyes anyway. She patted Trixie and then hugged her tightly.

"Is there anything I can do for you?" I asked.

She shook her head. "I'm so sorry. I didn't mean to make a scene." She gazed up at the high ceilings and the grand stairway. "There aren't many places for a private cry around here."

"There are a few nooks, but you have to know your way around. Could I get you a cup of tea?"

"That's very kind of you, but I'll be fine. This little girl was the perfect cure for what ails me."

Surprisingly, Trixie didn't squirm out of her grasp. She licked the woman's nose, which produced a big smile.

The woman looked up at me. "Thank you for your concern."

"Let us know if there's anything you need."

"Thank you."

I left her alone with Trixie. At the bottom of the grand staircase, I spied Casey.

"Is she okay?" he asked. "She's older than my mom. I didn't know what to say to her."

"It's fine, Casey. You did the right thing to call me." When Trixie joined me in the lobby, we headed up to bed. I wouldn't have known what to say to her when I was Casey's age, either. I barely knew now.

Except for the occasional emergency, like the guest on a crying jag, I was enjoying my break from early rising. Feeling quite the lazy bum, I rose at ten. I dressed in jeans and a Kelly green turtleneck, and carried a bulky sweater that I could don for outdoor duties. Trixie and I headed for the dining area of the Sugar Maple Inn before the early lunch rush. We walked down the stairs—the railings wrapped with lush pine garlands, red gingham bows, and chubby pinecones.

Twinkletoes, who must have left the apartment earlier through the cat door, raced up the stairs to greet me. She wound around my jeans-clad legs as I descended. Halfway down the stairs, I picked her up. She rewarded me with loud purrs and rubbed her head against my chin. "You're such an early riser," I said. "You don't want to miss a single thing." My curious kitty had no qualms about walking into guest rooms when the doors were open. She even had the nerve to jump into open bags and check out the contents of luggage.

On the main level, three small pine trees in staggered heights adorned each side of the staircase. Warm golden lights twinkled on them all day and all night. I loved living in an inn at Christmas. It was loaded with holiday bling and cheer from top to bottom. I had done a lot of the decorating, but that had been fun.

Twinkletoes squirmed and jumped from my arms. I stopped and watched as she darted down the hallway toward an elderly lady who walked with a stick. I worried that Twinkletoes might cause her to trip, but I could hear the woman cooing to Twinkletoes and watched as they stepped into the elevator together.

"Holly!" Shelley waved at me. She, Oma, and Zelda were seated at a table near the fireplace, where giant poinsettias were clustered on both sides. Lights twinkled on a tall Christmas tree, which we had carefully placed away from the fire.

Gingersnap, Oma's golden retriever and the canine ambassador of the inn who made it her job to kiss and greet everyone, lay on the floor and flapped her tail when she saw us.

I stopped to stroke her head.

My Oma always looked impeccable. Her hair fell into place in a sassy short cut. She didn't bother with makeup except for a touch of lipstick. Her dove gray turtleneck accented her silver hair and brought out the blue in her eyes.

She was far from drab, though, with rosy cheeks and a hand-knitted vest in red, decorated with swirls of silver Lurex and tiny beads that caught the light when she moved.

Shelley tucked her honey-colored hair behind her ears and her eyes lit up when she said, "Ava Schroeder saw Santa Claus at her house last night. She says at least eight reindeer were pulling his sleigh. Ethan Schroeder has suggested to his elementary school friends that Wagtail might secretly be the North Pole."

I laughed and took a seat at the table. "This is so much fun! In the past, I was always busy packing, shopping, and trying to finish up at work before I left. Everything was just a big mad rush. I didn't do anything to make Christmas magical for other people. I'm sort of ashamed of that now."

Zelda poked me. She nodded in the direction of a couple in their seventies. The woman was wrapping the contents of the breakfast bread basket in a large napkin. She tugged it around muffins, Danishes, and bagels, then jammed them all into her oversized purse.

I exchanged a look with Shelley.

"Should we say something?" asked Zelda.

"No!" Oma hissed. "But maybe we shouldn't give them so much bread in the future."

Her companion, a portly fellow with rosy cheeks and silver hair just long enough to curl on the back of his neck, placed a tip on the table and held out his hand in a gentlemanly gesture for the woman to leave first.

Gingersnap walked over to him. Smiling, the man patted her.

The woman, however, curled her hands under her chin and held her arms close to her as though she feared Gingersnap. She walked out and her companion followed.

Gingersnap returned to our table and sat next to Trixie.

"I hope they're not guests of the inn," Shelley said.

"Shh," Oma hissed. "They checked in yesterday evening."

The woman, who was gaunt but well-dressed in black slacks and a distinctive horizontally striped black and white sweater, returned to the table. She whisked the tip away in one smooth motion and marched out, stuffing the cash into her big bag.

Four

"Well, I never!" Shelley's mouth hung open. She pulled out her wallet and replaced the tip. "What is wrong with people? Doesn't she know we count on our tip money?"

Oma picked up the money and handed it back to her. "You are very kind, Shelley. I will cover the tip." Oma reached into her pocket and replaced the money. "The gentleman, Dale Thackleberry, is the CEO of a canine and feline attire company. He has been a guest before. We should not embarrass him."

Oma gave me a worried look. What was that about?

"Funny, she was skinny, but she didn't look like someone so desperate that she needed to hoard bread," I said.

When the waitress came for our orders, we all stopped gabbing and listened. "The breakfast specials today are gingerbread pancakes, brown sugar and apple oatmeal, and rib eye steak with eggs and hash browns."

Trixie gazed at me with hopeful eyes. "We should probably be good and have the oatmeal, but we'll splurge and try the gingerbread pancakes," I said. "We should know how they taste, right?" Trixie wagged her entire hind end in agreement.

Shelley and Zelda opted for the rib eye steak. Oma and Gingersnap had already eaten.

Oma smiled at us. "Our new doctor arrived in town last night. It is a big relief to have a doctor in Wagtail again."

"Is he single?" asked Zelda.

Oma leaned toward her like she was going to say something confidential. "Very single. And handsome, too!"

We all giggled like silly schoolgirls. And then I told Oma about Rupert and the Grinch.

"He cannot do this," she said in her distinctive German accent. She hated that it clung to her even though she had been an American since before my father was born. "I will go to see it for myself and have a talk with him."

I was about to warn Oma that Aunt Birdie had been very upset, when she showed up in the lobby. She stalked toward us in a chic burgundy and black plaid winter suit. If her eyes hadn't blazed with anger and her expression hadn't been so dour, she would have cut an attractive figure. The streak of white that rose from the middle of her forehead suggested that the rest of her hair might look that way if she didn't regularly color it black.

She paused for a split second, held up her right hand like a troop leader, turned, and shouted, "There she is!"

And then she marched toward us, full of fury, followed by two other Wagtail residents.

When she reached the table, Aunt Birdie looked so menacing that we all shrank back a little. All except for Oma. The two of them didn't get along very well, probably because they both knew how to stand their ground.

"Liesel," she hissed, "we have come to insist that you do something about that hideous inflatable Grinch this minute. Do you understand me? Not tonight. Not tomorrow. Not next Christmas. Right now."

A chubby fellow stood behind her. "Liesel, it's inflated again. I wouldn't mind it being up during reasonable hours, but listening to that song over and over again is driving me batty."

Another Wagtailite joined them. "I'm going to have to double my blood pressure medication if I hear it play 'Grandma Got Run Over by a Reindeer' one more time. It's . . . it's—"

"Grinch-like. That's what it is. Just plain mean!" said the chubby guy. "Although I noticed that he changed the words this morning. He must have recorded it himself. Now it's playing 'Aunt Birdie Got Run Over by a Reindeer.'"

I hoped the others weren't having as much trouble hiding their laughter as I was.

"No!" Oma wasn't laughing. "What can he be thinking? I will not tolerate such behavior in Wagtail. Excuse me, please, ladies. I have work to do."

Oma headed toward her office with Aunt Birdie and friends trailing along behind her. Gingersnap moved to her favorite spot near the front door. She was always on alert for someone to kiss.

After breakfast, Trixie and I took our shift at the Sugar Maple Inn's Christkindl Market booth, conveniently located close to the inn. "Let It Snow" played on outdoor speakers, and I hummed along as I replenished the supply of Christmas ornaments.

The glitter on a blown glass golden retriever caught rays of the sun as I slid it into place on a hook. From the location of our booth, I could see that Gingersnap had shifted to the porch, where she waited for people to fuss over her. Out of the corner of my eye, I caught a quick movement as a fellow dodged around the end of the booths and stood motionlessly with his back against the wall. Thirtyish, I guessed. Hair the color of coffee grounds fluffed as though it was naturally curly, but he'd clearly tried to coax it into behaving by brushing it back. Although he was slender, there was a gentle roundness to his chin, and he had a distinctive prominent nose that I'd bet was a family trait.

As furtive and potentially sinister as his actions were, I wasn't terribly worried. After all, it was the season of shopping and secrets.

However, if he didn't want to be noticed, he'd have been well-advised not to wear harlequin pants with a diamond pattern in bright colors. He peered around the corner and ambled over to our booth. He frowned as he gazed at our selection. "Don't you have anything tropical? A palm tree or a pink flamingo, maybe?"

Close up, I realized that he sported an amazing tan for the time of the year.

Wagtail was located in the Blue Ridge Mountains of Virginia. Snow covered the ground, and it was a brisk forty degrees outside. I responded as sweetly as I could. "We don't get a lot of call for tropical items."

His nose wrinkled, and he heaved a huge sigh. His gaze skimmed our wares. "Pinecones are so banal."

I thought they were pretty. In fact, I had used them rather liberally on the Christmas trees in the inn. Besides, we had a huge selection of blown glass ornaments in the shapes of dogs and cats.

While he perused our selection, I spotted a young woman watching him from a distance. She pretended to be interested in the wares of another booth, but I could tell she was actually observing my customer.

His expression brightened. "A German shepherd! That would be perfect."

He handed me cash with long fingers. His hands spoke volumes about him. Those manicured nails screamed city slicker. *Metrosexuals*, I thought they were called. His soft hands had never done a lick of hard work.

"Squee! It *is* the Blakester!" Two young women approached him from behind.

"We knew it was you!"

"And look at his pants!"

"Selfie!" they sang in unison.

The Blakester greeted them with enthusiasm. "You caught me. What's up, ladies?"

One of the girls produced a phone and held it out to me. "Would you mind?"

"Not at all."

The Blakester swung an arm around each of them and smiled as though he was used to posing with complete strangers. The girls kissed him, one on each cheek. The photos would definitely be cute.

I handed the camera back to them.

"Instagram!" they chimed.

"We are so cool, running into the Blakester."

Repeating *thank you* over and over, they ran off giggling and peering at the phone.

The Blakester shrugged. "Fans. Thanks for taking the pics."

"My pleasure." He was reaching for his purchase when Mr. Thackleberry, the round man from the dining room, sneaked up behind him and said, "Gotcha!"

The younger fellow's eyes opened in fear, but he soon smiled. "Gramps!"

"What are you doing here already, young rascal?"

"I've been traveling for two days. Flew in just this morning from the islands."

His grandfather's smile waned, and he stared at the younger man for a long moment. I had a bad feeling the young guy had been caught in a lie.

But Gramps recovered quickly. "How'd you like to be Santa's helper this afternoon?"

The younger fellow groaned. "I don't think so. In fact, I'm pretty sure I promised Mom that I would help her."

Gramps laughed and pointed his forefinger at his grandson. "You can't fool me, young Blake." And then he turned to me with the same winning smile. "Are you Holly Miller?"

"I am."

He held a pudgy hand out to me. "Dale Thackleberry. Thank you for making the arrangements for me. And there's Trixie!" He smiled and whistled to her. "I had a Jack Russell. For a long time he was known as the Thackleberry dog because he was in all our ads. I still miss that little guy."

I had been receiving packages for him all week. He was bringing his entire family to the inn for the holidays. No wonder Oma didn't want to insult him by scolding a member of his party for stealing a tip.

Oma had put me in charge of arranging for a sleigh at his request. Boxes upon boxes of toys had arrived at the inn for him to hand out to local children, dogs, and cats. "I'm so glad to meet you! The whole town is looking forward to your visit, Santa!"

His grandson shuddered. "No, Gramps, please. Not again. Does Vivi know about this?"

Dale Thackleberry studied his grandson. He placed his hand on Blake's shoulder. "Someday you will understand that the purest reward in life stems from bringing joy to others."

Blake grumbled, "Who said that?"

"Me." Dale chuckled with delight. "Now don't either one of you breathe a word about this to Vivi. You understand?"

I nodded along with Blake, even though I didn't know who Vivi was. I hoped she wasn't the woman who stole the tip he had left for the waitress.

Dale checked his watch. "I'll meet you in the lobby at four o'clock, Holly." He shot a glance at Blake. "And you, young sir—if you won't come with me, at least you could help load the sleigh."

They turned to walk away but not before I heard Blake

say, "Gramps, they have people to do things like that. Besides, I may need to distract Vivi."

Three children squealed as they ran past with their dogs, dodging around shoppers. A woman who must have been their mother chased after them yelling, "Santa Claus is going to hear about this!"

I couldn't help smiling. It was one of those rare times in life when everything was going my way. Holmes, my childhood friend who had grown up to be the man of my dreams, would be here anytime now. There was one teensy problem, though. Holmes was engaged. Try as I might, I hadn't been able to get the story from him, but there was some kind of complication. Maybe this time I could get him to tell me about it. I wasn't inclined to try to sway him, of course. Tempting as it might be, the last thing I wanted was to interfere in their relationship. I just kept hoping it would implode on its own. After all, Holmes had hinted that he would like to move from Chicago back to Wagtail. A plan I wholeheartedly endorsed.

It was going to be a wonderful holiday, and I brimmed with Christmas spirit. Trixie napped on a bed in the back of the booth. Her red collar adorned with frolicking elves suited my little girl, with her white fur, black ears, and a black spot on her rump. She had been my constant companion since I'd rescued her a little over a year ago. Unfortunately, she had a nose for trouble. More specifically, she had a habit of finding corpses.

A bald man strolled up and examined our wares. "I gather you are associated with the Sugar Maple Inn?"

"I guess our T-shirts for sale gave us away?"

His cheeks were ruddy, probably from the cold. "May I see the green velvet dog coat?"

I handed it to him. "Is it the right size?"

He examined the label. "Thackleberry," he said with

disdain, his nostrils flaring. He handed it back to me. "I don't buy Thackleberry products."

"Oh." I forced a smile, wondering what was wrong with them. The coat was adorable.

He leaned toward me and spoke confidentially. "Haven't you heard? There's something in their fabrics that's causing dog allergies. Makes them itchy and they lose patches of fur."

I frowned at him. We had quite a few of the products. In fact, Trixie's elf outfit was made by Thackleberry. She didn't appear itchy to me.

"Don't believe me? Look up *Thackleberry allergy* online." He gave a little wave and strolled away.

I knelt to Trixie and ran my hand over her fur. "Do you feel itchy?" I didn't see any patches of missing fur.

She gazed at me with bright eyes. Her ears pricked for a moment before she jumped to her feet and issued one yap.

I stood up, wondering if the man had returned, but it was Mr. Huckle who shuffled in our direction, bundled in an elegant navy blue wool coat. Oma had hired the gnarled gentleman when he lost his position as the butler to the wealthiest man in town. He had endeared himself to everyone who worked or stayed at the inn. Guests raved about him. He was always ready to walk dogs, brush cats, and make appointments for our guests and their pets.

"Miss Holly!" he cried as he approached. "Your grandmother should like to speak with you. I am to fill in until Miss Zelda takes over."

A nice-looking guy with brown eyes and dimples approached the booth. He smiled at me as I left and headed across the plaza toward the inn.

Trixie ran along in front of me as though she knew where we were going. Built as a mansion for a family in the 1800s, the stone-covered inn had been expanded and renovated by its many owners. We trotted up the stairs to the porch that ran the length of the original building. In spite of the frosty temperature, people occupied the rocking chairs, most with steaming mugs in their hands and dogs lounging at their feet.

We entered the main lobby, turned right, and walked along the hallway toward the reception lobby, where the inn office was located. I shed my plush sweater as I walked. My hair crackled with static electricity as I tugged it over my head.

Trixie barked.

In my disheveled state, I spied a woman about my age with brunette hair stepping off the elevator. She glanced in both directions, pushed back a strand of hair that was designed to hang along the side of her face in the latest trend, and said, "Excuse me. Which way to the main lobby?"

I smiled and pointed in the direction we had come. "It's that way."

"Wonderful, thank you!"

I admired her chic outfit. She looked so put together in her winter white trousers and matching sweater. Her nails were polished in a cheery Christmas red. I gazed down at my own nails, scrubby from handling pine and decorating. My jeans were okay for working at the Christkindl booth, but I couldn't help wondering if I had gotten a bit sloppy in my attire.

"Do you work here?" she asked.

"Yes. Is there something I can do for you?"

She pulled out a sheet of inn stationery. "I'm afraid my room is inadequate. I will need eight bottles of Mistletoe Cactus Dew and blackout curtains. I can't sleep if there's even a tiny hint of light in the room. And I need to be scheduled for a massage and a mani-pedi, and make reservations at some restaurants. I hope they're not all booked."

I was still stuck on her first request. "Mistletoe Cactus Dew?"

"Yes, they collect the rain that falls on the cacti in the rain forest. It's the purest water one can obtain because it

never even touches the earth. It's the only water that passes
my lips, and I use it for washing my face. You should try it."

We had some great stores in Wagtail, but I seriously
doubted that any of them carried Mistletoe Cactus Dew.
Maybe I could convert her for the length of her stay. "Wagtail is known for its spring water. People used to come here
just because of the water. You might want to try it."

She gave me the sad but tolerant look of a teacher with
a clueless student. "That touches the earth."

"I'll do my best on the rainwater. You can schedule
the massage and mani-pedi through Mr. Huckle in the
lobby. He has stepped away from his desk, but he'll be back
a little later."

"You really should try Mistletoe Cactus Dew. You won't
believe what it will do for your complexion."

I nodded and faked a smile as she sauntered away. She
looked terrific, but I never wanted to be that high mainte-
nance. She wasn't going to be happy if I couldn't find rain
forest water in Wagtail. Maybe I could melt some snow and
bottle it. I tried not to snicker.

But it wouldn't hurt me to schedule a manicure for myself. I walked on to the reception lobby, where Zelda greeted
me with a worried look.

"What's wrong?" I asked.

She avoided my gaze. "Um, nothing."

Right. She couldn't fool me. "Did Oma have problems
with Rupert?"

Zelda busied herself with papers.

"Hey, Zelda, have you ever heard of Mistletoe Cactus Dew?"

She stared at me, horrified. "I've heard of Mountain Dew.
I am getting so old," she whined. "Is Mistletoe Cactus Dew
a new rock group?"

I felt a little bit better about not having heard of it. "Apparently it's water." I stepped into the office.

Oma and her best friend, Rose Richardson, Holmes's grandmother, waited on the sofa.

In spite of her fondness for gardening and hiking, Rose's face showed precious few wrinkles for her age. She kept her hair blonde and had the same friendly blue eyes as her grandson, Holmes. But at the moment, she appeared as troubled as Oma.

My favorite applesauce cupcakes with caramel frosting and a tray of gorgeous iced sugar cookies in the shapes of doghouses, dogs, and cats rested on the coffee table.

Oma poured hot cider into a mug and handed it to me. "Sit down, *liebling*."

Trixie jumped up on the sofa between them and pawed at Oma, who promptly obliged her with a tiny dog treat in the shape of a Christmas tree.

Neither Oma nor Rose smiled. My heart skipped a beat. I could sense their discomfort. Something was wrong.

Five

"Holly," said Oma, "there is something we must tell you."

The button on her vest was going to fall off if she kept twisting it. I squirmed at her discomfort.

Rose tilted her head like a sad puppy and spoke fast. "Honey, we wanted to tell you this sooner, but we just didn't know how."

"You were so happy with your dreams of a Wagtail Christmas." Oma gazed at me with forlorn eyes.

"We meant well. Truly we did. Now we have no choice," Rose blathered.

"We should not have waited so long. The day has arrived. There is no time left," said Oma.

I watched them like a ping-pong game, my heart beating faster and faster in fear of what they were going to say. Was one of them ill?

A look flew between Oma and Rose, and Oma finally blurted, "The Thackleberrys have arrived."

What was wrong with that? "I met Dale a little while ago. He seemed very nice."

"We couldn't be sorrier," said Rose.

My eyes narrowed as I observed them. They weren't making any sense. Why would they be sorry about the Thackleberrys? I knew they were coming and had even received packages for Dale. Ohh, maybe it had something to do with the woman who had snatched back the tip? "You're making me a little crazy here. Could you be a bit more specific? What's wrong with the Thackleberrys?" I held my breath.

"Nothing," Oma spoke hastily. "Dale and his daughter, EmmyLou, have stayed with us before. They are lovely people."

"Lovely," Rose echoed as though she wanted to reinforce that image.

"Holly." Oma clasped her hands together and leaned forward, "The Thackleberrys will be Holmes's in-laws. His fiancée and her family are coming from Chicago to meet the Richardson family, and . . . they're spending Christmas here." Oma heaved a sigh so big that she shuddered slightly.

Holmes's fiancée? I felt like someone had punched me right in the gut. I wasn't sure I could breathe anymore. So that's how things were. Holmes was definitely going to marry that girl. I felt so stupid. "She's a Thackleberry?" I stammered. "I thought her name was Norma Jeanne Blume."

Rose cocked her head in sympathy. "Her mother was a Thackleberry before she married."

For a very long moment, I absorbed the news. And then I reached deep to pull up a smile. My voice didn't sound quite right when I said, "That's all? I thought one of you was sick!"

I stood up and called Trixie. Still faking a smile, I said lightly, "No big deal." And I left the room.

If I knew Zelda, she had been eavesdropping. She seized my arm when I tried to pass. "We could play pranks on her."

"No! Don't you dare do that." I hurried away because I really didn't want anyone to be sympathetic to me at that moment. I walked out the sliding doors and into the cold where I took some deep breaths.

I was *not* going to cry. I wasn't much of a crier anyway, but at the moment I was on the brink, and it wouldn't have taken much for tears to flow.

I walked along the Christkindl market booths, the noise and crowds and colors all a blur. My life was taking a major turn. Everything had changed. Nothing would ever be the same.

And then, as I stood at the base of the giant Christmas tree in the center of the green, drawing huge breaths of fresh air, I realized that I was wrong. Nothing would change. It had been silly and unrealistic of me to imagine that Holmes would ditch his fiancée and move back to Wagtail. It had been nothing but a dream. Just a bubble of fantasy that burst in one second and was gone. It didn't impact my life at all, only my wishful thinking.

All things considered, it was okay. I had anticipated something far worse. I was enormously relieved that neither Oma nor Rose were ill. I should be grateful that they were well. We would be fine. I had Trixie and Twinkletoes, and after all, the holidays were about making other people happy, not about living our dreams.

As my thoughts gelled, I watched the Schroeder children excitedly telling someone about the tree that Santa had left at their door. The death of their parents was a life-changing event, yet they were managing. Just seeing them made me understand that my silly dreams about Holmes had been nothing but fantasy.

Ethan Schroeder, a cute fellow with a mop of uncontrollable curls, ran toward me. "Holly! Holly!"

"Hi, Ethan." I expected him to tell me about the visit by Santa's elves.

"I need a job."

"You do?"

He glanced back at Marie Carr. "My sister and I want to get Granny Carr something special for Christmas. She never buys anything for herself, and she's been real good to us since . . . since . . ." His little head fell forward for a moment.

"I understand." He meant, but had trouble saying, *since his parents died.* "How much money do you need to make?"

"A lot!" He pulled a wad of bills out of his pocket and showed them to me. "The sweater we want to buy is sixty dollars, but all we have is nine dollars and—" he reached into his pocket again and pulled out coins "—forty-eight cents."

"I see the problem."

"I know how to sweep. And I could walk Trixie."

At the mention of her name, Trixie waggled and sniffed his hands for treats.

"I'll tell you what. I really need someone to help me in the Christkindl booth for a couple of hours. Do you think you could do that?"

"Sure!"

"Go tell your Granny Carr and make sure it's okay with her."

Ethan ran back to Mrs. Carr. After listening to him, she smiled at me and waved.

Ethan grinned as he returned to me. He chattered happily as we walked to the booth.

Ashamed by my childish reaction to the news about Holmes, I tried to focus on the here and now—the things in life that really mattered.

Mr. Huckle welcomed Ethan warmly. "I was going to offer to stay and help Miss Holly, but I see she has an excellent assistant."

While Ethan looked around the booth in awe, Mr. Huckle whispered, "Do you need a hand?"

I thought it far too cold for him to be outdoors any longer and shooed him back to the inn.

A sweet couple holding hands studied our wares. The girl shyly asked to see the blown glass wedding couple ornament. The groom was dressed in a tuxedo, and the bride wore a white gown.

Ethan climbed on a stool and handed it to her.

She beamed when her boyfriend paid Ethan for it. As I observed them, it dawned on me that this Christmas would be a very special time for Holmes and his fiancée. I would do my best to bite my tongue and keep any snarky opinions to myself, even if I thought she was completely wrong for him. I would hold my head high and be a cheerful little elf, because there were others whose holidays wouldn't be as lovely as mine. This Christmas was about Holmes, not about me.

I let out a long breath of air as I came to grips with the new development.

Two hours later, Zelda, bundled up in a vintage gray and white sweater with her long blonde braid hanging over her shoulder, scurried by the front of the booth and let herself in through the hatch in back.

"Have you met Norma Jeanne?" Her eyes were wide. "Holly, she's the spitting image of you."

"Who is Norma Jeanne?" asked Ethan.

I gave Zelda a sideways glance. "She's a brunette?"

"Well, yes. But that's not all. She's petite like you and . . . Wait until you meet her. She's not as pretty as you are, but the resemblance is uncanny."

I hugged Zelda. What a sweet thing to say, even if it most likely was a bald-faced lie. "She's just a visitor," I told Ethan.

While Ethan, a natural salesman, showed a woman Christmas collars for her dog, I whispered to Zelda, "Now you listen to me, Zelda York. This is the girl Holmes loves, so we're going to make this the best holiday ever. No being mean to her. Okay? We have to do this for Holmes."

"But he's making such a big mistake. We should stop him!"

"Zelda! We don't know that. If Holmes loves her, then she must be nice. Promise me you won't play tricks on her."

"Mmmf." Zelda chomped on a gingerbread cookie in the shape of a Santa boot.

Trixie jumped up and watched Zelda with a frantic look.

"Calm down, little one. I brought a cookie for you too, Trixie." Zelda bent to hand her a teensy dog treat in the shape of a bone. She straightened up. "Oma said not to forget to get the sleigh ready for Mr. Thackleberry."

I looked at my watch. "Of course." I had been so absorbed in thoughts about Holmes and Ethan that I had forgotten all about it.

"Ethan, you have done such a great job today. I think we sold more than ever! How about we go get that sweater for your Granny Carr before someone else buys it?"

"Really?" His cheeks had flushed red from the cold air, and he looked just like a painted doll.

"C'mon, Trixie." I waved to Zelda and the three of us left.

Ethan held my hand and skipped all the way to Houndstooth, an upscale clothing store. He ran directly to the sweater display and pulled out a red sweater. The saleswoman joined us.

"Do you know if this is the correct size for Marie Carr?" I asked.

"It is," she said. "But I think she might like this one in beige better."

Ethan looked at her in shock. "It *has* to be the red one!"

I shot the saleswoman a pleading look.

Fortunately, she didn't push him. We paid for the sweater and asked her to wrap it super festively. Ethan walked out carrying a box wrapped in glittering silver paper and a giant red ribbon. I had never seen a happier child.

Trixie and I walked him home to be sure he made it there safely. Not that we had that kind of problem in Wagtail. It

was still a town where kids could ride their bikes all afternoon without their parents worrying. But I was responsible
for him and wanted to be sure he actually went home.

When he was safely inside the house, we hurried back to
the inn office, where I had stashed the boxes Dale Thackleberry had sent ahead. I opened some, packed a slew of
toys in a huge red bag, and hoisted it over my shoulder.

It weighed a ton. I staggered out to the reception desk,
bent over under the weight, and was headed for the sliding
glass doors when I heard someone say, "Holly? Is that you?"

I knew that voice. Holmes! I swung around and found
myself face-to-face with Holmes and the woman who had
stepped out of the elevator and asked me for directions.

Holmes cocked his head to look at me in my twisted state.
"Norma Jeanne, this is Holly."

In spite of what I'd said to Zelda, I desperately wanted
to hate her. She was lovely in that winter white outfit. And
at the moment, I was hunched over like Quasimodo.

"I'm so pleased to finally meet you. Holmes talks about
you all the time," she said.

"Do you need a hand with that?" Holmes asked. "It looks
heavy."

"I'm good. Thanks," I lied, eager to get away from them.
"Nice to meet you, Norma Jeanne. Excuse me." I was about
to topple over, but I managed to deliver the bag to the green
sleigh with plush velvet seats that waited just outside the
door. Someone had tied a festive bow to the front of it.

The driver of the horse-drawn sleigh, Buck Bradon, was
dressed in red and green elf garb. He jumped off to take the
bag from me. "Whoa, Nellie, but this thing is heavy. I'm
surprised you could carry it. Is there more?"

I nodded and stretched my back. "The rest is in boxes.
Be right back."

When I returned to the reception lobby, Dale Thackleberry had joined Holmes and Norma Jeanne. From his shiny

black boots to his round belly, white beard, and sparkling eyes, Dale made a perfect Santa. No cheap costume store getups for him, that was for sure.

"Wow. You're the best dressed Santa I have ever seen."

"Thank you, Holly. I had this custom made for me at our factory. Always thought we should expand from dog and cat clothes to costumes for people."

A petite woman, frail with age, stood next to him, steadying herself with a cane. Her white hair was pinned up in a bun. She wore a red velvet dress with white faux fur trim that was worthy of any Mrs. Claus. An orange Pomeranian with bright, smart eyes peered out of her stylish green velvet purse.

Trixie danced below the bag, her nose pointed upward, eager to meet the new dog.

"And you must be Mrs. Claus?" I asked.

Dale beamed. "My mother, Doris, is coming along with me today. That's her favorite child in the bag, Muffy."

Doris laughed. "Don't you believe him! Although Muffy is usually better behaved than the rest of the family."

I wondered if she meant Blake, but didn't think I should point out his absence.

His grandfather clearly hadn't forgotten. "I had no idea *you* would have to load the sleigh." He shook his head. "Blake should have given you a hand."

"It's okay."

"No, it's not." He sounded like Scrooge. "My grandchildren have grown up having everything done for them. No one should think he's too good to offer a helping hand."

Norma Jeanne sighed and seemed bored, as though she had heard that line before.

On my next trip in from the sleigh, Blake had finally shown up with a short woman whom I guessed to be in her late twenties—the same woman who had been spying on him earlier in the day. Long dark blonde hair cascaded over her shoulders, and she had the same distinctive nose as Blake. She was nuzzling with Muffy.

Unlike Norma Jeanne, who looked like she was ready for a photo shoot, this girl wore a long baggy sweater over blue leggings that emphasized her pudginess. "Selfie with Santa," she cried, holding up her phone.

Blake groaned and raised his hands in protest. "Not me, Tiffany. This is so cheesy that I may perish. Thankfully, we are in the wilds at the end of the earth, where few will see us. The last thing I want is to memorialize this humiliating affair."

She made a snarling face at him. "You're such a snot, Blake. You used to be so much fun. Norma Jeanne?"

Norma Jeanne winced. "I'll take the photo, Tiffany."

I hustled to the closet for the boxes.

Holmes followed me.

When I bent to pick one up, he asked, "So what do you think of NJ?"

"NJ?"

"She hates her name. You know, the whole Marilyn Monroe thing. She prefers NJ, but her family insists on calling her Norma Jeanne. I know you're going to get along. She's a lot like you."

Not much, she wasn't. I immediately chastised myself for thinking that. "She seems very nice. Thanks for helping me with the boxes."

When we walked out of the office, Dale bellowed, "Blake, you've got two arms. Get over there and help them."

Blake's expression was priceless. "I'm sure they don't need me. Right, Holmes?"

Holmes clearly wasn't onto Blake's hands-off way of life. "They're right there in the office, Blake."

Holmes and I handed the boxes over to Buck. They embraced like old friends and agreed to meet for a drink. When we returned for more boxes I noticed that Blake had conveniently disappeared, but I said nothing.

When the sleigh was loaded, Dale hopped up into it and looked down at me. He whispered, "Blake better enjoy himself while he can, because he's in for a much bigger humiliation. I'm cutting him off."

"Because he's not helping you?" I asked in surprise.

"Naw. I'm not a petty man. It's because he's been lyin' to me and taking money on false pretenses. If there's one thing I don't abide—it's bein' lied to."

Six

Dale turned, faced forward, and shouted, "Ho ho ho! Let's go, Rudolph!"

Bells tinkled as the horses walked. Holmes, NJ, and Tiffany emerged from the inn to join Trixie and me. We waved as the horses pulled away with Santa Thackleberry and his mom, Doris, in the sleigh. Trixie didn't actually wave, but I held her up so she wouldn't get underfoot.

"Is he headed to the green?" asked Holmes.

I nodded.

Holmes looked down at NJ's high-heeled boots. "Are those made for walking in snow?"

Tiffany laughed. "They're not even made for *walking*, let alone snow. Can I go over with you, Holly?"

"Sure." The two of us and Trixie followed the short path past The Blue Boar Restaurant and walked toward the green. "I gather Dale is your grandfather?"

"In spirit, but not biologically. My biological grandmother, Vivi, married Dale. But he's the only granddad I've ever known."

"He seems like a great guy. So how are you related to Norma Jeanne?"

"Oh gosh. It's complicated. Dale and his first wife had a daughter named EmmyLou, who is Norma Jeanne's mom. My dad is Vivi's son."

"So you're cousins but not biological cousins?"

"Pretty much. Step-cousins, maybe? When Dale married my grandmother Vivi, our families kind of merged."

"All of you live in Chicago?"

"Everyone except my brother, Blake, who is going to med school in Grenada."

"That explains his tan!"

She gave me a sideways glance, but before she could say anything, a woman with short layered hair held out her arms. "There's my baby!"

"Hi, Mom." Tiffany hugged her mother. "This is Holly. She works at the inn."

"Holly!" She gave me a hug, too. "I'm Linda Kedrowski, Tiffie and Blake's mom. EmmyLou! Come meet Holly!" she called.

The woman who had been crying in the Dogwood Room joined us. "*You're* Holmes's Holly? My goodness but we've heard a lot about you. So you must be the famous Trixie?" She squatted to Trixie's level and petted her. "I hear you have quite an unusual talent."

Of course. I should have realized that Holmes would have told them about Trixie's knack for finding bodies.

"I am so excited about being in Wagtail for Christmas. Vivi usually insists on a cruise or someplace perfectly dreadful," said Linda.

"A cruise doesn't sound too bad," I said.

"Hah! One year we were afraid we would have to row

the ship." Linda laughed. "I don't know why we can't stay home for Christmas like other people. Of course, this year is an exception for Holmes and Norma Jeanne." She stroked her daughter's hair. "Tiffie, maybe you can find a nice boy like Holmes while we're here."

Tiffany stiffened. "I don't need to. As a matter of fact—" she checked her watch "—my boyfriend should be arriving in about an hour."

Linda clapped her hands against the sides of her face. "No! You really have a boyfriend?"

"You don't have to sound quite so astonished, Mom."

Linda hugged Tiffany. "I thought this day would never come. Why didn't you tell me?" She cast a critical eye over her daughter. "Shouldn't you go change?"

"What's wrong with this?" asked Tiffany.

"Don't you have something *prettier*?" Linda smiled at her daughter.

Tiffany appeared to be getting miffed. "No." She turned and walked away from her mother.

"Sweetie! Wait!" Linda ran after her.

EmmyLou sighed. "Holidays! Why did anyone ever think it was a good idea for families to reunite once a year? I guess you see a lot of this kind of thing at the inn."

Actually, I didn't, but to be polite, I nodded. After all, we did see quite a bit of unusual behavior.

At that moment, sleigh bells rang merrily. Children squealed and dogs barked. Dale and Doris smiled as the sleigh drew close to the big tree in the center of the green. They were clearly having fun handing gifts out to children, dogs, and cats.

My own little Twinkletoes surprised me by appearing in the crowd. But instead of nabbing a catnip toy, she jumped into the sleigh, hissed briefly at Muffy, the Pomeranian, and settled comfortably on Doris's lap, where she was rewarded with a cat treat.

But her fun didn't last, because Dale and Doris disembarked and handed out gifts as they talked to children. Trixie followed Twinkletoes's example and jumped into the sleigh. They snuggled together on the seat and watched the merriment from their perch.

When Doris and Dale returned to the sleigh, Trixie nabbed a giant stuffed toy in the shape of a squirrel and ran back to me, dragging it over the snow.

I debated retrieving Twinkletoes from the sleigh, but Doris appeared perfectly happy with her feline company.

Most of the dogs and kids were too interested in their goodies to get underfoot, but I appreciated that Buck made sure the sleigh pulled away slowly. Watching it glide over the snow with the bells ringing warmed my heart. Who could possibly be unhappy?

EmmyLou, for one.

I turned to look at her, but my gaze fell on Holmes laughing with Norma Jeanne, who had changed into running shoes.

It was like he'd stuck a dagger through my heart.

Seven

I literally shook it off. I was not going to be that way. Not, not, not!

I walked back to the inn. Trixie dragged her new toy over the packed snow, unwilling to accept my help.

The woman who had earlier taken the tip stood on the front porch as though she was guarding the entrance. I now suspected she was the evil Vivi everyone had talked about. Her arms were crossed over her chest, and she glowered at the world as though she was very angry.

Trixie bolted up the stairs and past her with the giant toy in her mouth.

I walked up the wide stairs, but Vivi didn't bother to step aside as most people would have.

Inside the inn, Shelley nabbed me. "Are you helping me serve cocktails and appetizers to the Richardsons and Thackleberrys in the Dogwood Room?"

"Sure."

"I'll handle cocktails if you can circulate with the appetizers."

I nodded my head in agreement. "Just give me a second to change clothes."

Outside, someone screamed. I ran to the door. The Thackleberry family clustered on the porch. I stepped outside. "Is everything okay?"

EmmyLou passed Vivi. She whispered to me, "Just the usual Thackleberry drama."

Vivi still held one arm across her chest. But the fingers of her other hand were now poised on her jawline, her long, pointy, bloodred nails tapping her face. "I heard that, EmmyLou."

"Vivi," said EmmyLou, "can't you just let him have his fun? It's Christmas!"

Vivi turned a hateful face toward her stepdaughter.

EmmyLou spoke in a soft, level tone. "Please don't spoil it for Dad. Or for Norma Jeanne. Just once, let us have a happy holiday."

EmmyLou walked past me. I stepped inside and closed the door, feeling very sorry for their family. But I had no time to linger. I shot upstairs to my apartment on the third floor of the inn. While I sometimes took the elevator, I figured walking up the two flights probably did me good. I had the top floor of the building all to myself, save for the huge storage room on the other end.

My holiday decorating binge had extended to my quarters as well. With trees all over the inn, it seemed silly to put up a tree in my living room, but I had anyway. This was the first time I could remember that I wasn't leaving home for Christmas, and I had always longed to put up a tree of my own. I had bought a small tree, gone overboard with lights, and scoured the Christkindl booths for just the right ornaments.

I paused briefly to admire it, then hurried on to my room

to change clothes. Not because of Norma Jeanne's chic style, I told myself. One really shouldn't serve food to guests in semi-grubby jeans.

It wasn't as though I didn't own pretty clothes. I had worked in fund-raising in Washington, DC, for years. Still, as I looked around my walk-in closet, everything seemed too dressy or too casual. I didn't want to look like I was trying too hard.

I finally settled on simple navy trousers and a white lace top with short sleeves. I added gold hoop earrings with a smattering of inset rhinestones for sparkle. I slid my feet into flats so I wouldn't trip while serving, and quickly brushed my hair back into a sleek ponytail.

Twinkletoes sat on the dresser, watching me. Her new catnip mouse, made out of a strong blue cotton fabric dotted with white snowflakes, lay at her feet. I slid a red velvet ruffle adorned with white lace edging over her head, expecting her to complain. Instead, she appeared to take pride in it and purred. I placed a matching one on Trixie, noting that they were made by the Thackleberry company.

With Trixie leaping ahead of me and Twinkletoes strolling with feline stealth, I rushed downstairs to an empty lobby. Everyone appeared to be outside watching the Yappy Hour parade. Everyone except Linda, who worked in the Dogwood Room, and Blake, who was sprawled in an easy chair, with one leg draped over the arm. He had changed out of the harlequin trousers. He now wore a white sweater accented with five wide vertical stripes in black. His trousers were cut short, exposing his bare ankles. He wore black velvet loafer-style shoes. Lazily lifting his right hand and flicking it, he said to his mother, "More to the right."

Two large trunks were open by the fireplace with tissue papers and ornaments spilling out of them. It looked as messy as it had when I was decorating the room.

Linda looked up at me when I walked over. "Hi! Your

grandmother said I could do this. It's just not Christmas without our stockings on the mantel."

Indeed, she had hung stockings for every member of the Thackleberry family, plus extras for Holmes and his family. The fireplace and mantel were huge, but there were so many stockings that they crowded it.

"That's a lot to travel with."

I was thinking about how much it must have cost Linda to fly with trunks of decorations when Blake said, "One of the perks of having a private plane. You won't believe what they wanted me to pay for an extra suitcase on my commercial flight."

"I hope you brought some normal clothes," said Linda without looking at him.

Blake ignored her. "That isn't the half of her stuff. She has a train set in that blue trunk."

"I love decorating for the holidays. Rose was telling me about her Christmas village that she didn't put up this year. She's bringing it over so I can set it up here!" Linda gazed around. "I don't know where it should go."

I didn't, either. "Maybe I can arrange something for you while you're at dinner tonight. How much space do you need?"

She went into a mind-bending explanation of the myriad ways she could organize the houses. With a hill or mountain, which she liked because we were in the mountains. Or entirely flat. It could start on the floor or be on a table. I was a little bit overwhelmed.

Blake smiled at me smugly, as though he found it all très amusing.

But there was one thing that worried me. "You do realize that cats and dogs run loose here. We can't be responsible if they break the lovely village pieces."

"Honey, I'm willing to take that chance. I'll replace anything they break. We don't usually stay someplace this nice for the holidays, and I want everything to be perfect."

"You always bring all this with you?"

"Decorating for the holidays is my joy during the season. Some people like to bake, some love the shopping, I decorate. And let me tell you, we've spent it in some spots where the only holiday décor was a head-bobbing Santa and some filthy gray tinsel on the registration desk. Vivienne believes in traveling on the cheap."

It wasn't any of my business, but I asked anyway. "What about your parents and siblings? Can't you make an excuse to celebrate with them?"

Linda closed her eyes for a long second.

Blake answered for her. "We've been shunned."

"Shunned? You're Amish?"

A grin crept onto Linda's lips. "No. But none of *my* relatives want to spend the holidays with us because—" she looked around before whispering "—they're afraid Vivi will come."

"She seems—" I searched for a gentle word "—complicated."

"She's a shrew and a miser is what she is. The woman *cannot* be pleased. Dale is the sweetest man you'll ever meet. None of us have the first clue what he ever saw in her. But we're not allowed to say a word to her about her boorish behavior because she has a heart condition. Contrary to what one might think, she's actually quite delicate. But it's so annoying that she gets away with saying and doing offensive things, and we just have to accept it." Her eyes widened. "Oh my gosh, here they come. Is there somewhere I can stash these trunks?"

"Sure." I grabbed one trunk, and she lifted another.

Linda followed me along the corridor to a housekeeping room. "Oh wonderful. It's not locked. You don't mind if I sneak in here like a little mouse to do some nighttime decorating, do you?"

"Make yourself at home." As soon as the words were out

of my mouth, I wondered about the wisdom of saying that to her.

When we walked out, Doris stepped off the elevator with Muffy, whose outfit put us all to shame. She wore a green dress decorated with rhinestones and matching green ruffles around her haunches. The ruffles were trimmed in red and glittered when Muffy moved.

Linda took Doris's arm and strolled with her to join the Thackleberrys.

Shelley headed toward me with a tray of hors d'oeuvres. She handed it to me and pointed to each item as she spoke. "The ones with the white dot on top are blinis with smoked salmon and a dab of crème fraîche. Those are mini flatbread white pizzas, and of course, these on the buns are pulled pork sliders. They're all canine-friendly. I'll be back with drinks."

Gripping the tray, I ventured through the mingling Thackleberrys and offered the selection to Doris, the family matriarch, who now sat comfortably in a French country armchair with Muffy in her lap.

Doris helped herself to a blini, promising Muffy a taste. Muffy did not seem reassured and had no qualms about extending her nose toward the blini. Smiling, Doris broke off a bite and fed it to her.

Tiffany knelt on the floor beside Doris and petted Muffy. "Can I dress up Muffy and walk her in the parade tomorrow?"

Doris was clearly delighted. "I brought a number of outfits for her. Would you like that, Muffy?"

Muffy only had eyes for the blini.

Behind me, I heard Blake speak in a snotty tone. "So where's this mysterious boyfriend, Tiffany? Shouldn't he be here by now?"

I presented the tray to Holmes and Norma Jeanne while listening to the chatter.

Tiffany checked her phone and cried out, "Oh no! His

flight was canceled. He's at the airport trying to book another one."

Blake laughed hysterically. "How convenient. That's the best you can do? Really, Tiff, you should have broken his leg. That way you wouldn't have to make up more excuses for your imaginary boyfriend."

Linda gasped. From her expression I guessed that she hadn't considered the possibility that Tiffany might have invented a boyfriend. "Honey, I'm sure he can catch another flight." Unfortunately, the uncertainty in her tone conveyed her doubt.

Tiffany glared at her brother. "He's very real. Which is more than I can say for you. Who dressed you in that costume?"

I glanced at him when I moved on and realized that his trousers flared out at the hips like riding jodhpurs.

"Those who get their clothes from Frumpy-R-Us are hardly in a position to judge."

"You mean your hind end is actually that wide?" Tiffany threw right back at him.

Linda seemed oblivious, but I didn't think it was a coincidence that she changed the focus of the conversation. "Norma Jeanne, will we all be gathering here in the summer for your wedding?"

Eight

Norma Jeanne smiled at Holmes, who seemed uncomfortable to me. "I don't think so, Aunt Linda. I had a city wedding in mind. And Tiffie will be one of my bridesmaids, won't you, Tiffie?"

Tiffany appeared surprised but hugged her cousin fiercely. "Of course I will!"

Blake raised his eyebrows and held his head high as though he was expecting an invitation to be a groomsman. None was forthcoming.

A man with a receding hairline plucked a white pizza off my tray. His beard was shot through with silver and kept very short to follow the contours of his face. "Norma Jeanne, I think you ought to consider a Wagtail wedding. It's beautiful in the summer. You could have it right here at the inn. I bet they host a lot of weddings. You could make a grand entrance on my arm right down that big staircase."

I gathered he was Norma Jeanne's father, Barry, who also

happened to own the architecture firm Holmes worked for. I'd been told he introduced Holmes to his daughter.

If anyone had asked me, I would have said Holmes was looking a little bit queasy. But maybe that was just my wistful imagination.

Norma Jeanne spoke with the confidence of someone used to getting her way. "Oh, Dad! I really have my heart set on the society wedding of the year. I've already picked out one of my dresses."

Now I thought her dad turned a little green.

"One?" asked her father. "How many do you need?"

"Three. One for the service, one for dinner, and one for dancing. And there's a wedding planner in Chicago who constructs ceilings out of flowers! Don't worry, Dad, you'll feel like you're in the great outdoors, only it will be even better."

Her father choked when he said, "A ceiling?"

Doris piped up from her seat. "Everybody makes too much fuss about weddings these days. Your great-grandfather and I were married in the church. My mother sewed my wedding dress by hand, and it's still the prettiest one I've ever seen. Afterward, we all went for lunch at my uncle Stan's Polish restaurant."

"Where did you go for your honeymoon, Grammy?" asked Tiffany.

"Niagara Falls. Your great-grandfather and I spent many happy vacations there."

I was having fun listening to their conversation when I noticed Dale beckoning me from the foot of the grand staircase. I scooted out to him, and he immediately nabbed one of the pizzas.

"Mmm. Delicious. Holly, I have a favor to ask of you. Your grandmother tells me you're up late every night helping Santa." He winked at me and handed me a stack of envelopes. "Could you sneak these into the stockings in the wee hours on Christmas morning?"

"Yes, of course. How did you know there would be stockings?"

"I know my family very well. Linda always hangs stockings. Blake is inherently lazy and complains about everything. Tim will have had too much to drink by now, Barry will do whatever EmmyLou tells him, and Norma Jeanne will always be the socialite drill sergeant. Just watch. You'll see that I'm right."

I stashed the envelopes in the lobby desk as fast as I could and was right behind Dale when he strode into the Dogwood Room bellowing, "Ho ho ho!"

"No no no," chanted Blake. He sighed and his face contorted with disgust.

Dale stared at his grandson for a long moment. He picked up a glass and a spoon and clinked on it. "My lovely family— what a joy it is for me to see you all here together. This has been a most interesting year for me." He stopped and gazed around at them with a big smile on his face. "In fact, it has been so remarkable that Santa Thackleberry will be bringing each of you a special surprise in your stockings this year." He raised a finger and placed it beside his nose just like Santa in *The Night Before Christmas*. "There is magic in the air, my children."

Norma Jeanne raised her wrist and tapped her diamond watch. "Sorry to interrupt your speech, Gramps, but we don't want to be late for our dinner reservation."

They began to collect coats and start for the door.

EmmyLou turned to her husband, Barry. "Would you get my coat and purse from our room?"

He passed me on his way to the stairs.

I overheard Norma Jeanne murmur to Holmes, "You know what will be in *my* stocking, don't you?"

Holmes tilted his head.

"A honeymoon in Bali, silly!"

If you asked me, Holmes turned nearly as green as the Grinch.

As they filed out the door, he placed a hand on my shoulder. "You're coming with us, aren't you? Oma and Rose are going to be there."

Having dinner with Holmes's future wife and her family was the last thing in the world I wanted to do. "Thanks, but I need to take care of a few things around here."

He looked at me with those kind blue eyes and nodded without saying anything. I had a bad feeling that he could see right into my head.

Smiling cheerfully, I whispered, "I'm baking a stollen for Oma. Shh. It's a surprise."

He blinked a couple of times. "Do you know how to do that?"

"How hard could it be?"

His serious expression vanished, replaced by a genuine grin. He didn't think I could do it!

"Save me a slice to try."

I would. I would do exactly that! I watched them file out with Rose, Oma, and Gingersnap. I dashed to the desk and retrieved the envelopes in case there was money or plane tickets to Bali or some other valuable item in them. I carried them into Oma's private kitchen. Not the one in her apartment, but the big, cozy room on the main floor that was reserved for family only. I lit a fire in the fireplace, pulled out the recipe for stollen, and read the instructions. Hmm. Didn't sound too difficult. There was a lot of rising time, which would give me a chance to take care of some other things. I chopped dried apricots and cherries, then poured rum over them. I tossed them and, since they had to sit to soak up the rum, left them on the turquoise island. With

Dale's envelopes in hand, I sprinted up the hidden stairway that led directly to my quarters.

Trixie ran up the stairs with me. To be on the safe side, I stashed the envelopes behind some books. Anyone entering my quarters wouldn't even know they were there. I changed into soft, stretchy jeans and a long-sleeved white shirt, with the cuffs rolled back. I was ready to work.

Back in the kitchen, I started the yeast and hit the refrigerator that Holmes claimed was magic. It wasn't, of course, but part of the inn's leftovers went into the fridge, which meant the refrigerator was always full of delicious food. The rest was shared with the less fortunate of Wagtail.

Trixie peered into the refrigerator with me, her nose twitching high in the air. I pulled out something labeled *Happy Howliday Feast for dogs* and looked inside. Tiny bits of steak were mixed with barley, carrots, and green beans. Trixie jumped up as high as she could to see it, which I interpreted to mean she wanted it for dinner.

Twinkletoes strolled in. She stretched and yawned before jumping up on the hearth and mewing very softly.

"Time for dinner?" I asked.

I opened a container marked *Divine Chicken Breast* and spooned some into a bowl. She ate it so fast that it must have lived up to its name.

The door swung open and Officer Dave peeked in. "Hey Holly, your grandmother around?"

"No. She went to dinner with Holmes and company."

"How's that going?" he asked.

I pretended to be cheerful about it. "Fine!"

"Yeah, right. It's me, Holly. I know it can't be easy for you."

"I want Holmes to be happy," I said, trying hard to side-step his question.

"I don't think he's very happy right now." Dave held his hands close to the fire and rubbed them.

"What do you mean?"

"One of the shopkeepers overheard Norma Jeanne telling her cousin, the one who wears the weird clothes, that she would sooner die than live in Wagtail."

"That's not terribly surprising, I guess. She's used to big-city life. Remember how much my old boyfriend Ben hated it here in the beginning?"

Even though I defended her, I knew that was trouble. It would break our hearts if we rarely saw Holmes. Was that the problem to which Holmes had alluded the last time I saw him? Norma Jeanne didn't like Wagtail but Holmes longed to return?

Dave studied me. "Most folks in town aren't being quite so generous about Norma Jeanne. She's fairly demanding. No one is going to snap your head off if you say what you think."

"If Holmes is in love with her, I think we should try to accept her." I was slightly surprised that I managed to sound so convincing when part of me wanted to do exactly what Dave suggested and complain about her.

A glimmer of a grin crossed Dave's lips. "You're a good actress, Holly Miller. I better get back out there. Tell your grandmother that we've had a little rash of burglaries. Ho ho ho, and 'tis the season, I guess. They've stolen an expensive down-filled dog bed, a hiking staff, four boxes of chocolates, and a thousand-piece jigsaw puzzle."

"Gifts for the dog, himself, his wife, the in-laws, and his kid?"

Dave smiled. "Could be. But Jed Kaine has been spotted in town. It's just like him to steal petty stuff. Let me know if you see him, okay?"

"Sure." Jed was a lowlife of the worst sort. When he wasn't peddling drugs, he was stealing. I knew of three stores in town that had posted his picture in a back room so employees could be on the lookout. He lived in Snowball, but once in a while something brought him to Wagtail. "Want some dinner?"

"Thanks, but I really need to get back to the stores and keep an eye out for this creep."

"Could be more than one person."

"And they could be long gone by now. See you later." Dave walked out the door.

I found leftover chicken breast in the fridge and whipped up a sandwich with mayonnaise, cranberry sauce, and heaps of lettuce on a batard.

When I was through eating, I mixed together all the ingredients for the stollen, kneaded the dough, and pushed the fruit into it. I was mighty proud of myself when I covered it with a kitchen towel and set it on the dining table near the fire to rise.

Addressing Trixie, who had watched me carefully, I said, "Now we'd better find a spot for that Christmas village." When we left the kitchen, I turned right and ventured into the inn library. It was a cozy room with a window seat and a fireplace. Shelley and I had decorated a rustic woodland tree with a red and black buffalo check ribbon, pinecones, hand-carved deer ornaments, sleds, fluffy white owls with big eyes, bright cardinals, bluebirds, and ornaments of woodland creatures of all kinds. The library wasn't large, though, and people passed through it to get to rooms in the cat wing, so maybe that wasn't a great choice for a village. Tiffany was the only member of her family who had requested a room in the inn's cats only wing, even though she hadn't brought a cat with her. I had to guess that she liked cats, or maybe she liked the idea of the screened porches that those rooms featured.

We returned to the main lobby, and as I gazed around, I spotted the corner on the right side of the lobby. We had debated what could go there and ended up leaving it fairly plain.

I walked down the hallway and stepped into the elevator.

Trixie balked and backed up. She had been afraid of small, confined spaces since the day I found her. Even now, the poor baby feared the elevator. I waved bye-bye as the doors closed.

In the basement, I half dragged, half carried a long folding table onto the elevator, then looked around for something sturdy but a bit shorter. A trio of long stacking tables seemed just right. I loaded them and took the elevator back to the first floor. Trixie sat in the hallway, waiting and whining.

She danced in circles when I stepped out and ran ahead of me when I brought the tables to the corner of the lobby. I set them in place, and when I turned, I realized that they were exactly opposite the huge Christmas tree in the Dogwood Room. Perfect.

I dusted myself off and returned to the kitchen where I washed my hands and put on an apron. When I uncovered the yeast dough, I was thrilled to find it had doubled in size. My love life might stink, but I appeared to have a knack for baking. Following the directions precisely, I punched down the dough, divided it in two, and left it on the table to rise for ten minutes while I washed bowls at the kitchen sink. Through the window above the sink, I could see solar Christmas lights aglow on the trees.

When I looked around for more items to wash, I discovered Trixie on the table, licking her chops, and part of the dough had disappeared.

"No! Oh, Trixie!" I screamed in panic. I was no veterinarian, but I knew raw yeast dough could swell in her tummy.

Nine

"Trixie!" I ran to her. "No, no, no!"

She scrambled to jump off the table in haste.

I reached for the phone and called the vet, who confirmed that eating unbaked yeast dough was an emergency, and told me to bring Trixie in immediately.

My next call was to Mr. Huckle. I kept it very brief. "I have an emergency, Mr. Huckle—"

He interrupted me. "I'm on my way."

My panic was spreading to Trixie who watched me with fearful eyes. I stashed the remaining dough in the fridge so no other dogs could reach it, picked Trixie up, and ran through the hallway to the reception lobby, where I picked up a golf cart key. Clutching Trixie, I ran the best I could to the golf carts parked outside. I placed her on the front bench with me, backed out, and gunned the golf cart.

If I hadn't been so panicked, I might have enjoyed the Christmas lights as I drove. But Trixie no longer sat up. She lay on her side and whined.

I couldn't remember having been so afraid. By the time we arrived at the animal hospital, Trixie was wheezing as though she couldn't breathe properly.

The veterinarian waited for us outside. She took Trixie into her arms and walked into the hospital very calmly, asking me detailed questions about what had happened.

My heart raced as I spewed the story to her. She disappeared into the back with Trixie, but a veterinary technician arrived and, in the same calm manner, asked me more questions. I repeated the tale, quivering inside.

She promised the doctor would be out to talk with me shortly.

Lights on a tree in the corner of the waiting room and little statuettes of dogs and cats in Santa hats did nothing to cheer me up. It was dark outside the windows. I stood in front of one, looking out at nothing and thinking about the day I had rescued Trixie. Someone had abandoned her at a gas station, and the sweet little girl had waited there in hope that the despicable person would come back to pick her up. A wet and muddy mess, she had jumped into my boyfriend's car, spilled coffee, and made a wreck of the carpet by tearing open a bag of cheesy chips.

The truth was that she had rescued me. If it hadn't been for Trixie and Twinkletoes, I might not have moved to Wagtail. I loved my life now in a way that I hadn't imagined possible..

How could I have been so stupid? I knew she was always ravenous. It was my fault. All my fault. Trixie was such a sweet little girl. She'd been through a terrible time early in her life. She deserved to have a good long life.

"Holly?"

I turned around, a lump of fear in my throat.

The veterinarian smiled at me and held out a plastic sheet with a pile of dough on it. "Does this look like what she ate? We gave her something to make her throw up."

Bits of cherries and apricots dotted the dough. "That's a lot!"

"It's a good thing you brought her in right away."

"I was worried about it expanding in her stomach."

She nodded. "Unbaked yeast dough can be deadly. Not only does it rise from the heat in their bodies, but it causes bloat. Plus, as the yeast ferments, it produces alcohol, which can poison the dog."

It was worse than I had thought. A chill ran through me.

She smiled at me reassuringly. "I think she'll be okay. But I'd like to keep her overnight so we can monitor her for alcohol poisoning."

"Thank you so much. Do you have someone here all night?"

"We're an emergency center and hospital, open around the clock. You don't have to look so worried, Holly. Some of the top specialists in the country work here. Trixie won't be alone. We have a few other dogs and cats whom we're monitoring. You go on home and relax. I'll call you in the morning."

I thanked her again and walked toward the door. I paused and turned around.

"Go home!" said the doctor. "I promise we'll do our best for Trixie."

She hadn't come right out and said there was nothing I could do for Trixie, but I got the message. Still, part of me wanted to camp out in the waiting room, just in case. I dragged myself out the door and into the golf cart. It seemed oddly empty without Trixie by my side.

On the way back, I noticed that someone had decorated a small pine tree with lights in the middle of nowhere. It stood alone in a field. I stopped the golf cart and said some fervent prayers for Trixie.

Feeling glum and lower than low, I headed home. When I walked into the lobby, Mr. Huckle jumped up from his seat in front of the fire in the Dogwood Room. "Miss Holly! What happened? Is it your grandmother?"

I told him the story.

"What a scamp that Trixie is! Don't worry, I'm certain that she will be fine. The veterinarians in Wagtail are excellent. Besides, 'tis the season of miracles, you know."

Miracles? I hoped Trixie wouldn't need a miracle!

"Now then, I should like to try this fabulous stollen that your grandmother loves so much. May I help you make it?"

"That's very sweet of you, but I think I'll pass on it this year. I don't really have the heart to make it now."

"You would disappoint your grandmother?"

"It's not as though she knows."

"I should very much like to bring her a slice with her morning coffee tomorrow." He cocked his head at me.

It wasn't as though I had anything else to do. I agreed. He accompanied me to the kitchen, where Twinkletoes stretched out in front of the fire. Mr. Huckle made hot chocolate while I threw out the cursed batch and started all over again.

He regaled me with tales of his childhood Christmases, including one just after World War II that was particularly sparse, but was made special because his father brought home a lost kitten he found on the street.

As I placed two stollen loaves in the oven to bake, Mr. Huckle casually said, "This must be a difficult holiday for you what with Mr. Holmes bringing his fiancée to Wagtail."

I tried to keep my cool. "I'm very happy for Holmes," I lied.

"Umm-hmm. And how happy are you for his bride-to-be?"

At exactly that moment, Holmes barged into the kitchen. "Smells great in here! Hey, do either of you know how I can join the elves?"

"It's a highly guarded secret," teased Mr. Huckle.

"Ask Oma," I suggested, playing along.

"She wouldn't tell me."

"Really? I think half the town knows by now," I said.

"Not anyone I know." Holmes turned his head just a little and watched me out of the corner of his eye.

"If you want them to do something special for someone, just write it on a slip of paper and stick it in the box in the lobby." I busied myself melting butter.

"No, no. You don't get it. I want to join them," Holmes insisted. "I want to be an elf."

I thought I had been handling the whole Norma Jeanne thing so well, but more than anything else, that cut me to the core. That was the Holmes I knew and loved. I turned my back to him so he wouldn't see my face and asked, "Where is Norma Jeanne?"

"She went to bed. She's a stickler about getting eight hours of sleep. Hey, did you ever find Mistletoe Cactus Dew for her?"

I gasped and flung my hand over my mouth as I turned to face him. "I forgot all about it!"

"Not to worry, Miss Holly." Mr. Huckle poured hot chocolate into a mug and offered it to Holmes. "She asked me for it as well. I called around town today. No one had ever heard of it. I stocked her room with Wagtail Springs water."

"Thank you, Mr. Huckle. I'm so sorry that it slipped my mind. Sorry, Holmes, but if it's that hard to find, maybe she should bring it with her when she travels."

"Aw, she'll live. We all drink Wagtail water. I'm sure she'll manage for a few days. Now about those elves . . ."

"You'd better talk to Oma. She's in charge."

"Argh," Holmes groaned. "You Miller women are so difficult. I feel like I'm going in circles."

I heard the door swing behind him as he left.

"It's not too late, you know," said Mr. Huckle.

I knew exactly what he meant, and he wasn't talking about elves. I pulled the stollen out of the oven and turned to face him. My eyes met his. "I respect your opinions, Mr. Huckle, but this time I fear you are wrong. It's far, far too late."

Just before midnight, dressed in my elf outfit, I tiptoed down the stairs. The Thackleberrys must have retired to their rooms. The Dogwood Room lay silent. But when I reached the bottom step, I heard murmuring voices.

I peeked in the library and spied Tiffany and her step-grandfather Dale. They sat in comfy chairs before the fire, their backs to me.

I hurried past them, left the inn, and walked through the snowy green to Rose's garage to collect our sleigh. Lights twinkled on houses as I drove through the streets to the inn. The Grinch loomed like an ominous dark cloud. Rupert must have figured out a way to turn off the lights and the music. I parked outside the registration lobby and stepped out of the golf cart.

"Well, well, well. If it isn't one of Wagtail's secret elves."

I shrieked in momentary shock and peered into the darkness because I had recognized the voice. It came from behind bushes that glistened with lights.

And now I heard chuckling. *Holmes.* "You sneak!"

He stepped out into the light. "I knew it!"

"You're wearing elf clothes." I looked closer. His shoes even had turned-up toes.

"I try to dress appropriately. Where are we going tonight?"

There wasn't a good reason in the world that he couldn't help us. "We're delivering Christmas dinner packages."

"Great! Where are they?"

"Inside. You're just in time to help us load them."

We entered the registration lobby and walked through the inn. No guests lingered on the first floor. I noted that even Tiffany and Dale had gone to bed. Shelley and Zelda met us at the inn's big freezers.

They teased Holmes mercilessly about his elf outfit. We loaded carts with boxes filled with turkeys, fresh cranberries, bags of potatoes and sweet potatoes, marshmallows, green beans, elbow macaroni, cheese, milk, butter, heavy cream, pumpkin pies, and gingerbread cookies. Even though the outdoor temperature was freezing, the items that could spoil were packed in coolers.

We rolled the carts through the silent lobby of the inn, with Twinkletoes riding on top of my cart, her tail twitching with anticipation.

Holmes suddenly stopped. "Hold it! Where is Trixie?"

I told them briefly what had happened.

"But she'll be all right, won't she?" asked Holmes.

"I hope so. Come on, let's get this done." I was already worried enough. I didn't want to discuss what could happen to her. She had been on my mind since I left her at the animal hospital. We loaded the sleigh, left Twinkletoes at the inn, and set off in the night, admiring the lights that sparkled in the dark.

Our first stop was a tiny bungalow close to the Wagtail Springs Hotel. We carried packages and a cooler up to the house and left them on the front porch.

When we climbed back into the golf cart, Holmes laid a hand on my arm. "Just a second."

We watched in silence as Vivienne trotted down the stairs of the Wagtail Springs Hotel and set off on foot through the green.

"Wasn't that the horrible woman we saw at breakfast?" whispered Zelda.

I waved my hand at her not to say anything more. After all, she was going to be Holmes's grandmother-in-law.

"What do you suppose she's up to?" Zelda continued.

She didn't understand my sign language message. I was going to have to come right out and say it. "She's Norma Jeanne's grandmother, Zelda."

Ten

I heard Zelda gasp. "I'm sorry, Holmes. I didn't mean to insult her but—"

Shelley interrupted, "She's a dreadful woman!"

Holmes twisted around in his seat. "Do me a favor and don't mention this to anyone, okay? I don't want to upset Norma Jeanne or her family."

"Think she's having an affair?" Zelda asked.

Shelley snorted. "Who would be interested in *her*?"

"Gee, Shelley. What did she ever do to you?" asked Holmes.

My eyes had adjusted to the dark enough for me to see the pained look on Shelley's face. "We'd better get going," I said. "We have a lot of houses to visit."

Zelda giggled. "You sound like Santa Claus!"

We delivered a few more packages around town, then headed up to some of the outlying farms and homes.

We were spotted by a little redheaded boy at an old

farmhouse. He wiped his eyes and yawned as he looked out the window. When we heard his yelp of surprise, we jumped off the porch as fast as we could.

The four of us laughed all the way back to town. Holmes and I dropped off Shelley and Zelda at their homes and parked the sleigh in his grandmother's garage. Holmes insisted on walking me back to the inn. We strolled through the green, which was blissfully empty in the wee hours of the morning. I missed Trixie running ahead in the quiet winter wonderland.

I couldn't help thinking there was a spring missing in Holmes's step as we walked. He was happy about having been an elf, though. I was a little bit jealous of Norma Jeanne. Maybe a lot jealous.

Holmes sucked in a deep breath of air. "Gosh, it's great to be back home. I really miss this place. NJ was teasing me about knowing everyone. Everywhere we went someone came up and said hello or congratulated us. This is going to sound stupid, but I feel like I'm part of something in Wagtail. Like tonight, for instance. If I dressed in an elf suit in Chicago and ran around leaving boxes of food on people's doorsteps, I'd probably end up at the police station, taken in for questioning."

I laughed. "I'm sure it's not that bad."

"There's a spirit here that I miss in the city. You must know what I mean. You lived in a city. I live in a high-rise and barely know my neighbors. A man in my building fell and died in his apartment. No one noticed until the odor started to bother the other residents. That could be me."

Did he really think that? It wasn't like Holmes at all. "Holmes! Norma Jeanne would worry. And surely your co-workers would notice your absence."

"Maybe, maybe not. I feel like part of the community here. That's something I don't have in Chicago. I'm just another working stiff there."

I understood completely. I had a circle of close friends in Washington, DC, but in Wagtail, I had a sense of belonging. Like I was part of the fabric of life.

We were nearing the inn when Holmes grabbed my hand and pulled me behind a park bench. "Squat down," he whispered.

Our faces were mere inches apart, and my heart raced. Was this a ploy for a kiss?

Apparently not. He paid no attention to me and raised his head just enough to see something.

"What is it?"

He pointed toward the inn. A woman bundled in a coat looked around furtively. The lights were bright enough to make out her face.

I kept my voice low. "It's EmmyLou."

Casey opened the front door of the inn for her.

We stood up. I looked at Holmes, who still stared at the inn.

"First Vivienne was doing something at the Wagtail Springs Hotel after midnight, and now EmmyLou is out in the middle of the night," he murmured. "Makes a person wonder what's going on."

"There must be some simple explanation," I said, trying to make it seem less suspicious. "Maybe they were meeting someone about a special gift?" But my voice trailed off as I spoke. That wasn't something people did in the middle of the night. There really wasn't a good reason for either of them to be out running around in the wee hours of the morning.

Holmes looked at me and chuckled. "You can't fool me, Holly Miller. You don't believe that for a minute."

"Okay, you're right. I don't. I was trying to be nice. After all, they're going to be your in-laws."

"Holly, don't say anything to Oma and Grandma Rose. Whatever Vivienne and EmmyLou are doing is their business."

I smiled at him. "Just like Oma taught us when we were kids and saw people sneaking around at night at the inn. No problem. I'll keep mum. Why don't you go home? That way EmmyLou won't see you if she's still in the lobby."

"Yeah. That's a good idea. Night, Holly. Thanks for letting me be an elf."

"Good night, Holmes." I walked across the plaza and up the stairs to the front door of the inn. I used my key to open the door, and when I was inside and about to close it, I saw Holmes watching me from the shadows. He waved at me, and I waved back.

I locked the door and turned around, only to find Casey watching me, his arms crossed over his chest. He raised his eyebrows. "Lots of sneaking about tonight, Ms. Elf."

I glanced around. "Where's Twinkletoes?"

"Haven't seen her in hours," said Casey. "I think your nighttime escapades have interrupted her routine."

"Casey, please don't mention anything about the ladies who came in late."

"You and your grandmother have made it very clear that what guests do is none of my business unless the cops show up. But is it just the ladies you don't want me talking about?" He winked at me.

"Men, too?"

"While you went over to get the sleigh." He mock zipped his lips. "That family is a bunch of night owls. Don't they ever sleep?"

I laughed at him and headed upstairs to bed. But when Twinkletoes wasn't in my apartment, I started to worry. I walked down the stairs again, calling softly, "Twinkletoes?"

I located her on the second floor. Twinkletoes lay facing a door, with her front paws tucked underneath her body. Her ears were erect and she was focused on the door.

Instead of room numbers, each of our guest rooms was assigned the name of a cat or dog activity. Twinkletoes was fixated on Sniff. I hoped that didn't mean a mouse had taken refuge there.

I wasn't far from the inn office. Out of curiosity and a little concern, I tiptoed downstairs and checked to see who was occupying Sniff. It was Tim and Linda Kedrowski.

Twinkletoes's behavior was peculiar, but it was the wee hours of the morning. Had it been daytime, I would have knocked to see if anything was wrong, but I couldn't exactly do that at this hour. Maybe one of them was having trouble sleeping. Valerian, a plant that a lot of people took to help them sleep, was a cat attractant, sort of like catnip. Maybe that was what she smelled.

I walked back by Sniff, picked up Twinkletoes, and carried her upstairs to bed.

I was sound asleep when my phone rang at eight in the morning. At the sound of the veterinarian's voice, I sat straight up.

"Good morning, Holly. I wanted you to know that Trixie had a great night. She didn't like being in a cage, but she was thrilled to have so much attention. Except for when we made her throw up, she thought she was having a fun night out at a party. You can pick her up around ten this morning."

I thanked her profusely and bounced out of bed, much too excited to sleep. I showered and threw on jeans. But memories of Norma Jeanne's polished look made me change my mind. I donned white tights, a short green skirt, a fluffy white V-neck sweater, and cute ankle boots. I didn't look city chic, but I didn't feel shabby like I had the day before. I picked up Twinkletoes. "Trixie's coming home!"

Twinkletoes didn't talk much but she mewed softly, and I had a feeling she had missed Trixie. She leaped from my arms and scampered to the kitchen. I knew what that meant. She was reminding me to feed her breakfast before I left.

I peered in the fridge at the dishes prepared by the inn just for cats. "Tuna Party? We *are* celebrating today."

I spooned it into a bowl, and from the way she snarfed her food, I knew I had made the right choice. She was still eating when I left. If she felt like socializing, the pet door that led down the back stairs to the private kitchen was open. She could come and go as she pleased. I walked down the stairs, only to be intercepted by Oma.

"You look festive." She held out her arms for a hug and whispered in my ear, "That wouldn't have anything to do with Holmes, would it?"

"Oma! Absolutely not." It was a lie, and we both knew it.

She winked at me. "Thank you for my stollen, *liebchen*. What a wonderful surprise! Mr. Huckle brought me two slices with my coffee this morning, and they tasted like Christmas. You were so thoughtful to bake the stollen for me."

I hugged her again. "Merry Christmas, Oma. I'm glad you like it."

"But our Trixie!" Oma held one hand against her cheek in dismay. "Mr. Huckle told me what happened."

"The vet just called. She'll be fine. I can pick her up in a couple of hours."

"You will bring her straight home so we can make a fuss over her, yes?"

"I will."

She leaned toward me, grasped my arm, and whispered, "I heard an extra elf joined you last night." When she released me, she raised her eyebrows with excitement.

I knew what she was thinking. My poor Oma was eager to see a romance between Holmes and me. Sotto voce, I said, "When Holmes heard about the elves, he had to join. Don't go reading anything into that. You know how he loves to surprise people. He's such a do-gooder."

"*Ja, ja,*" she said with a grin. "That is our Holmes. Did he bring the other woman with him?"

"Oma! No. NJ was not included."

"Rose and I are very concerned that she is wrong for him."

"That's because you're biased. And because you want him to move back here." I tried to sound like I meant it when I said, "We have to give her a chance. For Holmes's sake."

"It's not just Rose and me who sense this. I'm sure she is a nice person or Holmes wouldn't be interested in her. But she thinks we are beneath her."

"What? I'm sure that's not true."

"I fear it is. She and her cousin, the one who wears peculiar clothes, were overheard being quite critical of Wagtail and the residents. They are snobs, Holly, who think they are superior to others. This is not good for Holmes. I fear that her pretentiousness will cause problems in the long run. Our Holmes is a kind and forgiving man. I do not wish for him to end up in a marriage that he tolerates but that causes him great unhappiness."

"Oma! We hardly know her. Who overheard this conversation?"

"Our own Mr. Huckle."

Ouch. I wished it had been someone else. In spite of his protests to the contrary, Mr. Huckle was a gossip, but he was notoriously reliable and accurate. He wasn't in the least prone to drama.

"Let's say that's the case. Don't you think it would be better for Holmes to come to that realization on his own?"

"Of course," said Oma. "But he might need a little help getting there."

"Don't you and Rose dare pull any of your tricks." I said it with what I hoped was a fierce face. They were known to meddle.

"Me?" She feigned insult. "Would I do such a thing?"

"Yes." The smell of coffee wafted to me. "You and Rose better not spoil things for Holmes. He would never forgive you two for interfering." I went straight to guilt. "How would you feel if you ruined his chance for true love?"

Oma laughed. "Perhaps he would be eternally grateful that we saved him from misery. You, my *liebling*, are far too transparent. You pretend to support Holmes's choice, but it is no accident that you have dressed this way. Trixie doesn't care what you look like." She winked at me again and headed for the office.

I felt very much alone without my little shadow. I passed the Kedrowski family in the dining area. Linda and Tim were eating breakfast with their kids, Tiffany and Blake.

Linda wore a sequined Christmas sweater with a reindeer leaping across her chest.

I couldn't see Blake's full attire, but I thought I could get dizzy from looking at his jacket too long. It was a wild zigzag print of gold, white, black, and silver—the only calm spots for the eyes were the black lapels. His shirt underneath was equally busy, bearing a silvery print of what appeared to be llamas. I smiled at them and nodded a greeting to some other guests.

Instead of being waited on, I ventured into the commercial kitchen and snatched a piece of bacon to munch on while I poured coffee into a mug.

"Cranberry sweet roll?" asked the cook.

I eyed the spiral rolls with cranberries peeking out and a sugar drizzle on the tops. "Of course. What else do you recommend this morning?"

"Smoked salmon eggs Benedict." Cook smiled at me.

My plate loaded with eggs, salmon, and heavenly hollandaise sauce, I returned to the dining area where Twinkletoes usually sat on the hearth of the stone fireplace on cold mornings. Today she was nowhere to be seen. I settled at the table near the fire anyway.

I didn't mean to eavesdrop, but the Kedrowski family was seated nearby. It was impossible to avoid overhearing and watching what was going on. It was a public place, after all.

"I can't wait to plan your wedding, Tiffie." Linda stirred her coffee.

"Don't hold your breath on that, Mom." Blake sneered at his sister.

Tiffany shot him an annoyed look. "Well, I can tell you that I do not want a ceiling of flowers, nor do I wish it to be the social event of the year."

"I think Barry wishes Norma Jeanne would change her mind about that." Tim took a bite of a cranberry sweet roll.

"I understand Norma Jeanne," said Linda. "It's a once-in-a-lifetime thing. All women want their weddings to be special."

High notes tinkled, signaling that a cell phone was ringing.

Linda frowned. "Tim! Not at the table, please."

Tim glanced at his phone. "I have to take this, honey." He rose and walked toward the front door. It wasn't long before he returned.

"Tim, we talked about this. We're on holiday." Linda was clearly unhappy.

"It was work. I may not be there, but the Thackleberry plant doesn't close down in my absence."

I had just refilled my coffee when a tall man about my age loped in. His blond hair was cut short in the back and on the sides, but the front was long enough to hang down in his eyes. His black turtleneck and trousers emphasized his height and lankiness. With a long face and a pronounced nose, I wouldn't have called him handsome, but his height and confidence made quite an impression. He wasn't the type one would easily forget. He strode over to Tiffany, who jumped up to hug him.

"Austin! You're finally here!"

Blake looked on, his mouth agape.

"Mom, Dad, Blake," said Tiffany, "this is Austin Conroy, my boyfriend whose flight was delayed." She shot a satisfied smirk at her brother.

"Austin," breathed Linda. "We are delighted to meet you. Please join us for breakfast."

Tiffany's father, Tim, rose and shook towering Austin's hand. "Glad to meet you."

Austin pulled up a chair.

"And this," Tiffany crowed with glee, "is my evil brother, Blake."

The two men nodded at each other.

Austin studied Blake for a moment. "You look familiar. Have we met?"

A moment of panic crossed Blake's face. "I don't think so. Which agency did she get you from?"

"Agency?" asked Austin. "I'm sorry, I don't follow."

"He thinks I paid you to be here." Tiffany's eyes narrowed, and she glared at her brother.

Linda paled. "Blake! Don't be rude to Tiffie's guest." She leaned toward her husband and asked, "Is that possible?"

Tim nodded but smiled pleasantly. "What do you do for a living, Austin?"

"I'm a CPA with Schwoerer, Coxon, and Conroy."

Tim appeared surprised.

"I think I have heard of them. A CPA, and already a partner in that big company," Linda gushed, obviously very pleased.

"The Conroy in the name is actually my dad, so don't be too impressed."

Blake shook his head. "Amazing. Have you been on stage? You're a terrific actor."

Austin appeared uncomfortable, but Tiffany placed a loving hand on his shoulder. "Pay no attention to Blakey. He's just sore because now Mom will be after *him* to find someone."

"That's not true, Austin." Linda smiled widely. "Our Blake is in medical school. There will be plenty of time for romance when he's finished. Right, Blake?"

Tiffany regarded her brother with suspicious eyes.

Just then, Vivienne joined her family at the table and the introductions began again.

"Where's Dale?" asked Linda.

"I'm sure I don't know." Vivi grimaced. "He's probably out wasting money on some other ridiculous holiday event. I wish you wouldn't encourage him to do that kind of thing."

I finished the last bite of my eggs and felt totally guilty for wanting to eat the cranberry roll. But the white icing almost sparkled on top, and the red cranberries peeked out like jewels. It was like dessert at breakfast! I checked the time. Over an hour before Trixie would be sprung. I tried to eat slowly. Finally, I couldn't stand it anymore. So what if I showed up early to pick up Trixie?

I stood up but hadn't taken more than two steps when Norma Jeanne walked in. She looked directly at me and stopped mid-step. Her eyes widened. Her mouth opened. And then she let out a little scream.

Eleven

All eyes were on Norma Jeanne. For a long moment, I thought she might faint.

Austin stood up. "NJ? Is that you? I can't believe it."

Aha! Apparently she had *not* been looking at me. That was a relief.

He skirted the table and headed for her, his arms open wide. "What are you doing here?"

They hugged like old friends.

Tiffany hissed, "Noooo!" Her hands clenched into little balls.

"How long has it been?" asked Austin.

Norma Jeanne blinked at him as though she couldn't believe her eyes. "Eight years?"

Linda, who didn't appear to have noticed Tiffany's horror, called, "Norma Jeanne, come and join us."

Austin pulled up a chair for Norma Jeanne.

"How do you two know each other?" asked Linda, smiling and apparently still oblivious to her daughter's distress.

"Austin and I dated when we were in college." Norma Jeanne smiled sweetly at Austin.

But poor Tiffany looked like the life had drained right out of her.

I was walking away when I heard Tiffany declare in a very loud voice, "We're all having Christmas here this year to celebrate Norma Jeanne's engagement. Isn't that wonderful?"

I glanced back just in time to see Tiffany smile again rather smugly.

Maybe she had realized that Norma Jeanne wasn't a threat to her relationship with Austin after all. I cut through the private kitchen and walked up to my apartment for a warm jacket. I felt like a child anticipating her Christmas gift. I could barely wait to pick up my little Trixie.

I rushed down the grand staircase, hoping I wouldn't be waylaid by anyone. Trying not to make eye contact, I walked by guests quickly and stopped in the office to retrieve a golf cart key. I waved to Oma and Zelda and stepped outside. It was a beautiful day with clear blue skies and a lovely brisk nip in the air. I hopped into a golf cart and took off for the veterinary hospital.

On the way, I passed a group of visitors piling out of a Wagtail taxi. In addition to the green, which was a walking zone, Wagtail had limited access by automobile. Nonresidents parked outside town and were brought in via golf carts, known locally as Wagtail taxis.

When I walked through the doors of the veterinary hospital, I felt far better than I had the night before. One of the vet techs carried Trixie out to me. Her tail wagged nonstop, and she bestowed doggy kisses on the vet tech's chin.

When Trixie saw me, she wrestled like a wild tiger to be released. On the floor, she pranced around me in excited circles. I knelt on the floor and was soon covered in kisses. But suddenly something distracted her, and she ran past me.

I turned around in time to see Holmes sweep her up in his arms.

"What are you doing here?" I blurted.

"I had to make sure my favorite girl was okay."

I shot him a doubtful look. How could he have known to be here? Unless Oma had called his grandmother . . .

My thoughts were interrupted by the vet tech.

"Trixie was so much fun last night," she said. "Because of the holidays we don't have a lot of animals in ICU right now, so she got a lot of attention and seemed to love every minute of it."

I paid the bill while Trixie continued to dance around. When I opened the door, she shot outside, ran straight to our golf cart, and hopped onto the seat.

Holmes and I followed her.

"Need a ride?" I asked Holmes.

"Thanks, but I have Grandma Rose's golf cart."

He pointed at it. Boxes were piled on the back seat. "I'm supposed to deliver those to the inn."

"A surprise for Norma Jeanne?" My smile faded as I realized he might be in for a big surprise when he found out her old boyfriend had shown up. I wondered if I should mention it to warn him. Part of me thought I should mind my own business. Would I want to know if I were in his shoes? Yes. I would. I would want to be prepared.

I sucked in a deep breath. "Have you talked to Norma Jeanne this morning?"

"Nope. Grandma Rose barely gave me time to shower before sending me over here to help you."

I clearly didn't need any help. And she wouldn't have known that I was here at all unless a certain German Oma had called her. They were up to something.

Holmes frowned at me. "Do you have time for a mug of hot chocolate?"

"Don't tell me it's in the golf cart under those boxes."

He checked his watch. "Help me unload these at the inn, and then we'll sneak away for a hot chocolate. Just the two of us. I haven't eaten breakfast yet."

"Okay. I'd like that." If he happened to run into Norma Jeanne's old boyfriend at the inn, well, I couldn't really help that. Maybe I could break it to him over hot chocolate.

I hopped into my golf cart and gave Trixie a big hug. "We missed you last night," I whispered.

Her dark eyes were bright and her tail wagged. She yelped, which I interpreted as, "Let's go, already!"

I followed Holmes back. When Trixie ran through the doors to the reception lobby, a cheer went up. Zelda, Mr. Huckle, Oma, and Rose fussed over her and fed her little treats.

"No more eating Oma's stollen!" scolded Oma.

"It is delicious, though." Rose looked over at me. "I just had a slice."

Zelda, who had a side business as an animal communicator, said, "Trixie is very happy to be home and she says in the future, she will try to steal only things that have already been baked."

"Could you please tell her it's not nice to steal food?" I asked. I wasn't sure Zelda could talk to animals as she claimed, but it couldn't hurt to have her try to explain that to Trixie.

"She's resistant to that idea and says she'll consider it only if you give her more treats."

That sounded like Trixie. Maybe Zelda really could read her mind.

"So where do you want these boxes, Grandma?" asked Holmes.

"Those are my Christmas village houses. I was telling Linda that I didn't have time to put them up this year, and she's itching to do it here."

"I set up some tables for her in the lobby," I said.

"I saw them. An excellent spot," said Mr. Huckle, nodding his approval.

We loaded the boxes of houses, lights, bushes, trees, bridges, and fences onto carts and rolled them toward the lobby. The entire way there I hoped we wouldn't run into Austin. Maybe I should have warned Holmes about his unexpected arrival after all.

But my intentions were forgotten when Rupert marched through the front door, his face as ruddy as the inside of a blood orange.

He strode up to me and boomed, "Your crazy Aunt Birdie killed my Grinch!"

Twelve

"Killed it?" I repeated, making sure I had understood correctly.

"That's right. She done stabbed it to death. I never knew a woman so doggoned mean. She won't stop at anything to git her own way."

I swallowed hard. "Did you see her do it?"

Just beyond Rupert, I couldn't help noticing that Norma Jeanne seemed a little uncomfortable as Austin was introduced to Holmes.

So much for hot chocolate with Holmes. I waved goodbye to Holmes and forced myself to focus on Rupert.

". . . I didn't have to see her. I knew who done it."

"I'll have a talk with Aunt Birdie right away."

"Just so you know, I called Officer Dave already. She might be in the slammer by now."

I certainly hoped not! Aunt Birdie was a pill, but she didn't deserve to be in jail. I promised Rupert I would take care of it, poor language at best, since I didn't know what I could do about it. Leaving in haste, I stopped by Oma's office to let her know what was going on.

"Do you think Trixie should stay here with me and rest?" asked Oma.

Trixie seemed fine and happy, but after her treatment, maybe that was a good idea. I left her lounging comfortably on the sofa in the office and walked toward Rupert's house.

On my way, I phoned Dave, who was already at Rupert's inspecting the damage. No one had been arrested yet. I picked up my speed.

A small crowd had gathered at Rupert's house once again. Ironic, I thought. They had come when the Grinch annoyed them and now again for its death.

Rupert had returned and appeared to be relishing the attention. Were the previously angry neighbors sympathizing with him?

I made my way through them to Dave, who was inspecting slashes in the material. The poor Grinch had collapsed into an enormous heap. "How did you find the holes?" I asked. "This thing is huge."

He glanced up at me. "They were apparent when Rupert tried to blow it up again." He shook his head. "It took a really sharp instrument and some force to get through this material."

"Whew! Then I guess Aunt Birdie is off the hook?"

"Nope. Not saying that at all. Just making an observation."

"She wasn't the only one who was upset by the Grinch, you know."

A man whom I recognized from the bookstore said, "Those people didn't have any Christmas spirit. I thought it was the best decoration I'd ever seen. In fact, I'm going to try to fix him."

No! Oh no. The only good thing about someone slashing the Grinch was that the controversy would be over.

Dave shook his head. "Can't fix it yet. It's a crime scene."

"Nobody's dead," said the man. "I brought special wide tape made for repairing plastic like this. Lemme fix the Grinch."

A chant went up in the crowd. *"Fix the Grinch. Fix the Grinch!"*

There was no question that Dave was annoyed. "Now look what you started. I don't want you touching the Grinch until I get this matter resolved. Do you understand me? There may not be a body, but it's still destruction of private property."

I watched Dave carefully. Did he really think he was going to find the person who slit the Grinch? There wasn't a grown man in Wagtail who didn't have a fishing or hunting knife. Even the ones who didn't hunt or fish owned them. And there were plenty of talented cooks in town who surely had some scary-looking kitchen knives.

Rupert edged up to us. "What if I don't press charges?"

"It's still a crime to damage property."

"What if I done it myself?"

"And reported it as a crime?" Dave stared at him in disbelief. "That would be a different kind of crime."

"Drat you, Dave Quinlan!" Rupert shouted. "I wanna put the Grinch back up. I'm not waiting two years until you realize you ain't gonna pin it on Aunt Birdie. She may be a cantankerous old harpy but she ain't dumb. Besides, look at all these people who liked it. Now what do I gotta do to make that happen without breakin' the law?"

Dave seemed pained by his question. "Don't you think the person who did this will do it again?"

"Maybe Aunt Birdie don't want to go to jail, and she'll reconsider now that she got off scot-free once."

Fat chance.

"It's up to you, Rupert," said Dave. "If you want to put the Grinch back up and forget all about this, then in the spirit of the holidays, I'll just pretend it never happened."

He wouldn't, of course. I knew Dave better than that. But I was relieved for Aunt Birdie and wasn't about to object, even if it meant more complaints about the Grinch. They would be a small price to pay to keep Aunt Birdie out of the slammer.

"But," said Dave hastily, "only if you agree to the terms you arranged with the mayor. Lights off at midnight and music at a tolerable level. And no more playing "Aunt Birdie Got Run Over by a Reindeer."

Rupert grinned. "Shucks! That's my favorite Christmas song."

Dave couldn't hold back a smile.

We walked toward the street.

"You headed to Aunt Birdie's?" he asked.

"How did you ever guess?"

"Mind if I come along?" He kept pace with me.

"As long as you don't arrest her."

"I hope to heaven I never have to do that. You don't mind if I put a scare in her, do you?"

"Not a bit."

It wasn't far to Aunt Birdie's house, just around the block, really. No wonder the Grinch had upset her so much.

We strolled up to her house. Swags of pine with large lights hung from the roof of her porch. The steps leading to the porch were flanked by matching pots of greenery, with tall yet delicate red spirals reaching up from the middle. Round red ornaments had been artfully arranged to look like they were growing out of the pots. Boxwood wreaths hung on her windows, attached by red ribbons. In the corner of the porch, a live tree sparkled with tiny lights. I had to admit that she had one of the prettiest porches in Wagtail this holiday.

I knocked on the door.

Aunt Birdie readily swung it open. She wore a long black skirt with a bulky cream sweater. It was very basic, but it draped perfectly on her thin figure and set off her dark hair with the white streak in it. "Holly! What a surprise. No gift in your hand? And a cop by your side. Do you need bail money? I would be delighted to see you, but you never come around unless there's trouble."

"Good morning, Aunt Birdie." I skipped past her slights and tried to butter her up. "You are coming for brunch on Christmas Day?"

"I loathe spending the holidays with inn guests, but I suppose that's my only choice."

"Ms. Dupuy," said Dave politely, "someone cut holes in Rupert Grimpley's Grinch. Would you know anything about that?"

"Me? I hope you jest, young Dave. Have you run out of scoundrels and miscreants to accuse of such things?" Aunt Birdie did a good job of appearing to be shocked. She spoke with confidence.

"You realize that it's a crime to destroy someone else's property, no matter how much it annoys you." Although Dave phrased it as a question, he spoke as though it was fact.

"Are you implying that I had a hand in it?" Aunt Birdie scowled at me. "Is this why you came here? To berate me?"

"You live so close," I said. "We thought you might have seen or heard something." There, that would make her feel important.

Her expression softened. "Well, that's different. I whole-heartedly thank whoever did it. Rupert should never have been allowed to set up that monstrosity in the first place. And if you—" she pointed at Dave with a gnarled forefinger

"—had any guts, you'd have made him take it down for good the very first night."

Dave opened his mouth, but Aunt Birdie wasn't through. "And I've got half a mind to skip Christmas at the inn because your grandmother is in cahoots with Rupert. I know she's letting him carry on just to annoy me. Some Christmas gift!"

She slammed the door.

Dave massaged his forehead with one hand.

The two of us turned and walked away.

"Good job of scaring her," I said.

"Did you notice how she avoided denying any involvement?"

"Yeah." I sighed. "I sure did. She's lucky you're not pursuing it."

"Maybe I should keep an eye on it tonight."

I winced. "Please don't arrest Aunt Birdie."

"You know I can't promise that. She doesn't have any right to run around town tearing down things she doesn't like."

I shot him my best pleading look.

"I ran into Holmes last night," Dave said.

"You met Norma Jeanne?"

Dave shook his head. "He was by himself taking a walk around town."

"He told me he misses Wagtail."

At that moment, a little girl ran up to us. "I lost my doggy!"

Dave sounded reassuring when he said, "I'll help you find him." But before he walked away, he looked at me and said, "Wagtail isn't all he misses."

I strolled home with my heart beating way too fast. Surely he couldn't have meant what I hoped? That Holmes missed me, too? Still, a tiny ray of hope lingered in my head.

I made it back to the inn in time for lunch. In spite of my big breakfast, I was starving and knew Trixie would be, too. I picked her up at the inn office where Oma and Rose were discussing the recent rash of thefts in town. Trixie and I ventured toward the dining area.

In the lobby, the Kedrowski family and Austin were clustered around the Christmas village that Linda was arranging. In just a few hours, she had created a charming tableau.

"Linda, this is beautiful," I gushed. "I can't believe the details."

She had set up a little village with railroad tracks, stone bridges, and an ice-skating pond.

Linda beamed at the praise. "It's not finished yet, but I'm having such a fun time. I'm in my element."

Tiffany backed up and aimed her camera at it.

"Oh, please," moaned Blake. "This is the height of kitsch. Must you photograph it?"

Tiffany snapped the picture, stepped away, and turned her camera to capture him with the village. "Why are you such a Scrooge? It's so pretty, and Mom worked hard on it while you were out doing heaven knows what this morning."

"How is it possible that we're related?" Blake groaned. "You and Mom have questionable taste. Really, only Norma Jeanne and I appear to have gotten the gene for culture and style."

"I beg your pardon? Have you looked in a mirror, Blake? Your jacket shines brighter than the sun." Tiffany acted like a 1940s drama queen, holding her hand to her head in agony. "Oh, oh! I need my sunglasses."

"Honestly, it was so pleasant when the two of you were out running around," their father groused. "Can't you try to get along?"

They were adults, so I presumed they knew better than to behave so snarkily toward each other.

The front door opened. A German shepherd trotted inside, a small bandage on her front paw. She headed straight to Trixie, wagging her tail. They sniffed each other politely.

EmmyLou and her husband, Barry, followed.

Tiffany shrieked and ran to the German shepherd. "Maggie! I didn't know you were here."

EmmyLou smiled wanly. "She wouldn't miss Christmas."

"Where has she been?" asked Linda. "I wondered why you didn't bring her with you."

EmmyLou and Barry exchanged a look.

Thirteen

"Where is Norma Jeanne?" asked Barry.

"I haven't seen her. What's going on?" Linda frowned at them.

EmmyLou mashed her lips together and appeared to be on the verge of tears.

Barry placed an arm around her shoulder. "Maggie has been at the animal hospital having some tests done."

"She doesn't look sick," said Tiffany, "except for her leg. What happened?"

"Her leg is fine. The bandage is just where she had an IV. We can take that off in an hour or so," Barry explained. "They did all kinds of tests. We'll know more in a couple of days."

EmmyLou covered her mouth with her hand and walked slowly toward the elevator as though she were the one who was sick. Maggie followed, sniffing the inn as she went.

"Oh no, is it something bad? This must be devastating to EmmyLou," said Linda softly.

Barry nodded. "We'd appreciate it if you didn't say any-thing to Norma Jeanne. This is a special holiday for her. We don't want to spoil it for her. Norma Jeanne isn't crazy about Maggie anyway. We don't want Norma Jeanne's joyous time here upstaged by a dying dog."

Tiffany gasped. "Dying?"

"We took Maggie to our vet at home because she was limping. That turned out to be nothing, but an ultrasound turned up something far worse. He sent us here for more tests. We're going to pretend as though it's nothing for now. We want all of you to have a fun Christmas. EmmyLou and I will baby Maggie while Norma Jeanne and Holmes enjoy their engagement."

They all nodded in agreement.

He frowned. "Assuming that EmmyLou can stop crying."

I left them to their family matters and grabbed a quick lunch of macaroni and cheese with a to-die-for crunchy, salty topping. Trixie snarfed the spaghetti and meatballs. I felt a little guilty for indulging, but Trixie and I were going to spend the afternoon outside in the Christkindl booth. We needed sustenance against the cold.

The bald man who had told me about the Thackleberry fabric problem was eating by himself at a table near the fireplace. He nodded to me in greeting.

After we ate, I filled a thermos with sweet hot tea and dressed Trixie in a down coat. I wrapped up in a heavy sweater and a down vest. We walked outside and replaced Shelley, who was glad to see us.

"I've been spying on the Thackleberry family for you," she said.

"Shelley!" I scolded. But I wanted to hear what she knew.

"They're actually fairly nice people, except for that guy, Blake, who acts like he's some kind of superstar who is too good to mingle with us peasants. Norma Jeanne is a *big* shopper. She's visiting every store with Blake, but they can't carry their purchases. Everything must be delivered to the inn for them. Tiffany hates Norma Jeanne. You can see it in the way she looks at her."

I couldn't help laughing. "Oh, the horror! Cousins and siblings spatting with each other. And Norma Jeanne likes to shop! They sound fairly normal to me."

Shelley laughed and took off, eager for a warm lunch.

Trixie amused me by visiting the other stalls. I knew what my rascal was doing—begging for treats. After she made the rounds and came back to our booth, she stood outside on her hind legs, placed her paws against the glass cookie case, and gazed at them longingly.

"I'm quite sure you have had enough for the time being," I told her.

She wagged her tail and smiled at me hopefully.

I found the tiniest cookie we had, very thin and no bigger than the nail on my pinkie, and used it to coax her inside. "No more cookies for you, Miss Cookie Monster."

Around one in the afternoon, EmmyLou came by with Maggie. Much like Trixie had, Maggie placed her paws on the cookie display and gazed at them.

"Holly," said EmmyLou, "I want to apologize for being such a mess. I thought I would be able to hide my sadness, but as you know, that didn't work out."

"No problem at all, EmmyLou. I was a basket case last night when Trixie was sick."

"We're waiting for the report on the cells they extracted from Maggie's kidney. I don't know whether it's worse to wait or to get the bad news."

"I'm so sorry."

"Our doctor at home was nice, but his words, *you may not want to fix this dog*, keep going through my head."

"That's awful!"

"I know he didn't mean to sound so callous, but that's what he said. There are two major organs involved, a kidney and the liver, and, well, I know everyone expects the worst."

I sought something hopeful to say to her. "If anyone can help, it's the doctors in Wagtail. They're outstanding." They were hollow words, even if they were true.

EmmyLou nodded. "I know. That's why we brought her to a specialist here. My dad and I have been coming to Wagtail for a long time. Even before it became a pet resort. And now so many of the stores carry our products that we have a reason to visit. We always made a point of having at least one meal out on your terrace overlooking the lake. This is our first wintertime visit. Maggie loves coming here where she can run around off leash and go hiking in the woods."

"Which cookie flavor does Maggie like best?" I asked. "Peanut butter, gingerbread, carob, cheese, or bacon?"

"Definitely bacon!"

Maggie didn't seem one bit sick when she focused on the cookie and extended her head as far forward as possible to reach it. I handed over a bacon-flavored dog cookie in the shape of a Santa hat.

She munched it on the spot.

Tiffany strode up, carrying a stack of papers, and promptly hugged Maggie. "How's our favorite girl?"

EmmyLou did her best, but I could tell she was trying hard not to cry.

"EmmyLou, I'm glad I caught up to you. I know you have a lot on your mind, but I'd like you to take a look at this." Tiffany handed her the papers.

While EmmyLou examined them, Tiffany gazed at our wares. "Are those our dog dresses?" she asked.

"They are! I hadn't realized how many Thackleberry dog and cat garments I own. You definitely make the cutest ones on the market."

"Thanks! I'm glad to hear that." Tiffany glanced around

before asking, "Has anyone brought them back or complained about them?"

I thought it best to be truthful, even if it hurt. This was their livelihood, after all. "None have been returned, and I have not received any complaints. But a guy stopped by yesterday and said something about them making dogs itch and lose their fur."

Tiffany groaned.

EmmyLou handed the papers back to Tiffany. "I don't understand. How can animals be allergic to our fabrics all of a sudden? Did we change suppliers?"

Tiffany shook her head. "I talked to Grampy about it last night. The really bad news is that someone started a website for complaints. I checked with some stores in Wagtail yesterday. They're not sure if they'll reorder because people are refusing to buy our products."

EmmyLou wiped hair out of her forehead. "This is a nightmare. Have you seen Dad? I'd like to talk with him, too. This is the first I've heard of it."

"I spent the morning with Austin. If I see Grampy, I'll let him know you're looking for him."

EmmyLou checked her watch. "I'll see if I can find him. How about meeting us at three o'clock at Café Chat?" She and Maggie left immediately.

Tiffany sighed. "Can you believe this? A business crisis over our Christmas holiday *and* Norma Jeanne after *my* boyfriend!"

"But she's engaged. I'm sure you have nothing to worry about."

Tiffany eyed me. "You obviously don't know Norma Jeanne. There's nothing she wouldn't do to get what she wants."

Funny, I was under the distinct impression that what she wanted was Holmes.

Tiffany mashed her lips together. "Come to think of it, I

haven't seen Norma Jeanne or Austin for a while. Excuse me."

She passed Holmes on her way to the inn. I couldn't help noticing the difference in their attitudes. Tiffany appeared to be in a panic, moving swiftly, while Holmes loped toward me, stopping to greet people and grinning like the happiest man on the planet.

He finally reached the Christkindl booth. "This market is so cool. Grandma Rose says it's going to be an annual thing."

"It's been a lot of fun. Even though it's cold outside, it's great to get out of the inn and do something different."

"Holmes!" Norma Jeanne shouted from the porch of the inn. She waved, holding papers in her hand, and hurried toward him. "Honestly! I keep losing track of you."

"Want to amble through the Christkindl booths with me?" Holmes asked.

"We don't have time for that. After we missed each other this morning, I printed out a schedule for the day. We have facials at two and massages at three thirty, which will just give us enough time to change into dinner attire before Yappy Hour." She thrust a schedule at him.

Holmes frowned as he looked at it. "I was planning to see some of my friends. Why don't you do those things and then meet us at Hair of the Dog?"

"I have to go all alone?"

"Maybe Tiffany or your mom would like to go with you."

I felt a little guilty for listening to their discussion. But I was trapped. It wasn't like I could move away.

"Holmes!" She placed her hand on his jacket and made a pouty face. "This is our special time together. You'll spoil the whole holiday if you don't come with me."

"NJ, I think you know I'm not a facial kind of guy."

"You would love them if you just tried."

"I'm sorry, I promised some old friends I would meet up with them."

"You should have told me so I could have planned accordingly. You know how I hate to deviate from a schedule."

"Hair of the Dog. Anyone can tell you how to get there. Just come when you're ready."

Obviously miffed, she turned on her heel and marched away, her head held high.

"You're in big trouble," I joked.

"It's a little odd being told what to do on your own stomping grounds. I never gave her obsessive planning much thought in Chicago. But last night she didn't want to stop by to see my folks just because it wasn't on her schedule and hadn't been planned in advance. My own parents!" His eyebrows dipped in the middle. "Not sure I like this regimentation when I'm home. I'd like to kick back and visit with friends and family."

"She wants to be with you."

His lips pulled tight. "You're saying I'm being a jerk. I'm not going to stand up the guys. But I'd better be a gentleman and smooth things over. See you later, Holly." He ran after her calling her name.

Great job, Holly, I thought. They had an argument and somehow, I managed to convince him to settle it. I was beginning to think I was my own worst enemy and should do what everyone had suggested—pull pranks on Norma Jeanne.

At three thirty, Zelda relieved me so I could take a break. Trixie and I nabbed some cranberry scones and tea and settled at a table in the dining area of the inn to warm up.

I saw Linda first. She walked through the lobby slowly, as if she were looking for someone. When she saw Tim, they exchanged a few hushed words. Then Tim strolled through the dining area, gazing around, and walked into the library. Very peculiar.

I didn't see Tim, Linda, Holmes, or most of the Thackleberry clan for the rest of the day. The Christkindl booth and my duties at the inn kept me busy, and Rose had arranged for activities and a special dinner for the Thackleberrys. But I couldn't get Dave's words out of my head. Holmes missed something besides Wagtail. It could be his parents, or his old pals. It could be hiking or the mountains, which were oddly addictive.

Just before midnight, I changed into my elf suit again, dressed Trixie in hers, and headed for the golf cart sleigh.

It was the night before Christmas Eve. Many of the people who owned cabins on Wagtail Mountain had arrived for the holiday. At Christmas, cities were stunning with all the glam and glitter, but there was something special about the coziness of a cabin in the snowy mountains for the holidays.

Even though it was past midnight and the crowds had dwindled, couples walked hand in hand through the green, which was quite romantic decked out in snow and sparkling lights on the trees. Trixie ran ahead of me, showing no ill effects from her poor dining choice the night before. Tonight's elf mission was to deliver bulky necessities to seniors in need. The Sugar Maple Inn handyman had received donations from stores around town and stashed them in the sleigh so it would be ready to go. As I understood it, there were vacuum cleaners, at least two small garden tillers, a couple of humidifiers, a chain saw, four giant cat trees, and a puppy corral. They didn't seem like much, but they would be cherished by those who needed them.

On the way over, Trixie stopped, lifted her nose, and sniffed the air. I stopped too, and sniffed the air. Did she smell a fire? All I could pick up was the lovely scent of fireplaces in use.

She took off running.

"Trixie!" I called.

There was no stopping her. I ran after her awkwardly in my elf shoes. Fortunately, she was going in the direction of Rose's house, where the sleigh awaited us.

But then she veered west and kept going with me stumbling after her and calling her name. She led me straight to Rupert's house, where she barked at the Grinch. It stood tall and dark in the night. Rupert had abided by Oma's rule that he turn off the music and the lights.

The trouble was—that wasn't Trixie's ordinary bark. It was the bark that sent chills through me. The one I had come to know all too well. It meant something was very wrong. Dead wrong.

I hoped no one had hurt Rupert.

"Trixie, shush. You'll wake the entire neighborhood." She kept barking at the Grinch, running around it, and sniffing at the base.

I tried to grab her, but she pranced away from me and continued to bark.

"Trixie, there's nothing here. It's just a blow-up Grinch. You saw it before."

She didn't listen to my reasoning. She darted away from me every time I got near. But her focus never strayed from the Grinch.

Was it because the light wasn't on? Surely not.

"What's goin' on out here?" Rupert walked toward me.

"I'm so sorry. I hope she didn't wake you."

"Naw. I'm puttin' a mane on a rockin' horse."

I glanced at him in surprise. "You're like Santa!"

He gestured toward me. "You oughta know, Ms. Elf."

"I can't imagine what set her off."

"Maybe a critter got inside there and can't git out."

"Inside the Grinch?"

"Sure. That's where the lights and everything are. I'll get a flashlight."

He was back in a snap. "Let's have a look."

He led me around to a nearly invisible door and opened it. Trixie scrambled past our legs in her zeal to enter.

Rupert shone the light inside. I stepped over the rim of

the base to enter. Even in the semi-darkness, I could make out Trixie's white fur as she sniffed something.

A large, dark mound lay inside. Far too big for a wood-land creature, unless it was a deer or a bear, and that seemed unlikely.

Rupert stepped in behind me. "Watcha see, little Trixie?" He aimed the flashlight toward the middle.

Dale Thackleberry was sprawled on the bottom of the Grinch.

Fourteen

Dale lay on his back. I rushed toward him and dropped to my knees.

Rupert followed and shone the light on Dale's face. "You know him? I never saw this guy before."

"Dale Thackleberry. He manufactures dog clothes." I grabbed Dale's hand. It was as cold as the food in a refrigerator. It was probably too late for him.

"Looks like he's a goner," said Rupert. "Friend of yours?"

"He's—" I corrected myself "—he was staying at the inn."

Trembling, I pulled out my cell phone. Because of the mountains, Wagtail was notorious for dead spots. I hoped this wasn't one of them.

"I better call from my landline," said Rupert. He departed immediately.

I tried punching in 911 anyway but couldn't get a signal.

Overcome with sadness, I hoped he wasn't dead. I slid my fingers under Dale's turtleneck in a desperate search for a pulse. His skin felt cold. His pulse had probably stopped quite some time ago.

Trixie had quit barking. She sat down beside Dale as though she knew for sure what I didn't want to accept.

There was nothing to do but wait.

Dave arrived in a matter of minutes. "This is Dale?"

"Yes."

"His family reported him missing a few hours ago."

"They did? No one mentioned that to me. I think he's been here awhile." Much like I had, he checked for a pulse. He shook his head and sighed when he didn't find one. He gently tried to flex Dale's fingers. He sucked in a deep breath. "It was mighty cold outside. I don't know if his fingers are stiff from the cold or if rigor mortis has set in. I already called the rescue squad so we wouldn't waste any time, but it's way too late for this guy."

Dave crouched and eyed Dale head to toe.

"What are you doing?" I asked.

"I don't see any obvious cause of death."

Dave heaved his body slightly and rolled him away from us. His hands supporting Dale's back, he said, "Shine the flashlight on him, will you?"

I picked it up and aimed it at Dale's underside.

"There it is." Dave ducked his head to examine Dale more closely. "Aw man." Dave scowled. "At Christmas, too. What's wrong with people?"

Dale wore a lightweight winter jacket with leather on the collar and wrists. There was no doubting the blood on the back of it, even though the jacket was a dark gray color.

"What do you think happened to him?" I asked.

Dave rolled him back, stood, and reached out for the flashlight. I handed it to him, and he flashed the beam around the interior of the Grinch. "You touch anything in here?"

"Only Dale. I don't see anything else to touch except the walls of the Grinch."

Dave nodded. "He's been stabbed. More than once."

The rescue squad arrived just then, and Dave motioned for me to leave. I picked up Trixie and stepped outside to make room for them.

Neighbors had begun to wander out to see what was happening. Most had thrown winter coats or jackets over bathrobes. One woman wore curlers in her hair.

Lights flashed as photos were taken inside the Grinch.

The chatter among them was quiet but died down completely when Dale's body was carried out and loaded into an ambulance for transit to Snowball. From experience, I knew they would send him to the medical examiner in Roanoke for an autopsy.

Holmes ran up to me, breathless. "Everyone is looking for you. We were worried when you didn't show up at Grandma Rose's garage. What's going on?"

"I'm so sorry, Holmes. Someone murdered Dale."

"Thackleberry?"

"I'm afraid so."

Maybe it was my imagination, but I thought I saw a tremor run through him.

"Oh no." Holmes rubbed his forehead. "He was such a terrific guy. They'll be devastated. He was the backbone of that family."

"EmmyLou is going to take it very hard. Losing her father! Some Christmas."

Dave strode over to us. "I'm sorry, Holmes. I hear he was a friend of yours?"

"Almost my grandfather-in-law."

His hands gloved, Dave held up a wallet. "Looks like he was mugged. There's not a dollar in his wallet. No credit cards, either. I hope the idiot who took them uses them soon so we can arrest him."

Mugged and thrown into the Grinch? That didn't sound right to me.

Holmes sighed. "I hope you don't mind if I skip elf business tonight. I think I should be with Dave when he tells the Thackleberrys."

"Of course. I should probably go back to the inn to make some tea for them or something. Maybe we can do double elf duty tomorrow night."

On the walk back, as soon as we could get signals, Holmes phoned Zelda and I phoned Shelley to let them know what was going on and call off the elf excursion.

The inn was quiet when we entered. EmmyLou and Tiffany lingered by the dying embers of the fire in the Dogwood Room, probably too concerned about Dale to sleep.

Holmes and Dave walked straight to them.

I heard sobs before I made it to the inn kitchen.

Casey emerged from the private kitchen. "What's going on?"

I explained what had happened and enlisted his help in putting on coffee and tea, and searching for something to serve the family.

I found a glistening raspberry cheesecake and set it on a serving plate. I quickly spread the cook's fabulous pimiento cheese on bread for sandwiches, cut off the crusts, and piled them on a tray. While ham biscuits were heating and Casey was eating some cold ones, I arranged red velvet cupcakes with luscious cream cheese icing on a larger tray.

When everything was ready, I loaded it all onto a cart with cream, sugar, napkins, dessert plates, and mugs. Taking a deep breath to fortify myself, I pushed it across the lobby and into the Dogwood Room.

Members of the family were still traipsing down the stairs in their sleeping attire.

Norma Jeanne, I noted, wore a flowing silk bathrobe in a shade of pink that verged on nude. It was beautifully tailored and looked like something from a 1940s movie. Her matching slippers bore feather trim on the front and had little kitten heels on them.

Her father, Barry, wrapped in a hunter green bathrobe, hugged her mother, EmmyLou, to him. Maggie, the German shepherd, whined at EmmyLou's ankles. Tiffany cried. Austin seemed awkwardly uncomfortable, as if he didn't know what to do. He probably didn't.

Dale's mother, Doris, sat quietly in a chair, clutching Muffy. Her head bent forward over the dog.

Linda appeared to be in shock. Her husband Tim asked me if we had anything stronger than coffee to drink.

"Of course." I finished unloading the cart so people could help themselves.

As I passed the grand staircase, Blake nearly ran into me. He wore a silky short-sleeved top in blue with a loud dragon print and matching shorts. Over it, he had draped a black velvet robe that hung open. But I thought he could probably see better if he took off his sunglasses.

I took a minute to dash upstairs to Oma's apartment. I didn't usually wake her for these middle-of-the-night matters, not that they occurred often, but she knew Dale, and I felt she would want to know.

I knocked on her door softly. Gingersnap probably woke her. Oma opened the door, and Gingersnap barreled out, wagging her tail with delight at the midnight excitement.

I explained what had happened.

Oma sagged and retreated into her apartment to sit down. "Not Dale," she moaned. "Does Dave have any idea who would do such a terrible thing?"

"I doubt it. He's downstairs with the family now."

"I will come to help you. Give me a moment to change my clothes."

I left with Gingersnap, collected the cart, and went straight to our liquor selection. We didn't often serve liquor at the inn, but some events required it, so we kept a stash on hand. I wasn't sure what Tim had in mind, but I guessed it wasn't an after-dinner type drink. I loaded the cart with glasses, brandy, Scotch, and Tennessee whiskey, and rolled it back to the Dogwood Room.

Norma Jeanne clutched Holmes and cried on his chest. Not that I could really blame her. I would have too, under the circumstances.

Tiffany appeared to have given up on Austin and cuddled Twinkletoes in her arms. I was proud of Twinkletoes for understanding that Tiffany needed her. Most cats would have jumped away at the wet teardrops hitting their fur.

Gingersnap always seemed to know when someone needed comforting. She sat next to Linda, who ran her hand over Gingersnap's soft fur.

Oma had joined the grieving family. She had pulled up a chair next to Doris and clutched her hand. Muffy and Trixie roamed the room together, sniffing things.

I couldn't imagine their grief.

Vivi finally made an appearance. She strode in, stood in the center of her family, and observed them, her head held high. Not a tear stained her face. Her lips were drawn in a tight line, and I noted that she had taken the time to change into a sweater and trousers.

Dave watched the family, too. I couldn't help wondering how he saw them. Was he watching for signs of a killer? A cop must see everything in a different light.

He walked over to Vivi. "Mrs. Thackleberry, I am so sorry to intrude on your grief, but I'm afraid I need to ask you some questions."

She stared at him, cold as ice. "I know who did it. Her name is Birdie Dupuy."

Fifteen

I stopped breathing for a moment. I never expected *that*. My Aunt Birdie?

Holding his half-empty glass of Scotch, Tim sank into a big chair. "Oh no," he moaned. "Mom, don't start that."

"I'm not starting anything. Dale started it. She ended it by murdering him."

"Perhaps we should speak privately," Dave said in a very kind tone.

"I have nothing to hide. They should know what kind of man he was. All these years I've heard nothing but what a witch I am and how wonderful Dale is. Well, it's time they knew the truth. My husband was having an affair with Birdie Dupuy. Why do you think he liked to visit Wagtail?"

I was paralyzed. Oddly enough, Birdie and Vivienne were the same type in a way. Birdie would never steal a tip from anyone, but she was just as grumpy and querulous as Vivienne. They were both attractive women, about the same age. They were tough and stubborn.

I couldn't really imagine Birdie having an affair, though. But then, why not? She believed ghosts were living in her house. How many other secrets might she have? I had stupidly assumed her life was as staid as she was proper. What if that was all a facade?

What was I thinking? Even if she had an affair with Dale, Aunt Birdie wouldn't have murdered him. Would she?

EmmyLou's teary eyes narrowed and her chest heaved. "When is the last time *you* saw Dad, Vivi?"

Vivienne's lips tightened. "You won't pin this on me, EmmyLou. He spent the night with *her* last night."

"EmmyLou reported him missing only a few hours ago, at eight in the evening," said Dave, his tone a little incredulous.

Vivienne appeared unfazed. "Are you suggesting that I should have barged in on my husband and his mistress? A wellness check, so to speak? If you want to know where he was today, I suggest you inquire of Birdie."

EmmyLou gasped. "Dad has been missing since last night? Why didn't you tell me? You knew we were looking for him. All day long you made excuses that sounded like you knew where he was."

"I did know." Vivienne was defensive. "He was with his mistress."

Tim rolled his Scotch glass across his forehead.

EmmyLou asked, "Holmes, do you know this Birdie person?"

Holmes looked straight at me. *Gee, thanks!*

I took a step forward. "She's my aunt."

Norma Jeanne looked up at Holmes. "Your friend's aunt murdered my grandfather?"

"Now just a minute," I said. "We don't know that."

Norma Jeanne looked at me incredulously. "What planet are you living on? Vivi just made it very clear."

"Like I would believe a woman who steals tips in restaurants?" It slipped out. Had I thought about it first, I never would have said it. I could feel myself flushing crimson.

But Dave, Holmes, and Norma Jeanne were the only ones who reacted. The rest of Vivienne's family took it in stride.

Blake, who lounged in a chair much like his father, holding a glass of alcohol but more weirdly dressed, snorted and had to stifle a laugh.

"Blake!" scolded his mother.

Dave said very firmly, "Mrs. Thackleberry, I would like to speak with you privately. Now."

He gazed at me briefly. I nodded, assuming he wanted to use the inn office for a private interview as he sometimes did.

When they disappeared down the hallway, chatter broke out among the family members.

Tiffany declared openly, "I don't believe her. Who would wait all day without saying anything when her husband didn't come home? What kind of person does that?"

Linda gasped. "Tiffany, she's your grandmother!"

Doris broke her silence. "Someone who did not wish to be caught would do that."

Tim drained his glass. "Don't be ridiculous. Mom didn't murder Dale. We all loved Dale. It was probably someone he did business with in Wagtail."

"Was Birdie married?" asked Norma Jeanne. "Maybe her husband or another lover killed him." She avoided looking at me when she asked the question. Instead she kept her eyes on Holmes.

He gazed at me, though. I could tell he didn't want to answer.

EmmyLou saved him by walking over to the hallway and looking down the corridor. "What's taking them so long?"

Less than fifteen minutes had passed. What she probably didn't realize, but I suspected, was that we would be up all night as Dave interviewed each member of the family.

"So how did Vivi do him in?" Blake looked around at his family.

"What is wrong with my children?" Linda cried. "How can you be so crass? For heaven's sake, I'm ashamed of you! She's your grandmother! I can't stand her. She's argumentative and cheaper than anyone I have ever met in my life. Vivienne is the cause of a lot of strife and anger in this family, but she's still your father's mother, and if for nothing else, she deserves some respect for that."

Tiffany rose and helped herself to cheesecake and a cupcake. Austin joined her at the food but opted for a ham biscuit.

Linda tried to get Tiffany's attention, but it didn't work. She forced a smile at Austin. "Tiffie, honey, don't eat your emotions."

Tiffany shot a dark look at her mother. Her shoulders sagged. "How could you be so unkind at a time like this?"

"Here they come," said EmmyLou.

We waited as the footsteps grew closer.

Vivienne seemed none the worse for the interrogation. Either she hadn't killed Dale or she was made of ice. I suspected the latter.

Dave took EmmyLou to the office next.

Blake sat up straight. "Hey. Dale's death makes us the rich side of the family. Vivi, you'll inherit everything." He jumped up, loped to her, and embraced her.

"Let go of me you little money-grubber. As I explained to the cop, Dale was worth more to me alive than dead."

"You see?" Linda bestowed a smile on Vivienne. "That's a very sweet sentiment. I'm sure all of us feel the same way. He enriched our lives, and we are poorer without him."

"Linda, you are such an idiot," said Vivi. "I signed a prenuptial agreement when we married. On his death, I get ten thousand dollars. That's it. Forevermore. Nothing else. I'm sunk."

Everyone stared at her in surprise.

Norma Jeanne let go of Holmes. "So the money stays on our side of the family?"

"What about the house?" asked Blake.

Vivienne's lips pulled tight again. "I have no rights to it."

"I don't understand," said Blake. "EmmyLou gets everything? Our side of the family is broke?"

I couldn't help noticing that Tim looked straight at EmmyLou's husband, Barry. The conversation continued, but Tim stared at Barry.

"The jet is ours, too?" asked Norma Jeanne.

"I am *not* giving up the jet." Blake sounded outraged. "You can't imagine how awful it is to take public transportation."

"It's too late." Tiffany spoke softly, not looking at anyone. "None of us have use of the jet any longer. Grampy sold it. The ride here was the last one. It flew on to its new home."

Vivienne's eyes widened. "That rat! He didn't say a word about this to me. How can I be the last to know?"

From their stunned and depressed expressions, she wasn't the only one who didn't know. A glance around the room suggested strongly that Tiffany was the only one aware of these developments. Even Tim and Barry appeared to be stunned.

Vivienne eyed Tiffany with suspicion. "Well, well, Tiffany. I had no idea that you were so close to your *Grampy*. Perhaps Officer Dave should be considering *your* motives for murdering Dale."

Linda gasped and jumped to her feet. "How dare you? Everyone rolls over backward to accommodate you, and you would turn on your own grandchild? Your own blood? You're a miserable wretch, and I, for one, am through indulging you."

Tim rose to pour himself another drink. He took it neat, not diluted. "You can live with us, Mom."

Linda looked at her husband in horror. "Tim!"

I understood Linda completely. It would be worse than having Aunt Birdie move in with me, and that would be a nightmare.

Linda grabbed Tim's arm and hustled him to a corner, where she whispered.

Vivienne said loudly, "That idiot cop put a stop on all Dale's credit cards. I can't even pay for my flight home."

Tim, still in private conference with Linda, looked over at her. "Don't worry, Mom. I've got you covered. I'll pay for whatever you need."

"Just look at you," said Doris. "One day without Dale and you're all acting like heathens."

Blake stretched. "It's not his absence that's the problem. It's the lack of money. I banked on being wealthy the rest of my life. I'm going up to bed. If the constable would like to speak with me, though I don't know what the good of that would be, tell the good man that he may come to my room."

Blake sauntered toward the stairs still wearing his sunglasses.

Linda's mouth dropped open, and she held her hands out like she couldn't understand her son.

When Dave returned with EmmyLou, he announced that he would be speaking to everyone else in the morning. Given the hour, I was glad they would be going to bed.

"Wait! I want to talk with you." Tiffany jumped up from her seat and hurried to Dave's side.

He nodded. "Okay. I'll see the rest of you tomorrow morning."

The family rose and filtered up the stairs. I rushed to collect glasses and dishes, keeping my head down so I wouldn't see what would probably be a good night kiss between Holmes and Norma Jeanne.

Oma started to help me, but I shooed her up to bed. I pushed the cart to the kitchen, where Casey helped me clean up. We put leftovers in the magic refrigerator and ran the commercial dishwasher so everything would be ready for use when the cook arrived to start breakfast.

Holmes walked in. He leaned against the counter and closed his eyes.

"You okay?"

He rubbed his face with both hands. "Sometimes things just don't work out like you planned. I wish I had called off Christmas with the Thackleberrys."

"I'm sorry. This will be a very sad holiday for all of Dale's relatives."

He gazed at me for a few seconds. "Why would anyone murder Dale?"

I hugged him—a big mistake! His arms curled around me and held me tight. I could feel his breath on my hair and longed to stay in his arms. I backed off right away. "I can't imagine. Dale seemed very generous and jolly." But as I said that I remembered what Dale had said to me about Blake. He was cutting him off financially. I thought I had better tell Dave before I shared that detail with anyone else, even Holmes.

I saw him to the front door and said good night. But instead of locking the door behind him, I peeked in the private kitchen where Casey had retreated to let him know that everyone had gone to bed and that I was going over to Aunt Birdie's house.

Even though I was exhausted, I felt the need to warn Aunt Birdie. Phoning to inform her that her lover had died was just too cold and cruel. I pulled on my puffy winter coat and helped Trixie into her down coat. The two of us set off to Aunt Birdie's. We passed the Grinch on the way. Lights glowed in Rupert's yard as cops from Snowball combed it in search of clues.

Aunt Birdie hadn't turned off her Christmas lights. Strolling up to her home was a true treat. I wished I had better news. I knocked on the door.

After a few seconds, I knocked again.

A light went on in the house. I heard her walking down the stairs.

"It's Holly, Aunt Birdie!"

She opened the door. "It's four in the morning! Have you lost your mind?" She frowned at me. "This better not be about that Grinch."

I stepped inside. I had to give her credit. She even dressed well to sleep. Her robe wasn't as glamorous as Norma Jeanne's, but it was a silky white fabric, quilted everywhere except the lapels. "Aunt Birdie, did you know Dale Thackleberry?"

Sixteen

Aunt Birdie's head jerked back a bit in surprise. She looked at me curiously. "What a strange question. And why is it in past tense?"

"I'm so sorry to tell you this, but Dale was murdered."

"What?!" She staggered backward and inelegantly flopped onto a bench. "When? What happened?"

So she did know him. "Trixie found his body tonight. No one knows exactly what transpired yet."

Her hand trembled as she covered her mouth. I sat next to her and placed an arm around her thin shoulders.

She leaned her head on me, pulled a tissue from her pocket, and dabbed her eyes. "He was such a gentle soul."

She sobbed for a few minutes. I didn't know what to do, so I just sat there with her. Trixie appeared to understand this wasn't a time to be rambunctious. She lay quietly on the floor with her head down.

Aunt Birdie wiped her nose and sat up straight. "It was Vivienne. I told him years ago that he should leave her. That woman is the most inconsiderate, vile being on this planet. The hawks that chase my beautiful songbirds are more decent than she is."

How interesting that the two women immediately pointed their fingers at each other. I wondered how long Aunt Birdie had been seeing Dale. She never should have had an affair with a married man, of course, but none of that mattered now, except that it certainly made her a suspect.

"She's a cold person, for sure. I wonder why Dale married her and stayed with her. She must have had some redeeming qualities. Right?"

"Wrong! She's a hateful witch. She tricked him into marrying her—"

"Tricked, Aunt Birdie? You mean she claimed she was pregnant?"

"I mean she lured him. Like a siren. And only after everything was signed did she show her true personality. She was miserly! Did you know that he had to hide money from her? She wouldn't let him spend his own money. She bought lavishly for herself but denied him everything. More than once he told me stories about having to trick her. He was loaded, Holly. I mean the kind of person who flew around on his private jet. His home is a mansion."

Not anymore. But I didn't think it was the right time to talk about private jets.

"How did you meet Dale?" I asked.

"He was an avid collector of hand-carved Americana and folk art. Someone in Wagtail sent him my way. He was very knowledgeable and so charming."

Aunt Birdie was Wagtail's resident expert on antiques and local lore. She even wrote articles for magazines and was considered something of an authority.

"Aunt Birdie, Dave will probably be by tomorrow to question you. I want you to be sure to tell him all this."

"You bet I will! He'll be very interested to know that Dale was leaving her."

"Are you sure? They acted like a couple."

"He filed for divorce five years ago."

"Shouldn't they be divorced by now?" I asked.

"Vivienne has a heart condition, and he was always afraid of triggering a massive heart attack. According to Dale, the smallest thing could set it off and she would be gone. It was just like him to be kind and not want to harm her in spite of her viciousness. I'm telling you, Vivienne knocked him off."

"She says she gets very little," I mused.

"Then she's up to tricks. Vivienne cannot be trusted."

"Birdie, do you need to have a lawyer with you when you speak to Dave?"

Her expression was priceless. "Law, child! I didn't kill him. No, I don't need a lawyer, but Vivienne's going to need a good one."

I hugged her before I left, and when the door closed, I could hear her crying. That was more than his wife had done.

Although it was dark when Trixie and I walked home, Wagtail was waking up. Lights were on in the bakeries, and a few coffeehouses were already open for early-bird business.

At the inn, I spied Mr. Huckle on the front porch with Maggie. I stopped Trixie from running to them.

We paused close enough to hear Mr. Huckle speaking.

"It's okay, Maggie." Mr. Huckle stroked her gently. "You see, heaven is a lot like Wagtail. All your pains and illnesses will be gone, and you'll be able to run and leap like you did when you were just a pup. Years from now, EmmyLou will come to join you. And when she does, you'll be first in line to greet her and show her around."

I wiped tears from my cheeks. Trixie wasn't willing to wait anymore and shot ahead to see her new friend, Maggie.

"You're up early, Miss Holly," said Mr. Huckle.

"I haven't been to bed yet." I gave him a swift rundown of Dale's murder.

"He was a fine gentleman. What a tragedy. It shouldn't be too difficult for Officer Dave to pinpoint the culprit."

"What do you mean? Do you know something?"

"I don't think he'll have to look beyond Dale's immediate family. They're quite a selfish bunch."

Mr. Huckle and Maggie accompanied us into the inn. Christmas lights glimmered on the grand staircase, and the scent of coffee wafted to me as I walked up the stairs, Trixie and Twinkletoes springing a few steps ahead of me. Just before the second-story landing, Twinkletoes stopped and retreated, crouching just below the step. I grinned about the fact that her ears and the top of her head would give her away.

Seconds later, I stopped in my tracks too when I heard murmuring voices and saw Norma Jeanne running along the hallway, her beautiful robe flowing behind her. I was fairly certain she didn't see me.

I walked up the next flight, wondering what she had been up to. It was amazing any of Dale's relatives could sleep at all.

I unlocked the door to my apartment. The only thing I wanted at that moment was to fall into bed. I changed into an oversized T-shirt. Thinking that my sleep attire was considerably less impressive than Norma Jeanne's, I placed my elf clothes in the hamper for the cleaning woman to pick up. One of the luxuries of inn life.

Ten minutes later, Trixie, Twinkletoes, and I were snuggled in bed.

I didn't feel guilty for sleeping in. When I stretched, I found Mr. Huckle had brought me tea and a chocolate croissant that he wisely hid under a dome. Teeny crumbs lay nearby, which caused me to suspect dog and cat cookies might have been on the tray as well.

I eyed Trixie. "Did you eat Twinkletoes's cookie?"

Trixie flipped over on her back with all four feet sticking straight up in the air. That was an avoidance maneuver, if ever there was one.

I sat up in bed and enjoyed the hot tea. Trixie looked at me, suddenly alert when I bit into the croissant. She rolled over and inched ever closer to me, her tail moving like a pendulum that was out of control. I tore off a tiny bite for her from a corner that hadn't touched chocolate.

But the peaceful moment was marred when I remembered what had happened to Dale. He had come to Wagtail so full of life and kindness. He had even brought toys to make Christmas merrier for others. Mr. Huckle was right. It was hard to imagine that anyone would want to harm him, let alone murder him. And with a knife! Wasn't that a sign of anger? Of rage? Even more so than other types of murder? It hadn't been an accident, that was for sure.

It was Christmas Eve day. Holmes's parents were throwing a party for Holmes and Norma Jeanne. I wondered if it would be canceled.

After a shower, I stood in my closet thinking of Norma Jeanne and remembering the lovely feeling of Holmes's arms around me. Norma Jeanne would be dressed in city chic again. I finally decided on a soft and fluffy hand-knitted sweater color-blocked in blue and green with matching blue trousers. It was simple enough but just a bit dressy.

Twinkletoes was nowhere to be seen. She must have scampered downstairs, probably irritated after Trixie ate her breakfast treat. It was lunchtime when Trixie and I made an appearance.

Crowds thronged through the lobby. There was a waiting line to be seated in the dining area. It was a zoo!

Mr. Huckle walked toward me with a tray while people called to him from the dining area.

"What happened?" I asked. "Where did all these people come from?"

"It's the last shopping day before Christmas. Santa Paws is on the green today. People bring their little ones, furry and human alike, to see Santa. They pour through the stores. The whole town is like this. It's chaos, I tell you!"

"Can I help you?"

"Thank you, Miss Holly. Would you take this tray into the Dogwood Room for the Thackleberrys?"

"Of course. No problem."

How could I have slept so late when all this was going on? I wound my way through the throngs to the Dogwood Room, which someone, probably Mr. Huckle, had the good sense to rope off with a sign that said *Private Party*.

Hoping I wouldn't drop the tray, I unlatched the rope with one hand and let myself in. A brunch buffet had been set up for them with crispy potatoes, pork sausages, bacon, scrambled eggs, a fresh fruit platter, and a variety of breads.

"Finally," muttered Vivi. "I hope that's my eggs Benedict."

I set the tray down and lifted one of the lids. "Looks like it." I handed the dish to Vivi.

Lifting the next dome, I found a second order of eggs Benedict. "Who else is having it?"

Blake sprawled across a large chair with his legs hanging over the arm. He lazily raised his hand with his forefinger pointing up but didn't look at me, as though I were invisible. I brought him his plate, along with utensils wrapped in a napkin. He didn't even sit up straight to eat.

EmmyLou held a balled-up tissue in her hand. She squeezed it so tight that her knuckles had turned white. "I've been receiving condolence messages. Someone even started a hashtag for *DaleThackleberryRIP*." Her face contorted and she sniffled. "But that worm Steve Oathaut had the nerve to e-mail me an offer to buy Thackleberry. What kind of person does that? Dad isn't even in his grave yet."

"Bah!" Doris scowled and shook her fist. "Stevie Oathaut is a toad just like his father. The Oathauts have tried to buy us out for years, but they will never own Thackleberry. Never!"

"They've made offers before?" asked Blake. "Maybe we should consider it. How much did they offer?"

"Slow down there, son." Tim settled into an armchair. "Just because you're going to be practicing medicine doesn't mean the rest of us are ready to give up the family business. EmmyLou, would you like me to respond to Steve Oathaut?"

"That would be very kind of you. I hardly know what to say to anyone at the moment. I feel sort of shell-shocked."

Vivienne glowered at her. "Shouldn't that be up to me as Dale's widow?"

EmmyLou barely glanced at her. "I'm sure you will be receiving plenty of condolences when we get home."

"So how would that work?" asked Blake. "If EmmyLou inherited everything from Dale, do any of the rest of us get a cut when Thackleberry is sold?"

Tiffany's face flamed with outrage. "Is that all you can think about? Grampy just died and all you can talk about is money. Well, let me tell you how it works. We're all broke. No more private jets or Swiss ski trips or medical school tuition. Is that clear enough for you?"

Every member of the Thackleberry clan focused on her.

"What are you talking about?" asked Norma Jeanne.

Tiffany wiped her eyes roughly with her fingers. "The company is on the verge of bankruptcy. Grampy was pumping money into it to keep it afloat. The house is mortgaged to the hilt. He dumped everything he had into the business."

She had everyone's attention.

Norma Jeanne gasped. "How serious is this, Tiffany? Are we all going to be out of work?"

Tiffany looked grim. "I don't know what will happen to the Thackleberry company yet. But there's a good chance it will shut down and go out of business, especially now that we're coping with this rumor of animals itching and losing hair from our garments."

Doris rose from her chair. Her wrinkled face was tearstained. "No! I will not permit this to happen. My husband and I worked too hard to create the Thackleberry company. I will not allow you to destroy it."

For the first time since I had met her, Vivienne smiled. It was more of a wry grin, actually, and then she began to laugh hysterically.

"What's so funny?" asked Tiffany.

"I was distressed about my future. But all you spoiled brats who have had everything handed to you—the trips to Europe, the debutante balls, the expensive schools, and the cars that cost more than most people make in a year—now you'll find out what it's like to count your pennies!" She laughed again, in the most wicked way I had ever heard.

Norma Jeanne turned to her father. "Thank goodness you don't work for the company business. At least *we'll* be all right."

Worry lines creased his face between his eyebrows. "EmmyLou? You haven't said a word about this. Seems like you would know if the company was in such dire straits."

EmmyLou appeared to be stunned. "We're dealing with the itching rumor but so far we haven't found any reported cases. Let's not jump to conclusions about the demise of Thackleberry yet. First we should mourn Dad. Look how we're falling apart without him."

"How do you know this, Tiffie?" asked her father.

"I found an irregularity and took the information to Grampy. He was looking into it. In the meantime, he lent pretty much everything he had to the company. If it goes under, it's all lost."

For a long moment, they were silent.

"I say we blow this place," said Blake. "Christmas is ruined anyway. I'm getting out of town as soon as I can get a flight."

"Good luck with that. It's the day before Christmas. There won't be a seat available anywhere," said Tiffany.

Blake flicked his hand in the air. "We have friends with jets. We'll just make some phone calls."

Linda seemed pained by his response.

"I don't often agree with Blake," Vivi declared, "but I'm all for that. We can take Dale's body with us. It's over."

Norma Jeanne, wearing black leggings that were way too tight, knee-high boots, a gold tunic, and a scarf big enough to circle her neck and still hang over her arms like a wrap, said, "I'm all in. Given the circumstances, I think we should just pack up and go."

EmmyLou spoke up. "Norma Jeanne, Holmes's family went to a lot of trouble to entertain us and arrange for a party tonight in honor of you and Holmes. And I should point out that Dad's body has been sent somewhere for an autopsy. I'm not leaving without him."

Tiffany sniffled. "It doesn't feel right going to a party when Grampy just died."

EmmyLou sighed. "I know, honey. I miss Dad more than I can tell you. Great-Grandma Doris and I discussed the awkward situation this morning. It would be a real blow to the Richardsons. And Dale would have been the first one to tell us to carry on. He loved all his grandchildren and would have done anything for you."

Blake choked on his coffee.

Vivienne's lips pulled tight. "Now listen here. I am the head of this family now. We no longer have the options we once did. Those days are over. You either come with us, or you find your own way home."

"You are not going anywhere, you ungrateful beasts!" Anger shone in Doris's eyes when she rose from her chair again. "If I could stand without this crazy thing, I would shake my stick at you. Blake, you are not an octopus. Sit up like a human being," she growled.

His eyes opened wide, but he twisted around and plopped his feet on the floor.

"You dreadful people have treated me as though I'm some kind of incompetent for years now," Doris continued. "I have had enough." Her voice lowered in volume but not in strength when she muttered, "How is it possible that you degenerates are my family? You have had every advantage in life, and now that Dale is dead, all you can do is grouse about money. Let's get a few things straight. Vivienne! You are *not* the head of this family. Norma Jeanne, the earth does not revolve around you. No one cares whether the wedding invitations will be ivory or ecru. And it would do you good to drink regular water like normal people."

Doris paused and glowered at them, her eyes moving from one to the next. "One of you murdered my son, and none of you are going anywhere until we know which one of you it was."

Seventeen

Doris's words hung in the air. The sad fact was that they all probably suspected one of them had murdered Dale. Not a single one of them appeared to be shocked. Some of them squirmed a little bit, and I thought I saw some shame.

Doris raised her bony hand and shook it. "Anyone who leaves before we know who killed my son will never receive another penny from me. Do you understand?"

Grandma Thackleberry certainly knew her brood well. They hadn't been one bit startled to hear that she thought one of them murdered Dale. But they were clearly horrified by the fact that they might not inherit from her, with the notable exceptions of EmmyLou and Linda, who looked at their children with rather worried expressions.

Tiffany's face remained surprisingly placid. She smiled at me. "Could we have a refill on breakfast breads? Someone—" she glared at Blake "—was a big piggy."

I nodded. Reluctant to leave the drama, I weaved my way back to the kitchen, where I filled a basket with muffins and croissants. Carrying a pot of coffee and the bread basket, I ran into Oma in the lobby.

"Good morning, *liebchen*. What a night we had. Such a sad one. Mr. Thackleberry will certainly be missed. Holly, there has been a change of schedule. When you are through with the Thackleberrys, can you relieve Shelley at the Christkindl booth, so she can eat lunch? Then, Shelley will cover for you at the market from two to six. Dale Thackleberry had asked to play Santa Paws in the gazebo this afternoon. We have found a replacement for him, but with these crowds we need an elf to help keep the children in line and give each of them a gift. You don't mind, do you?"

I didn't mind at all and readily agreed.

"Oh! And our little rascal, Trixie, was carrying this. I wouldn't have noticed, but Gingersnap wanted it. I suspect it's not a dog toy."

She handed me a wool felt Jack Russell terrier. About two inches high, it had been meticulously hand sewn.

"It looks a lot like our Trixie, no?"

"It does. Except for the brown fur around the eyes. I wonder where she got it."

"Someone will be missing it. I will hang it on the tree in the dining room. That way we will know where it is if anyone is looking for it."

I continued on my way, brought the bread basket to Tiffany, and filled coffee cups for the family members, who appeared to be much more sober now. No one spoke of leaving anymore.

When they had finished eating, I cleared the dishes, grabbed two muffins for my lunch, and realized I had put my elf clothes in the hamper.

I shot upstairs in search of the housekeeper, Marisol. I spotted her cleaning cart parked on the second floor. The door to the Stay guest room was open. Trixie and I walked inside.

"Marisol! Good afternoon."

"Hello, Holly."

"I left some elf clothes in my hamper this morning, but now I'm going to need them at two o'clock. Have you already put them in the wash?"

"Oh! I am sorry. They are in the machine right now."

Marisol was a good egg. "Nothing to be sorry about. I'll have to hope they're dry in time."

She patted my arm. "I will do my best."

I knew she would. I was thanking her when a white paw reached out from under the bed and swatted my shoe.

"Twinkletoes!" I hissed. "Are you snooping again?"

Marisol laughed. "She is my constant companion. Did you know that she waits for me to arrive? Every day she is by the door looking for me. Then Twinkletoes goes from room to room with me. I've never met such a nosy cat. None of the guests can have any secrets from her."

Trixie wriggled under the bed to join her.

I knelt on the floor. "Come on, you two. Out of there."

Twinkletoes was holding on to something and kicking it viciously with her back feet.

"Twinkletoes! No!"

She didn't relinquish it. I reached under the bed for her. Even when I pulled her out, she clung to her toy—a pill bottle. No wonder she had been attracted to it. It rattled and rolled.

Trixie emerged from under the bed, eager to sniff Twinkletoes's toy.

I examined the prescription bottle to be sure it had not been damaged and that my little rascals hadn't ingested the contents. The childproof cap held tight. In spite of Twinkletoes's rough treatment, the plastic bottle looked fine.

The label on the bottle read *Doris Thackleberry. For sleepless nights. Take one capsule.*

I glanced around. A lady's blue sweater hung on a chair. A small bottle of perfume stood on the dresser next to some

Christmas gifts that looked so perfect they had to have been wrapped in the store.

Hoping that Twinkletoes wouldn't attack the pill bottle again, I placed it neatly on the bathroom vanity.

"Holly? Is everything all right?" asked Marisol.

"Yes. Fine, thanks. I'll see you in an hour or so."

We were short on time. I dashed down to the kitchen, grabbed a bowl, a serving of Liver It Up Pup, and a banana, and dashed out to the Christkindl booth.

"Thanks for coming." Shelley collected her thermos and gloves. "It's been a madhouse. On the bright side, there won't be much to pack up after today."

I looked around. A lot of the ornaments had been sold as well as dog and cat gifts like collars and bandanas.

Shelley hustled off, and I served Trixie her overdue brunch. My first customer bought a dozen ornaments and nearly wiped me out of dog cookies. I texted Shelley that we needed more dog cookies and to bring them with her when she returned. Masses of people passed by, and many of them bought gifts and stocking stuffers. The hour passed so quickly that I really didn't have time to ponder the situation of Dale's murder.

As soon as Shelley returned, I headed to the inn basement to find my elf costume. It hung on a hanger, clean and dry.

I took the elevator upstairs to the third floor, while Trixie raced up the stairs. She met me at the door to our apartment. In my quarters, I changed as fast as I could, pulled my hair back into a ponytail, and dressed Trixie in her elf coat and hat.

Twinkletoes finally made an appearance. She stretched and yawned.

"Do you want to come with us?"

I tried a little cat elf hat on her. The green hat with red trim bore the Thackleberry label inside, reminding me again of what had happened. The hat was well thought-out for a cat, with little spaces for her ears to fit. She didn't object until I added the coat. No matter. The hat was enough. Her long fur would keep her warm.

With Twinkletoes in my arms and Trixie running ahead, I left the inn for elf duty.

I could see why Santa Paws needed help. The line of children, animals, and parents stretched well away from the gazebo. Santa Paws was already there, and when he turned around, I recognized the job for exactly what it was—a setup.

"Holly!" Holmes seemed happy to see me. "What are you doing here?" He reached out for Twinkletoes, and I could hear her purring in his arms.

"I suspect two sneaky grandmothers arranged this."

"Ahhhh. I think you might be right." He lowered his voice. "Grandma doesn't care for Norma Jeanne."

"I'm sure that's not true." I said it to be kind, even though I knew he was correct.

"Really? Then why did she arrange for the inn cook to teach Norma Jeanne to make shrimp and grits?"

I had to laugh. "Because your grandmother loves you and you like shrimp and grits."

"Norma Jeanne has never cooked anything but instant coffee in her entire life. And she makes that in the microwave. It about killed her to be in a hot kitchen."

I rather relished the image, but didn't think I should say so. "Ready, Santa?"

He climbed into the red velvet chair in the gazebo. Twinkletoes jumped on the railing and couldn't have looked cuter. I even heard an adult wondering if she was real or part of the decorations.

One by one, I led children and dogs up the steps to Holmes. Some of the cats walked on leashes, but most preferred to be treated like royalty and carried. I snapped pictures with an assortment of cameras. And when they left, I gave each one the item a parent had selected from our assortment while Santa Paws had their attention. Not a bad arrangement. The parents knew the allergies of their children, dogs, and cats and could avoid inappropriate treats.

Some of the children and cats balked and fussed about posing with Santa. Not a single dog feared him.

But when Ethan Schroeder turned up without Marie Carr, I wondered what was going on.

"Holly! Are you an elf?" asked Ethan.

Oh boy. "Shh. Don't tell my secret, okay? I'm an honorary elf. Sometimes when the other elves are very busy, like today because they have to finish the toys and load the sleigh and everything, well, then Santa asks me to fill in and help him here in Wagtail."

He eyed me with uncertainty. "For real?"

Holmes boomed, "For real! Now come up here and tell me what you want for Christmas, young fellow!"

Ethan whispered something to Santa Holmes. For a moment I worried that he would recognize Holmes. Then it dawned on me that he had been born after Holmes left for Chicago.

When I helped Ethan down the stairs, I asked where his Granny Carr was. "Over there." He pointed at Café Chat. "I told her I had something important to tell Santa."

"Okay. How about you pick out a treat for you and your sister. Does she have any allergies?"

"Nope."

He hung around after the next kid was on Santa's lap. "Holly, can you tell me something?" A worry line creased his little face between his eyebrows. "Will my parents have Christmas in heaven?"

His question took me aback. I hurried to answer without giving it much thought. "Sure they will. The best Christmas! But you know what? They'll be having Christmas with you and your sister, too. Tonight when you go to bed, look out the window and find the biggest twinkling star in the sky.

That's them waving at you to let you know they're always with you, no matter where you go."

"How do you know that?"

"I'm an elf. And I'm older than you."

He seemed to accept that absurd logic. When he walked away, Holmes brought down the child who had been on his lap. Smiling, Holmes reached out and high-fived me. "Well done! We have a little problem, though. He wants to be adopted for Christmas."

"How sad." It broke my heart to know that was his Christmas wish. "Some things even an elf can't fix."

Holmes grinned with a sparkle in his eye. "He also wants a BadBoyz 8000 blue and green Monster bike for Christmas."

"Think Marie got him one?"

"I doubt it. They're fairly pricey. Plus it's in a big display in the window of Mountain Trails, the mountain bike store. I saw it there yesterday. I doubt that there are two BadBoyz 8000 Monster bikes in Wagtail."

I couldn't help laughing. "You're still coveting toys for Christmas?"

"There happened to be a very cool leather jacket next to it."

"I'll text our handyman and have him pick up the bike for tonight's elf delivery."

Holmes looked around the gazebo. "Think you can get a connection here?" he asked.

"It's been a while since you lived here. Café Chat has Wi-Fi. I bet I can pick it up." I texted our handyman immediately, and added a little something else to my request. He texted back and knew exactly what I was talking about. Apparently every man in town liked that store. I had never paid it much attention.

It was dark at six o'clock, when I put up the *Closed* sign.

"Want to grab a drink, Elf Holly? We haven't gotten a chance to sit and talk."

I couldn't help laughing. "Now how would it look if people saw Santa and one of his elves drinking on Christmas Eve?"

He laughed so hard that he almost doubled over, except the big fake belly was in the way.

"Besides, don't you have a party to go to?" I asked.

"Oh yeah. How could I have forgotten about that?" He ran a hand over his face. "It's going to be awkward. I tried to get my folks to cancel it this morning."

"If something had happened to Oma or Rose, we wouldn't be in a partying mood. I imagine the tone will be subdued."

"You're coming, aren't you?" he asked.

Gack. I reminded myself to try to be supportive. "I'm not sure. I may pull inn duty."

He looked at me for a long moment. "I believe it's mandatory for elves. I'd better get going. Hope I see you there, Holly."

He took off at a fast clip.

Behind me, someone said, "You're not going to the party?"

Eighteen

I turned around. "Dave! How is the investigation coming?"

"Aunt Birdie is a pill."

"I already knew that. Did she tell you—"

"She wants me to call her so she can be there when I handcuff Vivienne and haul her off to death row. That's almost a quote."

I cringed.

"The Thackleberry heirs aren't much better. A rather astonishing lack of sorrow in some of them."

"Does that make them suspects?"

He tilted his head. "Maybe. But sometimes it's the killer who puts on an act and cries the hardest, you know?"

"But you think it's one of them?"

"Not jumping to any conclusions yet. I know better than that."

"How about the weapon? Did you find it?"

"It has not been found. In fact, there was nothing of particular interest inside of that Grinch. Initially, I thought the killer must have dragged him inside it, but there are no signs of anything being dragged across the snow. Nor is there any indication of blood on the snow. It appears someone convinced Dale to go inside and then stabbed him to death."

"So it was probably someone he knew. Not a stranger."

"Most likely. Although I gather he was a fairly inquisitive and friendly guy. A stranger might have enticed him with the notion of going inside that thing. Quite a few people have expressed an interest in seeing the interior."

"Dave, on their first night here, Dale told me that he was going to cut off Blake financially. He said Blake was lying to him. Something about false pretenses, I think."

"That Blake is something of an odd duck."

"You mean his clothes?"

Dave shook his head and snorted. "Do you think he realizes how he looks? What I meant was his disdain for everything. His family embarrasses him. The inn is tacky. Wagtail is primitive because there's no Starbucks or a nightclub. The food isn't Manhattan chic. Nothing is good enough for him."

"He, Vivienne, and Norma Jeanne wanted to leave this morning, but Doris put a quick stop to that."

"Vivienne resents Doris, and Doris despises Vivienne. Doris says that EmmyLou's mother, Dale's first wife, was an angel. Vivienne moved in on Dale a few years after he divorced his second wife. She convinced him to marry her in one of those quickie ceremonies in Vegas. Doris is just thankful Dale had the good sense to have her sign a prenup. She's been wicked ever since. It's a lovely family," he said sarcastically. "So, how come you're not going to the party tonight?"

"Oma will probably go. I may need to mind the inn."

Dave studied me. "It can't be fun for you to see Holmes with another woman. But I think he would appreciate your presence. And so would I."

I felt like I was twelve again and talking about boys. "What? How do you know that?"

Dave massaged his forehead. "If I were Holmes, I know I'd feel better if you were at the party. But all that aside, can you go to the party for me? I'll drop in for a few minutes, but people won't speak openly if they know I'm there."

"You want me to spy?" I giggled at the thought.

"Hey, someone in this town committed a brutal murder. I hope his or her animosity doesn't extend beyond Dale, but I don't know that it doesn't. I'd like to get a lead on this as soon as I can."

I wasn't giggling anymore. "Sure. I hadn't thought about it that way. I've been having fun with all those adorable, excited children and cute dogs and cats. Meanwhile the killer could have been standing among them."

"I certainly hope not."

I promised to phone him with an update, collected Twinkletoes, called Trixie, and walked back to the inn. Twinkletoes had been a trooper, but she seemed very happy about it when we were back in the lobby and I removed the hat from her head.

It was always quiet at the inn in the late afternoon and early evening because we didn't serve dinner. Oma thought people should go out to patronize the restaurants. Happily, the crowds were gone.

Oma's high heels and Gingersnap's claws clicked on the floor as they approached.

Oma wore black velvet trousers with a matching top that was beaded and burned out, creating a semi-transparent lace design in the fabric at the neckline. Gingersnap's collar matched Oma's outfit. The black velvet stood out against her golden red fur.

"Don't you look elegant!"

"You are coming tonight, *ja*? Rose and Holmes would be offended if you did not attend."

I wrinkled my nose. "Who's watching the inn?"

"Casey. And please wear the red dress."

Oh no. I loved that dress, but plain black would probably be better for fading into the background. Not just to listen in and spy, but so I wouldn't look like I was trying to compete with Norma Jeanne.

My reaction must have shown on my face, because Oma said, "You know she will dress in something very fancy."

"That's exactly why I don't want to."

"*Liebling*, the time to win Holmes over is *before* he marries. This may be your last chance. Don't squander it."

I felt a little rotten about the fact that everyone knew I was crazy for Holmes. They were all feeling sorry for me. I didn't care for that one bit.

Down the hallway, the elevator doors opened and Doris stepped out. Her cane tapped along the floor as she walked toward us, with Muffy racing ahead to greet Trixie.

Muffy wore what I assumed was a Thackleberry dress. It was black with flouncing ruffles. On the back, written in rhinestones, was *Santa, is it too late to be good?*

"Holly," whispered Oma, "Doris would like to speak with us. Do you have a few minutes before you change clothes?"

"Sure." I was in no hurry to get to a party celebrating Holmes's impending marriage.

Oma led us to the kitchen where Doris, the Thackleberry matriarch, took a seat in a big armchair and rested her feet on the fireplace hearth.

Oma claimed the other big armchair, and I pulled up a chair.

"Thank you for meeting with me." Doris gripped her walking stick as though it gave her a sense of security. "I need your help."

Doris turned teary eyes toward me. "Holmes says you have uncovered the identity of a few murderers."

Uh-oh. I knew what was coming. "I just got lucky."

"This shouldn't be too difficult," she said. "I'm very sorry to say that the suspects are limited to members of my family. If I were younger, I would do the snooping myself. But these days I can't keep up with them." She paused and took a deep breath. "Worst of all, I'm afraid I could be next."

Doris swallowed hard. Her hands shook a tiny bit. "Initially, I was convinced that Vivienne murdered Dale." She paused and dabbed her nose with a handkerchief. "He was a wonderful son. Always so thoughtful toward my husband and me. But more than that, and I don't just say this as his mother, Dale was the most kind and giving person I have ever known. Always looking out for other people. Always trying to make life better for everyone in his family, and even total strangers. His first wife, Norma Jeanne, embraced his giving nature."

I thought she might have misspoken.

"Norma Jeanne?" asked Oma gently.

Doris glanced at her. "I haven't lost my marbles yet. In her family, it was a tradition to name the first daughter after her maternal grandmother. A lovely gesture. That's why EmmyLou has such a Southern name. Her maternal grandmother came from Texas. After his wife's death, I suppose Dale was lonely. EmmyLou was an adult, and the house was empty. He married again, briefly, but it didn't work out. Then he made the mistake of marrying that shrew, Vivienne. To Dale's credit, he tried to make the marriage work. For far too long, if you ask me. It was something of a shock to him after his loving first wife. The second wife was tolerable until she began catting around. I don't think he was prepared to deal with the likes of Vivienne. Oh my, how he tried to make her happy. But as far as I can tell, her discontent and constant vexation with everyone and everything is ingrained in her. She never even tried to overcome it. Dale asked her to seek counseling, but she refused, claiming nothing was wrong with her. She has lived her life thinking only of herself, never giving the tiniest bit of consideration to anyone else. She is a user of people. You know the kind? She takes what she can from them, and when she no longer has any use for them, it's as though they no longer exist."

"It must be hard for all of you to have a family member like that," said Oma.

"I often wished Vivienne would just stay home and let the rest of us enjoy ourselves. But I think it bothered her to imagine that we might have fun without her. Of course, it backfired, because we avoided family gatherings. I had to meet my own son secretly so she wouldn't come along. She wanted to micromanage everything we did. We didn't have anything to hide, but she was always unpleasant. I'm not surprised that he sought comfort in the arms of another woman."

"But you have changed your mind?" I asked. "You no longer think Vivienne murdered Dale?"

"I don't know. There are other family members who worry me as well. When Dale was born, his father and I worked long days and every weekend to build our business. Our success led to a good life. We could afford luxuries. We had the money to pay for Dale's education, and, of course, he had a job at Thackleberry the minute he graduated. Some things in life came easy for him, but he never took them for granted. He always tried to help other people get a leg up in life. EmmyLou was raised the same way. She is generous and giving to a fault. But the fourth generation worries me."

She stopped speaking.

"Norma Jeanne, Tiffany, and Blake?" I asked.

"They appear to have grown up in a bubble. It's as though they have no concept of anything outside of their own lives. I don't understand it, really. I suggested to Dale that it could be the result of having everything given to them as soon as they thought of it. It breaks my heart."

She heaved a great sigh before continuing. "Dale was quite disturbed by their attitude. Cars, condos, trips, they expected it all." She paused. "Blake has dropped out of medical school. Dale was paying his tuition and found out quite by accident. I don't think Blake's parents even know yet. That boy—" her mouth bunched up in anger "—he's a man, not a child anymore, was pocketing his tuition money and living a life of leisure. What kind of person does that? It's not normal for a young man to be lazy like that. He should have dreams and goals. If that's not a sign of being overindulged, then I don't know what is. Did he think we would never notice that he didn't finish school? Or did he plan to come home and play doctor on the social circuit without any credentials? I have no idea, but that young man makes me very angry. He's able-bodied and intelligent. There's no reason on this green earth for him to lounge around at his grandfather's expense."

"Dale mentioned it to me," I said. "Not the details, but he told me he was going to cut Blake off. You think Blake might have killed him because of that?"

"It's possible." She clutched her hand to her chest. "You can't imagine how terrible I feel about suspecting members of our family. It's the last thing in the world I ever expected. But I'm terribly afraid that one of them killed my boy. My sweet Dale."

Oma looked at me and raised her eyebrows.

How did I get into these messes? I gazed down at Trixie, who appeared so innocent and unconcerned. It was her nose that had landed me in this position. What could I say? I had already agreed to snoop for Dave anyway.

Doris Thackleberry gazed at me. I wished I couldn't see the fear in her eyes.

Nineteen

Poor Doris was scared for her own life. Who could blame her? She was frail and elderly, and couldn't walk without her cane. It would be too easy for an unscrupulous person to make her death look like an accident. What if it were my Oma who was afraid someone wanted to kill her?

"I don't know that I can do much, Mrs. Thackleberry, but I'll try on one condition."

Her expression brightened, but she remained cautious. "A bargain?"

"You have to tell Officer Dave that you're afraid." He needed to know. What with investigating Dale's murder, I had no idea how he could manage to protect Doris, but that was his job. It was up to him.

Oma smiled at Doris. "That's actually a very good idea. You should definitely do that."

Doris nodded. "It's a deal."

Oma added, "This should remain private between the

three of us and Dave. We don't want to trigger any aberrant behavior."

The two of them seemed relieved, which I found distressing. Doris had to be very careful. Just discussing the matter didn't mean it had been resolved.

Oma checked her watch. "You better hurry and dress, Holly."

"You two go ahead. Don't wait for me." I started for the back stairs that led to my apartment.

"Holly!" called Oma. "Don't chicken out!"

I might have if Dave hadn't mentioned the importance of gathering information and if Doris wasn't afraid. The truth was that Dale's death would surely be discussed in hushed circles at the party. Maybe I could pick up on something.

In my apartment, I hung up my elf outfit and donned the big, fluffy Sugar Maple Inn robe. Trixie looked up at me. "I know. It's not chic like Norma Jeanne's robe."

I was hungry. I peered in the fridge, which was well stocked with cat and dog foods but a bit meager on the human side. I fed Trixie and Twinkletoes, but I had to settle for yogurt.

After a quick shower, I swept my hair up in a loose twist and pinned it. I debated between dresses for a moment and finally stepped into the red one to please Oma.

It had a fitted waist. The top part was sleeveless, and the neckline curved down a bit daringly in the front. I wasn't used to showing quite so much cleavage. The skirt featured two inverted pleats in the front so that it flared a bit. It was actually a simple dress, but the vibrant color packed a punch.

It didn't need much in the way of jewelry. I added dangling earrings that would sparkle when they moved, but nothing more.

Trixie sat on the floor watching me. Twinkletoes had disappeared, probably ready for a long nap.

I checked the big chairs in my living room. She was nowhere to be seen. I grabbed a coat and left with Trixie.

As we stepped on the second-floor landing, Trixie tore down the hallway. Once again, I found Twinkletoes nestled with her front paws tucked under the chest, staring at the door of Sniff.

I picked her up, but she made such a fuss that I placed her on the floor again. She groomed her fur, as though she was insulted by the smell I left on her.

"Have it your way," I said.

Trixie and I continued to the lobby. "We can't have Gingersnap show you up." I led the way out to our Christkindl booth. It felt a little bit eerie that the booths would soon be taken away. Our handyman had already begun to box up the few items that remained. "Do we still have some of the red collars with the sparkles on them?" I asked.

He pulled one out. "Like this?"

"Exactly." It glittered in the light of the booth. Even though it was probably meant for a poodle, I fastened it on Trixie's neck. "There's no reason a Jack Russell can't wear bling," I told Trixie. "Are you coming tonight?" I asked the handyman.

"Wouldn't miss it. Casey said the whole family is appalling."

"I wouldn't go that far. But they were very concerned about their inheritance."

"Is it true that Aunt Birdie is a suspect?" he asked.

"Rumors travel fast in this town!"

"Don't evade the question, Holly Miller!"

"I don't think Dave has any suspects yet." That was true enough.

He made a face at me.

"I'll pay for the collar at the inn gift shop."

He gave me a thumbs-up. "See you at the Richardsons'."

Trixie and I walked along the plaza where it abutted the

inn. We entered through the registration entrance. When we neared the desk, Twinkletoes shot out to surprise us.

Trixie barked in alarm and chased her a few steps.

When I unlocked the gift shop door, Twinkletoes dashed underfoot into the store. I deposited payment for the collar in the cash register. She didn't stick around though. Boxes were piled on the floor. We had a lot of work ahead of us.

But not tonight. I locked the gift shop door, and for a moment, I thought I had locked Twinkletoes inside. She mewed her soft little *meh*. I peered through the glass windows of the store but didn't see her.

Trixie barked at something, her head tilted so that she was looking up.

Twinkletoes strolled along the second-floor railing, her tail high, prissy as could be, as though she were showing off. I hated when she did that. It was how she had gotten her name. Nevertheless, I still held my breath every time, terrified that she would fall. They say that cats right themselves and land on their feet, but I had heard of some that hadn't.

She leaped off the railing, and I thought she hurried along the corridor where the rooms were.

I grabbed a golf cart key and walked out to the Sugar Maple Inn golf carts. As I drove to the party, I considered my thought regarding Trixie's new collar. I felt like Norma Jeanne was the flashy poodle, and I was just a simple Jack.

I scolded myself for feeling that way. No person or dog was worth more than another. I truly wanted Holmes to be happy. And if Norma Jeanne was the one who made his toes tingle, then I should be his best friend and support him. I didn't tell Trixie what I was thinking. I suspected she wouldn't agree with me.

Golf carts lined the street in front of the Richardson home.

When Holmes's father had a serious heart problem a few years before and required a ranch-style home without stairs, his parents had gutted an older house in their favorite Wagtail neighborhood. While it looked like the same beautiful stone house from the outside, the interior had lofted ceilings and massive rooms for entertaining, all on one floor.

Trixie and I walked into the mother of all Christmas parties. Little girls in frilly dresses ran from little boys in Christmas sweaters. A long table was loaded with tempting food, and a smaller one contained bowls of dog and cat party treats. I was about to nab a cheese cookie for Trixie, but she saw some of her dog pals and scampered across the room, abandoning me.

Holmes's grandmother Rose kissed my cheek and took my coat. She winked at me. "You look beautiful, sweetheart. There's a bourbon cranberry punch on the table that you have to try. It's my new favorite. And I can wholeheartedly recommend the peppermint martinis."

I thought I'd better eat something first. "Everything looks wonderful, Rose. Holmes must be so happy."

She frowned at me. Into my ear she whispered, "Of course he's not happy. How could he be happy with that girl? Just look at her."

I gazed across the room. Norma Jeanne looked like she belonged on a fashion runway. Her black dress with a round neckline showed no cleavage at all. But the skirt turned into a see-through material at her panty line and spiraled around her to make the bottom of her dress. It ended just below her knees and flowed behind her, not unlike a tail. It was stunningly space-age and eye-catching, but you couldn't have paid me to wear it.

I had been wrong to even imagine that I might compete with her.

But Blake upstaged everyone, even Norma Jeanne. He wore a black—well, I wasn't quite sure what it was. A dress? A garment at any rate. On his shoulders and torso, it appeared to be a fabric that decayed into strings. The middle featured glitzy triangles. Just above his knees, it appeared shredded, so that glimpses of his bare legs showed. It ended just below his knees, revealing his legs, black socks, and short black boots. It was the most curious thing I had ever seen.

What I noticed next though was that Norma Jeanne was watching Austin with Tiffany and her parents. He appeared to be getting along with her dad, Tim, particularly well.

"It will kill me if Holmes marries into that family," whispered Rose. "Who ever heard of intentionally wearing rags to a party? Now, if that were all he had, I would be the first to be sympathetic, but it's just weird if you ask me. It looks like something a cat shredded. Excuse me, honey. I believe I'm needed."

She hurried off, and I made a beeline for the food. While I noshed on Swedish meatballs, stuffed mushrooms, and crab crostini, I drifted around the room, listening to snippets of conversations.

All the locals were talking about the murder.

I think Rupert must have done him in. If it had been anybody else, someone would have noticed something.

It can't have been easy to get that guy in there. He had to be a good two hundred and fifty pounds or more. Nobody picked him up. That's for sure. You think there could have been two murderers?

Have you met his wife? I'd have stabbed myself in the back if I had to go home to her every night.

His granddaughter's awful pretty. I'm not surprised that Holmes is smitten with her.

"Holly! Holly!"

I turned to see a local girl I knew from Café Chat where she was a waitress.

"Would you mind taking our picture with the Blakester?"

"Not at all." I took her phone and snapped shots while Blake posed with her and a young man.

She retrieved her phone. "I heard the Blakester was in town, but I didn't believe it. You think he's the real Blakester?"

I assured her that I had no idea. When Blake moved on, I asked her who he was.

"Are you kidding me? He's like the most awesome trendsetter in the world. You know, one of those people who turn up at all the glamorous events in New York and LA."

So he was using his med school tuition money to play the wealthy socialite? "Maybe it's not him," I murmured.

She pulled a website up on her phone and showed me a picture. It was Blake. I had no doubt about it.

The very next moment I heard Linda say, "You what?" loud enough to silence the chatter in the room.

Twenty

Norma Jeanne's eyes went wide, and she glared at her aunt.

Sheepishly, Linda said a general, "I'm sorry," to no one in particular, and the murmur of voices rose again.

I edged toward them, stopping to add a sausage roll to my plate full of food.

"Young man," said Linda, "I most certainly hope that you were joking about quitting medical school. Honestly, you could give me a heart attack just saying things like that."

With a smug expression, Tiffany handed her mother a phone. "I knew you were up to something. Who dresses like that?"

Linda gasped. "Blake! This is you. What does it mean?"

Her husband, Tim, gazed at the phone over her shoulder.

Blake flashed his sister a look of daggers. "It doesn't mean anything, Mom."

"It must mean something. This site is all about you," said

Linda. "And that girl whom you don't even know wanted a picture taken with you. Now explain yourself."

"I'm an influencer."

"I have no idea what that means," said Tim. "Is it a computer thing?"

"It means that a lot of people are influenced by what I do. I set the trends."

"Why?" asked Linda.

"Because I'm cool."

"Is that why you insist on wearing these strange clothes?" Tim gestured toward his son's attire.

"Dad, you have no fashion sense. This is a very expensive garment. Where's Norma Jeanne? She would understand."

"Honey, are you doing this for money? Is that it?" asked Linda. "Your grandfather wasn't sending you enough?"

"Grampy sent him plenty," said Tiffany. "That's why he was going to cut him off."

Linda's gasp drew stares.

"Mom," said Blake softly, "can we please talk about this back at the inn?"

Vivienne, who had been standing nearby listening, calmly threw back a cup of punch before saying, "Did you think he wouldn't cut you off if you killed him?"

When Vivienne laughed and strode away, Linda said, "Don't you worry, Blake. We'll get this all straightened out."

Tim gave his son a pat on the back, which caused the loose strings of his outfit to wiggle, which caused dogs to bark at Blake.

Most people who saw it broke out laughing. Blake was clearly mortified and left in a huff.

"Wow! You clean up pretty well for an elf, Miss Holly Miller." Holmes smiled at me. "Have you tried the bourbon punch? I can recommend it."

I couldn't tell him I felt like I had to keep my wits about

me so I could listen in on conversations and observe people. "Not yet. Are you having a good time?"

"It's amazing. The whole town turned out. There are people here whom I haven't seen in years."

"A lot of people in Wagtail care about you."

It was the wrong thing to say. His smile faded. I felt awful and sought something else to distract him. "Maybe they really came to see what Blake would be wearing."

"Never a dull moment around that guy. Speaking of which, any news on Dale?"

"Not really."

"We should put our heads together. We make a pretty good team."

Norma Jeanne strolled up. "Holly, I've been admiring your dress. Who is it?"

It took me a second to understand what she was asking. "I really don't know."

She nodded as though I confirmed what she suspected. Wrinkling her nose, she said, "It's so *red*. It's the next best thing to a Christmas sweater."

I was fairly sure that was a slap in the face. With a cheery smile, I said, "I heard you learned how to make shrimp and grits."

Norma Jeanne's smug expression faded. "Never again. And no more hiking, either. Did Holmes tell you that his buddies took us on a hike? It was the most excruciatingly boring two hours of my life, and my feet are covered in blisters. I swear I'm going to have to go to a spa to recuperate. No more hiking for me. The only hiking I plan to do is on sidewalks from store to store."

"This isn't really the best time of year for hiking," I said. "Although the snow is pretty."

"That's not all. Did you tell her?" asked Norma Jeanne.

"My aunt invited her to go riding." Holmes's eyes turned up toward the ceiling.

I thought he was bracing himself.

"I swear that horse bucked me off intentionally," Norma Jeanne declared.

"Oh no! Are you all right?" I asked.

"He didn't buck, NJ." Holmes spoke in a level tone.

"He threw me off of him. I call that bucking. I can't imagine what my mother sees in Wagtail. I think I'm a city girl, through and through."

She was. And while I was getting to like her less and less, I didn't think it was fair of us to judge her for it.

Trixie ran up to us and placed her paws on Holmes's legs. He bent to pet her, but Norma Jeanne drew back.

"She won't hurt you," I said.

"I don't do dogs." Norma Jeanne wrinkled her nose again.

I was in shock. "But your mother has a dog. Maggie. And your great-grandmother has Muffy."

"Isn't it awful? I could not believe they brought them on this trip. Even if I don't touch them, I end up with fur all over my clothes."

Holmes's brow furrowed, as though it was the first time he'd heard her speak that way.

I was done being nice. I was through being supportive. "Excuse us."

Right in front of her, I grabbed Holmes's hand and tugged him through the crowd and out the door. Trixie came with us.

When we were away from people, under the starry velvet sky, I came right out and said it. "You cannot marry her."

Twenty-one

"Holly Miller!" Holmes scolded me. "I thought you, of all people, would understand. You dated Ben, who is the same way. He doesn't like cats or dogs."

I held out my palms. "And do you see me marrying him? If you recall, I turned him down. Trixie and Twinkletoes had a lot to do with that. I didn't want to live my life without animals. No—I *couldn't* live my life without animals." I tried to lower my voice and be more sympathetic. "And I don't think you want to do that, either."

Holmes sighed and rubbed Trixie's ears. "The odd thing is that I fit into Norma Jeanne's life in Chicago, but it's painfully apparent that she doesn't fit into my life."

As much as I hated to admit it, I sort of understood. Life in the city was different. I had loved it. I had been to the grand parties, gone to the theater, shopped in the fancy stores, and taken advantage of all that city life had to offer. But even back then I had done it with a dog. Just because *I* had elected to live in Wagtail didn't mean Holmes had to do the same thing.

"I guess you made that choice when you proposed to her," I said.

"Actually, Norma Jeanne was the one who wanted to get married. She suggested it one day and . . . Why do you think this engagement has dragged out so long? I knew there were problems." He sucked in a deep breath of the cold air. "When my dad was sick and I had to keep coming back here, I realized how much I missed it. For crying out loud, Holly, her family makes dog clothes! You'd think she would fit in here, wouldn't you? That she would love living in Wagtail."

"I think Dale and EmmyLou would fit in. But—" I couldn't bring myself to say it. He knew what I meant. He was surely thinking it himself. Norma Jeanne would hate life in Wagtail. It wasn't her thing. No one cared about haute couture here. And there were dogs everywhere. I had serious doubts about anyone who *didn't do dogs*, but I couldn't say that to Holmes. *Could I?*

"Sometimes we make sacrifices for the people we love," I said softly.

He squinted at me. "So if I truly loved Norma Jeanne, I would give up on my dreams to come back to Wagtail?"

Actually, I had meant it the other way around. If Norma Jeanne truly loved Holmes, she might agree to live in Wagtail to make him happy.

And then he grabbed me in a big bear hug. "Holly, you're absolutely right! I've been trying to talk this out with Dave and some of my buddies. Even with Grandma Rose and Oma. And in one sentence, you set me straight. It all seems so clear to me now. Thanks. You're the best."

I had no idea what he meant and was more than a little afraid that he might have misinterpreted what I said. But he seemed very relieved and smiled like his old self.

"I'm glad I could help." I said it weakly since I had a bad

feeling I had actually made things worse. But then I wondered—worse for me or for Holmes? In the end, he would do what his heart told him to do, and it wasn't up to me. For someone who had been determined to support Holmes and his decisions, I had made a mess of things. I never should have butted in.

At that moment, Norma Jeanne tottered out on heels that weren't meant for snowy paths. "Holmes, honey? What are you doing out here in the cold?"

"It just got a little bit hot in there," he said.

She looked from him to me and back again. "Looks like it's getting hot out here."

On some level, I supposed I deserved that. But our little chat couldn't have been more innocent. Okay, so I *had* told him he couldn't marry her, but it wasn't like we were smooching or anything. "We were just catching up, Norma Jeanne," I said. "Holmes has been so busy that we haven't had time for a chat."

"Holmes, would you mind terribly if I headed back to the inn?" she asked. "What with Grandpa's death, this has been the worst holiday ever. And I haven't gotten any sleep since I've been here." She glared at me. "Apparently there's not a decent pair of blackout curtains in this entire town or any potable water, either. My skin is already the texture of sandpaper."

She was awful! All those not-so-subtle jabs were like slaps in the face. I reminded myself not to stoop to her level. I had to be kind. After all, her grandfather had been murdered and the whole family had been roused in the middle of the night. I would be a basket case if I were in her shoes.

"But it's Christmas Eve," said Holmes. "You'll miss the carols and the ringing of the bells."

Not to mention that the party had been thrown in their honor. I didn't mention that, though. It was their issue, not mine.

"Right now I don't care if Santa Claus himself comes from the North Pole to ring bells. I'm going back to the inn." She shot a sly look in my direction. "It's not like you won't have plenty of company, most of whom will be telling you lies about me."

Whoa! How deftly she planted that seed in Holmes's head. Very practical. No matter what might be revealed, she could say we were lying.

I had tried my best to be supportive of Holmes, but in that moment, she revealed the true Norma Jeanne. She was calculating and manipulative. I was done trying to like her.

Holmes walked her into the house and I followed. He was offering to get her a Wagtail taxi, and then, right behind her, a party host's nightmare commenced.

Aunt Birdie and Vivienne saw each other. They stood four feet apart. I knew it was trouble with a capital *T*.

"You have some nerve coming to a party in honor of my family," said Vivienne.

"I was invited." Aunt Birdie held her head high.

"If I had murdered someone, I believe I'd be keeping a low profile." Vivienne leveled a cold gaze on Aunt Birdie.

"Perhaps you should take your own advice."

"Holmes, do something," spat Norma Jeanne.

"I'll take Aunt Birdie," I said.

Holmes tried to get Vivienne's attention by flattering her, while I took Aunt Birdie's arm intending to steer her away. But we were too late. Vivienne tossed an entire glass of bourbon cranberry punch at Aunt Birdie, who stepped aside with amazing dexterity. The full force of the liquid hit Norma Jeanne in the face and splashed down her dress.

The room went silent. *Oh no!* I cast about for something, anything, to say.

One of Holmes's buddies broke the tension. "Funny, I thought the bourbon punch was delicious."

I walked away with Aunt Birdie fast.

"He had filed for divorce," she said. "He didn't love her."

I placed my hand on her arm. Poor Aunt Birdie.

She watched the commotion surrounding Norma Jeanne. "Can you believe that he stayed with her for years because of her heart condition? He put her well being before his own happiness. He finally decided he had to move on. He didn't want to live the rest of his life with her. But he never got the opportunity to enjoy life without her again. She was such a harpy. He thought it would be the last time the family gathered for the holidays. That witch must have been waiting for him outside my door, and when he left, she stabbed him."

"That's so creepy. She was stalking him?" I shivered at the thought.

"She must have been. How else would she have known where I lived?"

"It's not that hard to find addresses on the Internet anymore."

"And I suppose she could have asked just about anyone who lives here. I'm fairly well-known in Wagtail."

"I'm sorry, Aunt Birdie."

"Are you, dear? That may be the nicest thing you have ever said to me. But I'm not leaving. I have more right to be here than she does, and I would like to have a word with your grandmother."

I watched her walk away as though nothing had happened. Aunt Birdie might be an obnoxious, opinionated character, but she had a lot of pride.

After Norma Jeanne left, Holmes found me and handed me my coat.

"What's going on?" Tiffany whispered.

"It's Christmas Eve," he said, as though that explained everything.

We weren't the only ones leaving. There was a mass exodus from the party. People piled out of the house and walked along the street. Holmes and I joined Oma and Rose.

Trixie and Gingersnap romped ahead on the street as Wagtailites emerged from their homes and merged with the crowd.

All the homes glittered in their holiday finery. I turned to look at the Grinch. He shone brightly, looking over the rooftops a couple of blocks away.

In short order, we arrived at the old Wagtail church. Children gathered at the front, all wearing red cloaks. Each one held a candle.

Ethan Schroeder stood next to his sister and waved at me, calling, "Hi, Holly!"

Mrs. Carr looked over and smiled at me. "Thank you for being so kind to Ethan. This holiday is especially hard on him."

"He's such an adorable little guy. I can't believe no one has adopted them yet."

"There's an adoption pending. I was hoping it would go through before Christmas, but you know how slowly these things move. The children don't know yet."

"Who's adopting them?"

"They won't tell me! Isn't that awful? But I'll miss those darling faces. I hope they stay in Wagtail. They'd have a built-in babysitter in me."

"You didn't want to adopt them?"

"Oh, child. I love them to bits, but they deserve a young, active family, not an old lady like me."

"You're not that old!" I protested.

"Old enough. Little ones are a handful. I'm ready to be the granny, not have full-time responsibility for them."

I understood. They were so sweet standing in front of the church, squirming and fussing. But most of the parents were a good thirty years younger than Marie.

Rupert tended to a little girl, sliding red gloves over her hands. Three other children demanded his attention.

Teenagers handed out candles to the people who had

come to watch. Each dog and cat received a light that could be attached to a collar with a carabiner-style clip. They glowed in the shapes of stars.

A bell rang once, silence fell over the crowd, and the children sang "Away in a Manger." And "Jingle Bells." And even "Rockin' Around the Christmas Tree." Not a single person in the crowd didn't smile as they continued their performance.

At midnight, the church bells in the bell tower rang out, just like I remembered from my childhood. It was Christmas Day.

The procession of candles and darting stars as people and their furry friends walked home was almost as special as the children singing.

Rupert introduced me to his four children and whispered, "This is my first Christmas with them in three years."

One of his daughters boasted, "My daddy has a Grinch!"

I hadn't given much thought to Rupert's holiday, but it all made sense now. Five stockings, four smaller Christmas trees, the baking, and the giant Grinch—Rupert had gone all out for his children. He might be a little rough around the edges, but he clearly loved those kids.

It was a charming and lovely end to the evening. Oma and I had both brought golf carts, so we gave our guests rides back to the inn.

In the main lobby, there was some kind of fuss going on.

The Kedrowski clan stood in the middle of the lobby. Tim tossed his sport coat over a chair and loosened his tie.

I heard Austin say, "No wonder you looked familiar! You're the Blakester!"

"I knew it," Tiffany boasted. "I knew he couldn't possibly arrive before us from medical school when he had to change planes three times from the islands."

"Blake! Darling, you can't drop out of med school,"

Linda said in a totally matter-of-fact tone, as if it wasn't even a possibility. "You're the smart one in the family."

Tiffany stared at her mom. Her jaw dropped before she said, "Thank you, Mother," and turned away.

"Now don't throw a snit, Tiffie. You know perfectly well that Blake was an A student. He was valedictorian of his class, for heaven's sake. You have other strengths, sweetheart." Linda rubbed the side of her face. "Good grief, say something, Tim!"

Tim slowly raised a glass to his mouth and took a gulp of bourbon. "What exactly is it that you've been doing?"

"I dress in all the latest designers' fashions."

"Do they pay you to do that?" asked Tim.

"Well, no. But I get into the trendy nightclubs."

"Do you get free drinks?" asked Tim.

"No."

Tiffany burst into laughter.

"That's not a job," Linda blurted.

"Then you're not making a living doing this?" asked Tim.

"I will be."

Linda held her hands on the top of her head like she was afraid it might explode. "I'm afraid to ask how you've been paying your expenses."

"Mom!" Tiffany shook her head incredulously. "Don't you see? He's been living off the money Grampy sends him for med school tuition."

Blake's parents gasped simultaneously.

Speaking calmly, Tim said, "That must provide you a comfortable life in the islands."

Tiffany crossed her arms over her chest. "Tell them, Blake, or I will."

Blake gazed around like he was looking for an escape. Apparently resigned to his fate, he muttered, "I live in New York most of the time."

"Most of the time?" His mother's eyes widened.

"Sometimes I just feel like going to the beach."

Linda narrowed her eyes. "I don't understand. You're a model?"

"I'm a trendsetter, like the Kardashians. People send me things to wear and invite me to fancy events."

"Like those ridiculous trousers and the absurd dress? Honestly, I was embarrassed to admit you were my son tonight."

"Mom, this retails for a couple thousand dollars."

Tim spewed bourbon.

Linda glanced in his direction. "Listen to me, Blake. You will not always be young and cute. One day you will look like your father."

They all gazed at Tim. He raised his glass in recognition but showed no sign of irritation.

Linda continued, "And then you'll wish you were a doctor."

"Mother! You just don't have an eye for high fashion."

Linda tried to hide her amusement by placing one hand over her mouth. She pointed to his bizarre getup with her other hand. "Is this supposed to be high fashion? Honey, argyle trousers are what clowns wear, and the pants that jut out at the hips are jodhpurs for riding horses. There's nothing new or fashionable about either one. And honestly, rags have never been in fashion."

Blake looked shocked, as though he had just realized the truth in what she had said.

"Your father will pull every string he has and get you back into that medical school."

Blake sagged. "How am I going to pay for med school?"

"Oh, honey! Don't worry," said Linda. "We'll find a way. Don't they give loans to med students? You'll get one, and we'll help you out."

Blake tented his fingers in front of his nose, his eyes wide. "A loan? I can't deal with loans. I shouldn't have to. I'm a Thackleberry heir."

After that, they settled quickly for the night. Given the death of Dale and the fact that the Thackleberry family hadn't slept much the previous night, maybe it wasn't so surprising that they all headed up to bed.

I changed into my elf costume for the final time this season. Trixie didn't mind when I dressed her. No sign of itching or allergies from her Thackleberry outfit. "We have some very big deliveries to make tonight. Are you psyched?"

She kissed my nose. I figured that meant *yes*.

I fed Twinkletoes something called Smitten Kitten that smelled of tuna, and the three of us walked down the hidden staircase to the private kitchen.

Holmes sat in front of the fire.

"What are you doing here?" I asked. He was already dressed as an elf.

"I thought I would pick you up. Rose wanted me to bring some gifts to put under the tree for tomorrow.

"I'm surprised she remembered with the party. It was lovely."

He nodded. But he made no move to leave.

I sat down on the hearth and faced him. "What's going on?"

"Would it be awful of me to break off my engagement to Norma Jeanne on Christmas Day?"

I nearly fell over. But part of me wanted to stand up and dance with joy. I tried to compose myself. "It's not the best choice of days."

"Everyone has gone to so much trouble on my behalf."

"I wouldn't worry about that too much."

"No one likes her, do they?"

I figured he would feel better if he knew the truth. "Not really."

"Seems kind of mean to do it on Christmas, you know? And on top of Dale being murdered. How much can one person take? Maybe it would be best to wait until we get back to Chicago."

It might never happen if he did that. But I understood and appreciated his concern and kindness toward Norma Jeanne. I opted not to say anything more. What I wanted him to do wasn't relevant.

Casey poked his nose in the kitchen. "Looks like a quiet night."

"Casey," I said, "the night of Dale's murder, you said a lot of the family members were out late. Do you remember who?"

"Sure. Dave already asked me the same thing. That mean Vivienne woman, EmmyLou, and Linda and Tim. Oh! And Blake. He asked me where there was a nightclub."

Holmes's eyes opened wide. "That's a lot of restless people. What time do you lock the door?"

"The sliding doors in reception are locked at midnight. But anyone can leave. That's a fire safety thing. They just can't get back in."

"You mean you can't lock those doors?" asked Holmes.

"There's an override button we can push to open or lock them in an emergency. But after midnight, they have to walk around to the main lobby. I usually lock that door around two thirty or three. That gives people time to get back here after last call at the bars."

"So it could have been any one of them," I said. I poured hot chocolate in a large thermos and grabbed a few disposable cups to take along in the mock sleigh.

"Are you ready to go, Holmes?" No sooner had I asked than a scream rose upstairs.

Twenty-two

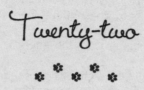

Holmes, Casey, Trixie, Twinkletoes, and I bounded up the back stairs to the second floor. Doors opened and people stepped out to see what was going on.

The screaming stopped the moment Holmes arrived on the scene.

A bare-chested Austin struggled into jeans in the hallway. Norma Jeanne was wrapped in a sheet, which she clutched to her chest.

Tiffany, wearing bright pink pajamas with a colorful cat print, pointed her hand at Norma Jeanne. "My own cousin! How could you do this to me?"

"It's not what it looks like," said Norma Jeanne.

"Really?" Tiffany crossed her arms over her chest. "This should be priceless."

Norma Jeanne cast a desperate look at Austin.

Austin had turned the color of beets, right up to the tops of his ears. "She was, uh, helping me, um, wrap your Christmas gift, Tiffany."

From the back of the crowd, Norma Jeanne's father said in a dry tone, "Norma Jeanne, put some clothes on. Austin, zip your pants." He walked away.

"Norma Jeanne!" Linda glanced at her daughter, Tiffany. "How could you? I mean, it's bad enough to cheat on Holmes, but with your own cousin's boyfriend?"

I looked at Holmes. His head tilted like a puppy who was trying to understand what was happening.

Norma Jeanne said, "Holmes, I was so depressed. I had to seek comfort somewhere."

"Gee, thanks, Norma Jeanne." Austin's expression suggested he'd been blindsided.

"Please, Holmes." Norma Jeanne nearly lost control of the sheet she wore when she reached out to touch his arm. "We have to talk. Everyone here hates me. It's all because of them. You know that. Holly, especially, has been simply awful to me. She's the one who has driven this wedge between us. She didn't even get me the Mistletoe Cactus Dew that I need. Don't you remember all the good times we had in Chicago? Let's go home and put this nightmare behind us."

Holmes's eyebrows drove downward, and his mouth twisted to the side. "It's far too late for that, Norma Jeanne."

"Please," she wailed. "At least give me a chance. Let's talk this out."

"I don't think so. There's not really anything to talk about."

Holmes walked away. Norma Jeanne started to chase after him but stepped on her sheet and fell flat on her face.

Austin helped her up. He ran his hand through his hair. "I apologize to everyone. I'm pretty embarrassed at the moment."

"As you should be!" Linda scolded. "And on Christmas. Really? The two of you couldn't have at least waited until you were back in Chicago?"

"Aunt Linda," said Norma Jeanne, "you've forgotten what it's like to be young and in love."

I couldn't help myself. "You're in love with Austin but you want Holmes to give you another chance?"

"It's all your fault, Holly," she spat.

"Norma Jeanne! That's enough." Her mother, EmmyLou, scowled. "You were engaged to Holmes. I presumed that meant you were in love with *him*. And Austin is dating your cousin! Of all the despicable things to do. I have been brokenhearted about my father being murdered, and worried sick about Maggie, and now you have to shame the whole family with this kind of behavior? Go to your own room."

Norma Jeanne's jaw tightened, but she did as her mother said.

I probably would have done the same just to avoid any further unpleasantry. Christmas morning was going to be very interesting.

Linda and Tim walked downstairs with Tiffany.

I followed them. "How about some spiked hot chocolate with whipped cream and marshmallows?"

"That's so nice of you, Holly." Tiffany looked like she was on the verge of crying. "Do you think there are any doughnuts or cupcakes?"

"Honey," said Linda, "you don't need to put on weight because of this."

"For Pete's sake, Linda. Will you leave her alone?" Tim blasted his wife. "You eat all the cupcakes you want, Tiffie." He shot Linda a dirty look. "And I'll have some with you."

"Mom! Why are you always so mean to me? Do you really think I haven't noticed that you call Norma Jeanne *the pretty one* and Blake *the smart one*?"

"Oh, Tiffie. Don't you see? I understand you better than anyone. You're just like me. I was never the brainy one, or the athletic one. I was just there. Plain Linda. Where do you think you got that nose of yours? It's just like mine. All I want is for you to be happy, sweetie."

"I'll have Casey check on goodies," I said. "He'll bring them right in to you."

They settled in front of the fireplace in the Dogwood Room.

I popped into the private kitchen and told Casey what the Kedrowskis needed. There was no sign of Holmes.

Trixie ran to the front door and gazed back at me impatiently. On a hunch, I looked outside.

Holmes stood on the porch, looking at the Christmas lights of Wagtail.

I joined him and asked softly, "Are you okay?"

"I'll be fine. Life in Chicago will be a little awkward and weird, since I work for NJ's dad. But I'll manage."

"Better to know before the wedding. Right?" I asked.

"There wouldn't have been a wedding. I was waiting until after the holidays to break off the engagement because I didn't want to be a jerk." He flashed a sad look at me. "I figured this trip would be a make-or-break deal. I couldn't quite figure out what was wrong with our relationship." He rubbed his face with both of his hands. "This trip has been very revealing. I was desperate to have the relationship end, which is why I was asking about doing it tomorrow."

"They say you learn a lot about people when you travel with them."

"I'll say! I saw sides of Norma Jeanne that I didn't know she had." He looked down at the porch floor. "It was usually fun when we were together, and then we went our separate ways, which I guess was the breather we needed from each other. My mom says I would never survive Norma Jeanne's regimented scheduling."

"That could get old."

"It never bothered me in small doses. I just saw it as one

of her quirks. There's nothing wrong with being on time and having a schedule, but when we were out with some of my old buddies, it was like she had set a timer on fun. I'm sure she wanted to leave because she wasn't enjoying herself, but she didn't understand that she was being rude. And she just couldn't imagine being an elf."

Holmes looked at me. "She wouldn't go sledding with me. She didn't want to spend time with my parents or Grandma Rose or my friends. Maybe those aren't reasons to call off a marriage, but everything added up, I guess. You set me straight last night. I realized that she was more in love with the idea of a wedding than she was with the reality of marriage. It would have been a disaster as soon as the wedding spotlight was off her."

"I'm sorry, Holmes." I wasn't sorry that the engagement was off, but I was sorry that he had been hurt. "If you don't want to come with us tonight, we would understand."

"Are you kidding? I wouldn't miss it for the world. It's exactly what I need to take my mind off NJ."

We walked to his grandmother's house, collected the sleigh, which was loaded with items for delivery, and picked up Zelda and Shelley.

First stop—Marie Carr's house. Holmes and I lifted the BadBoyz 8000 blue and green Monster bike out of the sleigh and carried it up to the porch. Zelda and Shelley followed with gifts for Ethan's sister.

While Wagtail slept, we drove around town delivering presents. It was about the closest a person could ever come to feeling like Santa Claus. In spite of his terrible experience, Holmes was cheerful and seemed fine. I didn't tell Zelda or Shelley what had happened with Norma Jeanne, and neither did he. It would get around fast enough, and I figured it was up to Holmes to tell them if he felt like it. Apparently, he didn't.

At five in the morning, Holmes walked me back to the inn.

"Thanks for letting me play elf with you, Holly. It was the bright spot in my Christmas. You know what bothers me more than breaking off the engagement—Dale's murder. I've been so self-absorbed that I haven't followed up on it like I should have. Dale was a great guy. I feel like I owe it to him."

Fat snowflakes began to float lazily from the dark sky.

"You know the Thackleberry family better than anyone else around here. Who do you suspect?"

Holmes looked up at the falling snow. "My money would be on Vivienne. I don't have any evidence, but do you recall seeing her at the Wagtail Springs Hotel in the middle of the night? I can't help wondering if it was a murder for hire. I'd be very interested in what she was doing there."

"I wonder what time Dale died. We saw her around one in the morning, right? And then the next day, she didn't bother reporting him missing, which sounds like evidence of guilt to me. You might be onto something."

"What do you say we take a little walk over to the Wagtail Springs Hotel later today and ask some questions?"

"Sounds good to me. Let me know when you're free. Are you okay walking home alone?" I asked.

"I love to walk in falling snow, and it would do me good to walk in the cold air. I have a lot to sort out. Lesson number one—never date your boss's daughter."

"Barry seems like a nice guy. If anything, he's the one who will be ashamed and find it awkward. You didn't do anything wrong."

"Awkward at work every day?" Holmes screwed his mouth to the side. "Less than ideal circumstances, don't you think?"

"It's the kind of thing people get over. It's not like Norma Jeanne works there."

He looked down at his boots. "I guess I feel a little guilty, too."

"Why? You've been a complete gentleman. Haven't you?" Uh-oh. What if there was someone else that I didn't know about?

"Because I've been wracking my brain for a reason to break off the engagement." He mussed his sandy hair. "I'm a crumb. Since we set foot in Wagtail, all I've done is think of reasons to break up with Norma Jeanne. That's almost as bad."

"You're inventing guilt! She just handed you the best reason ever."

"But would she have done that if I had been more attentive?"

"Holmes, it doesn't matter. When did you get to be so wishy-washy? You didn't create this situation. I was there the day Austin walked in and she saw him. I knew there was still something between them."

"You're just saying that to make me feel better."

"Would I do that?"

"Yes."

Okay, that was true. I would. "Not this time. Their eyes met and it was obvious."

"My family went to so much effort," he griped.

"Why don't you pay for the party and the Thackleberrys' bill at the inn?"

"I could do that! Grandma Rose and my folks were going to pay for their lodging. What a great idea. That would make me feel a lot better." He swung his arms around me in a big hug. "Merry Christmas, Holly."

I swear there was a new spring in his step as he crossed the green on his way home.

I tiptoed up the stairs for my final duty as an elf. I retrieved the envelopes Dale had given me. With Trixie and Twinkletoes at my feet, I carefully checked the names and deposited them in the appropriate Thackleberry stockings.

* * *

I woke early to a winter wonderland. Snow covered everything. Wagtail sparkled in its finery. It clung to the branches of the evergreens and blanketed the rooftops. The sun shone in a vivid blue sky, and the world seemed crisp and clean.

After a shower, I dressed in a white sweater and a flared red skirt. I slid a red velvet collar with white accents over Twinkletoes's head. She sat proudly, as if she knew it was special.

Trixie wore her sparkly red collar. Feeling quite festive, we all went downstairs to the early brunch.

Gingersnap greeted us first in a green velvet collar, her tail wagging nonstop.

"Want to come, Gingersnap?"

The *Closed* sign hung on the front door. It was the first time I had ever seen it used. Our buffet was only for inn guests, invited friends, and the inn family today. I walked outside into the brisk morning with the dogs. The sidewalks had been cleared. In spite of the snow, or maybe because of it, most people were walking their dogs off leash. They bounded through the green, jumping and playing with glee.

It wasn't easy to coax Trixie and Gingersnap back inside. But the promise of cookies did the trick.

Many of Norma Jeanne's relatives clustered around the tree in the Dogwood Room. Norma Jeanne wasn't there yet. I wondered if she was hesitant to show her face after her scandalous behavior the night before.

Blake lazily made his way down the stairs. For the first time, he wore regular clothes—a forest green turtleneck and matching green trousers.

"Merry Christmas!" I called to him.

"Yeah, yeah. Merry Christmas," he mumbled.

He went straight to his stocking and unceremoniously

dumped the contents onto a chair. His long fingers zeroed in on an ordinary white envelope. He ripped it open and pulled out a sheet of paper. As he read, his complexion went ashen.

He reread the note, turned, and said loudly to his family, "Is this some kind of joke?"

Twenty-three

Tim raised his coffee in a toast. "Merry Christmas."

"This must be Vivi's idea," said Blake. "Where is that Scrooge?"

"She hasn't made an appearance yet." Tim looked exhausted, as if the steam had gone out of him.

EmmyLou and Maggie approached me. "Holly, I have spoken with your grandmother, but I wanted to apologize to you, too. I can't imagine what Norma Jeanne was thinking last night, and I can only hope that Holmes will forgive her and that they will reconcile. I hope you will forgive us, too. Her behavior has been simply abominable."

"No need to apologize, EmmyLou. You'd be surprised how often things like this happen in an inn."

Her eyes opened wide. "I guess you do see a lot of inappropriate dalliances here. There's something about getting away from home that makes us lose sight of our morals.

Please don't think ill of Norma Jeanne. Her grandfather's death has her so rattled that it impaired her judgment."

I doubted that, but I wasn't about to say so to her mother.

EmmyLou smiled wanly. "If you'll excuse me, I should go see if my grandmother, Doris, needs any help."

It wasn't easy to tear myself away from the drama in the Dogwood Room. But Rose seized my arm when she saw me. "Is it true?" she whispered.

I didn't know exactly what she had heard, but I nodded. "You mean about Norma Jeanne?"

She picked up two glasses of mimosas, handed me one, and clinked them. "This is the best Christmas ever!"

"Shh. They'll hear you."

"Holmes was there?" she asked. "He saw with his own eyes?"

"I'm afraid so. He took it pretty well, though." I didn't know how much I should tell her. If Holmes wanted to share the fact that he would have broken off the engagement anyway, that was up to him.

Rose looked at the ceiling and raised her glass like she was toasting. "Christmas wishes do come true!"

Shelley and Zelda arrived with Dave and gushed to Rose about the party thrown by the Richardsons the night before. I hustled to the kitchen to help Oma and the cook.

I carried dishes out to the buffet and arranged them—honey-glazed ham, peppered country bacon, smoked salmon, biscuits hot from the oven, wilted winter greens with citrus, individual spinach and red pepper quiches, a wreath of praline French toast with syrups, fresh fruit salad, scrambled eggs, Cointreau mimosas, an assortment of bagels and breakfast breads, chocolate mousse, and—could it be? Was that really Fluffy Cake?

My mouth watered.

"No turkey?" asked Tiffany.

Oma overheard her question. "We will have turkey, goose, and stuffing for dinner tonight at The Blue Boar."

A blast of fresh air hit me when Holmes arrived with Mr. Huckle. Much more cheerful than Blake, Holmes said, "On my way over I saw Ethan outside showing off his new bicycle. The sidewalks look pretty good. It's a little icy to ride on them yet, but he couldn't stop parading the bike around. You've never seen a happier kid! This is a holiday that he'll remember."

I had a feeling we would remember this Christmas, too. But not for the same reasons as Ethan.

Tim and Tiffany were the first to sit down at the tables. EmmyLou helped Doris to a seat. Tim watched them, then raised a mimosa glass to Doris. I retrieved bowls with Christmas brunch for Muffy and Maggie. The dogs were having scrambled eggs with fresh salmon, wilted winter greens, and a sprinkle of bacon.

I had to coax Trixie away from their food. "I'm bringing you a bowl, too. I promise!"

The tables in the dining area had been arranged in a big rectangle so everyone could fit and there would be no division of families.

I suspected the Thackleberrys might not like eating Christmas brunch with a cop, but Dave had been invited long before Dale's murder.

Aunt Birdie arrived, wearing a red plaid dress and bearing an armful of gifts.

There was a long moment of awkwardness as Norma Jeanne and Austin chose seats. Norma Jeanne sat near her mother, but poor Austin appeared to be at a loss.

I suspected he wouldn't be comfortable with Tiffany and wasn't sure how well received he would be by Norma Jeanne's family. Feeling for the poor guy, I ushered him to a seat near Dave, Zelda, and Shelley.

Holmes, his parents, and Rose sat close to Oma and me.

I finally fetched Christmas brunch bowls for Gingersnap, Trixie, and Twinkletoes. They dug in right away.

Christmas carols played softly in the background, loud enough to spark the holiday spirit but not so loud that people couldn't hear one another speak. A fire blazed in the big fireplace, and lights twinkled on the tree.

When most people were seated, two chairs were empty, but I couldn't put my finger on who was missing.

Oma rose from her seat. "Thank you all for joining us at the Sugar Maple Inn this holiday. You may notice that we have left one chair empty in remembrance of Dale Thackleberry, who was taken from us far too soon. I like to think he is here with us today in spirit. May we all find peace and joy in our hearts in spite of his absence." She lifted her mimosa glass. "Merry Christmas."

It was a somber way to start the meal, but EmmyLou mouthed her thanks in Oma's direction. It had been the right thing to do.

While our guests helped themselves, Oma leaned toward me and whispered, "Is it true that Norma Jeanne was playing hanky-panky with Austin?"

"I'm afraid so."

Oma smiled and threw her hands in the air. "What a relief! She was not the right woman for our Holmes."

"Don't get too excited. Norma Jeanne's mother hopes they will reconcile."

"No! We cannot allow this to happen."

Everyone appeared to be having a great time. The food was delicious. I wasn't sure I'd ever had French toast and ham on the same plate, but it was a combination that I gobbled up. Before venturing toward the Fluffy Cake, I made rounds filling mugs with coffee and tea. As I refilled coffee for the Kedrowskis, it finally dawned on me that it was Vivienne who had not come down to brunch.

I leaned over to her son, Tim, and spoke softly. "Is everything all right with your mom?"

Linda overheard me. "Maybe we should check on her, Tim. It's not like her to miss free food."

Tim sighed. "You know why she's not here. How could she show her face after what she did?"

I was itching to ask what exactly she had done, but it probably wasn't any of my business.

"I'll face her," said Tiffany. "I'm not afraid of her."

Linda nodded. "I'll come with you, but if I know Vivi, she won't answer the door."

"I can open it if you're worried," I offered.

Linda glanced at Tim, who shrugged. "Maybe that's wise," she said. "That way we won't worry if she's just sitting there being grumpy."

They followed Trixie and me to the inn office, where I fetched a ring of room keys in case we needed them. We walked up the stairs to the Swim guest room.

I knocked on the door. "Mrs. Thackleberry?"

There was no answer.

I tried again, rapping as hard as I could to wake her. "Mrs. Thackleberry?"

Still nothing. I slid the key into the lock and turned it. Pushing the door handle down, I swung the door open.

Twenty-four

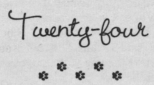

The bed was made perfectly. The curtains were open.

"Either she's meticulous about making the bed or she didn't sleep here last night," I said.

Linda and Tiffany said simultaneously, "She would never make her own bed."

"What did she wear to the party? Do you remember?" I asked.

Linda blushed. "She didn't make a point of telling you all about her couture dress that she bought from the designer at a fashion show?"

Tiffany scowled. "It drives me batty that she spends so much on clothes for herself but she threw a fit when Grampy gave to charities."

"She puts Scrooge to shame," said Linda, "and takes miserliness to new lows. For years I packed extra gifts so you kids wouldn't think she had forgotten you."

"I didn't know that," said Tiffany.

"Dale used to sneak them under the tree with your names on them. When you were older, he started giving the envelopes, which bypassed her entirely. Your grandmother is a pill. Do you know why you call her Vivi? She didn't want anyone to think she was old enough to be a grandmother. Can you believe it? Most women take pride in their grandchildren. Not Vivi."

I peeked in the bathroom quickly to be sure she hadn't fallen. "I guess we might as well go back and have dessert." That gorgeous Fluffy Cake was uppermost on my mind.

Linda nodded. "Vivi will have to turn up eventually to face what she did."

As we walked along the hallway, I asked, "Should we mount a search for her?"

"Goodness, no." Linda laughed. "You wouldn't come to Christmas brunch either, if you had taken away all the gifts and left the stockings empty."

"I don't understand. I saw Blake's stocking. It was full of goodies."

"That's because I filled them. If it had been up to Vivi, we wouldn't have received Christmas gifts at all. But Dale always gave each of us something special," said Linda as we walked. "A trip or a new car, something sort of pricey. But this year, the envelopes contained notes welcoming us all to the real world."

"Everyone has been cut off," Tiffany explained. "In addition to gifts, each family member received extra annual income from the profits of the business. But not anymore. Even if the company survives, we're entirely cut off."

Uh-oh. Those envelopes were from Dale. I had inserted them into the stockings myself. Unless Vivienne removed them and replaced them with her own, they were from Dale. I wondered if I should mention it to them but thought better of it. I left it with a simple, "I see."

"She'll have to come back eventually. By then, we will

have adjusted to the disappointment." Linda wrapped her arm around Tiffany's shoulders.

We were walking down the grand staircase when Linda said, "Tiffie, would you run ahead and tell your dad that Vivi isn't here?"

As soon as Tiffany was out of earshot, Linda placed her hand on my arm. "We had a very special gift for Tiffany, but it disappeared this morning."

Uh-oh. Not an allegation of theft. I hated when that happened. "When did you last see it?"

"She, actually. We've lost her a couple of times. I guess we feel so at home that we leave the door ajar and she runs out."

"She?"

"A kitten. A special white kitten. I can't tell you how hard it is to search this inn. There are a million places a kitten could go. Tim and I have had to sneak around the inn a couple of times in search of that sweet little baby. We didn't want to spoil the surprise for Tiffie."

"So that's what you were doing!" That explained Tim and Linda's odd behavior. Unfortunately, I had a feeling I might know who was helping the kitten escape. Twinkletoes had parked herself outside of Tim and Linda's room because of the kitten inside.

"She could be anywhere. But let me check one place. If I find her, should I bring her to your room?"

"May I go with you?"

"Of course. Come with me." I led the way up to my apartment.

When I unlocked the door, Linda said, "This is where you live? Silly me. I never thought about where you and your grandmother might be at night when we're all in our rooms."

I went straight to Twinkletoes's favorite cushy armchair. Sure enough, she was cuddling a white kitten and washing its head.

I crooked a finger at Linda.

She peered over the back of the chair. "If that isn't the sweetest thing! She's acting like she's the kitten's mother."

It was a darling scene. I hated to take the kitten away from Twinkletoes. Reluctantly, I lifted the kitten and handed her to Linda.

While Linda hurried out, I spent a few minutes with Twinkletoes telling her what a lovely cat she was to take that kitten under her wing—so to speak.

I returned to the dining area, but before I sat down, Tiffany whispered to me, "Thank you for seating Austin away from me. I know I invited him, and he's my guest, but after last night, I wouldn't mind if he fell through a hole in the floor and vanished."

When the last of the Thackleberry clan had finished eating and drifted away from the dining area, Shelley said, "I don't mean to hurry things, but I'm due at my sister's house in Snowball in a couple of hours. Let's clean up so we can get to gifts!"

"And I have a dog communicating appointment this afternoon," said Zelda.

"On Christmas Day?" I asked.

"They want to know how he feels about his Christmas presents," Zelda explained.

I could usually tell if Trixie and Twinkletoes liked their toys. Maybe the people had bought Thackleberry clothes and wanted to know if their dog itched.

I was clearing dishes when Aunt Birdie gasped. She stood before the tree in the dining area. "Holly!"

I set the dishes down and strolled over. "Is something wrong?"

Aunt Birdie's hand trembled as she pointed to the little felt dog. "Where . . . where did you get this?"

"Trixie found it. Looks kind of like her, don't you think?"

"I do *not*. It looks like Iggy, the Thackleberry dog."

"Dale mentioned having a Jack Russell. I bet someone in his family had this made for him."

Aunt Birdie removed the ornament from the tree, closed her hand over it, and clutched it to her chest. "I made it for him. I gave it to him the last time I saw him."

Chills raced up my arms. That was the night he was murdered. "Are you sure? Maybe it just looks like the one you made."

She turned her head slowly. Her sad eyes met mine. "I think I would know the dog I hand stitched. See? There's a tiny heart right here on his collar. And I made sure he appeared to be smiling."

"Then how did Trixie get hold of it?"

Her eyes narrowed. "That's what I would like to know."

I went back to work clearing the dishes and moving the leftovers to the magic refrigerator. There was plenty of Fluffy Cake left, and I had my eye on it. When the commercial dishwashers were running, I brought a selection of cookies to the Thackleberrys in the Dogwood Room. The red raspberry jam on the Linzer stars stole the show on the platter. Chocolate-laced Florentines would be popular, I thought. Traditional iced sugar cookies were in the shapes of dog and cat items like doghouses, bones, and mice. Gingersnaps and vanilla-chocolate pinwheels rounded out the platter.

Shelley rolled in a cart with coffee, tea, and hot chocolate carafes so they could help themselves.

Not surprisingly, the Thackleberrys were somber. I noted a few little gag gifts, but there were no smiles. No one laughed or giggled. Norma Jeanne wore a pearl and diamond necklace that she had not worn at brunch. I was about to comment on how beautiful it was when it dawned on me that it had probably been meant for her wedding.

Muffy tore at the wrapping paper on a tall and slender package. When Trixie, Gingersnap, and Maggie came to investigate, Muffy growled and showed them her teeth, establishing her claim on that gift very clearly.

"Muffy!" scolded Doris. "We do not behave that way." To us she said, "Muffy is an only dog and thinks everything belongs to her. She has never had to share toys or anything. They tell me it's quite common for Pomeranians to be possessive. But you'd think she would have more sense than to challenge a bigger dog like Gingersnap or Maggie."

All breeds could be possessive, I thought. But I didn't recall Muffy acting that way about her food. Maybe there was a scent on the gift that attracted her for some reason.

Moving carefully, Tiffany edged over to the gift. "Looks like it's for you, anyway. Maybe Muffy could sense that."

Tiffany carried the gift to Doris, which sent Muffy into a barking fit.

"Muffy," Doris said quietly, "calm down. We're about to see what's inside."

Muffy couldn't wait. She ripped the paper, grabbed the tag, and scampered off with it, growling when she passed the other dogs.

Doris slid out the contents. "A new walking stick. This is wonderful. It looks like it's made of oak." She set the bottom on the floor and stood up. "My, it's so long and there's no handle to lean on."

Shelley said, "It's a hiking stick."

"Oh?" Doris admired it. "I had no idea there was a difference. But I must say I rather like it. I don't feel like an old fuddy with this. Do I look athletic? Who is this from? I love it!"

No one answered.

As the moment dragged out, we all realized who must have given Doris the hiking stick she liked so much. A pall fell over the room again.

Doris sat down as though her legs had given way. She

held on to the walking stick like she might never let go. "That's why Muffy was protecting it. She smelled Dale on the wrapping paper."

Shelley and I left the family to their grief and returned to the dining area.

"Was that the saddest thing you ever saw?" Shelley dabbed at her eyes. "I don't know how they can function. I think I would go to bed and hide under the covers."

We joined Oma, Mr. Huckle, and Zelda in the private kitchen, where a fire crackled and Christmas lights twinkled on the mantel and in the window. The change in atmosphere was striking. They were jolly and laughing about something.

"Our numbers have diminished," I observed. "Where is everyone?"

"Rose, Holmes, and his parents went home." Oma looked at me when she said, "Now that the engagement is off, it's a little bit awkward for them to be here with Norma Jeanne's family."

"What about dinner tonight?" I asked.

Shelley snorted. "Zelda, Mr. Huckle, and I will serve as a buffer zone again. The one I feel sorry for is Austin. Apparently he called all over this morning, trying to get a flight out, but everything is booked, and the airports are closed because of the snow, so even if he finds a flight, it will probably be canceled. Poor guy was considering going to the airport and sleeping in a chair there until something opened up."

"He brought it on himself." Mr. Huckle clucked disapprovingly. "One doesn't engage in a tryst with a bride-to-be, much less with the cousin of one's girlfriend."

"But now he's stuck here with them and persona non grata to both sides of the family." Zelda tried to hide a grin. "We'll take him into our little buffer group tonight. Or maybe we'll seat him next to Norma Jeanne!"

It was wrong of us to chortle about it, but we did.

"What happened to Dave and Aunt Birdie?" I asked. "I thought they would be here with us when we opened gifts."

A look flashed between Mr. Huckle and Oma.

"Officer Dave received a most mysterious call," said Mr. Huckle.

"He was very polite and thanked me." Oma stroked Gingersnap. "He apologized for his abrupt departure, claiming *duty called*. And then Aunt Birdie left in a huff as usual."

Oh no. I would surely hear about some kind of imaginary transgression.

For the next hour, we tried to keep our laughter and fun quieter than normal as we tore open beautifully wrapped packages, giggled over gag gifts, and admired cashmere sweaters.

Trixie carried around a stuffed slice of cake as if she wanted to show it to each of us, but no one was allowed to touch it.

Twinkletoes hid under discarded wrapping papers and pretend-swatted Trixie and Gingersnap when they investigated the twitching papers.

With hugs and kisses and shouts of Merry Christmas, our friends scattered. Many of them were off to noontime celebrations with family. I caught a breath of fresh air on the porch as they departed. The blue skies and the sun had vanished, and the air held that special stillness that came before snow.

My cell phone rang, and I glanced at it. Aunt Birdie. I should have expected her call. I was tempted to let it roll over to voice mail, but guilt got the better of me. "Hi, Aunt Birdie," I said cheerfully.

"They've come to get me!"

Twenty-five

I'd never heard Aunt Birdie screech quite like that before. "What? Aunt Birdie, what are you talking about?"

"Help! They're swarming through my house!" The line went dead.

I told Oma what had happened, bundled up Trixie, pulled on my own coat, and left. I didn't expect so many people to be walking around in Wagtail on Christmas Day. A few of the cafés were open, and some people had brought their dogs to the fenced playgrounds on the green. The smaller Christkindl booths had been removed. Only two of the largest ones still stood to serve food and beverages during evening festivities. Even on Christmas Day, there was plenty going on in Wagtail.

But most of the action was at Aunt Birdie's house. She stood on her porch, shivering and screaming at police officers as they paraded in and out.

"Aunt Birdie!" I ran up the steps, took off my puffy coat, and flung it around her shoulders. "What's going on?"

"They think I killed Dale!" She reached out to grab the sleeve of a policeman. "That's my computer. You can't take that. You have no right to it."

"Listen, lady," he said, "you're not going to need this where you're going."

I gasped.

"Did you hear that? Did you?" Aunt Birdie's hands trembled.

"Is Dave here?"

"Yes, that miserable rat is here. I'm sure this is all his fault."

I walked into her house. Police were combing through drawers and closets. I watched one of them bag her kitchen knives.

"Dave!" I yelled. "Where are you?"

I heard his very calm voice. "In the pantry."

I was not as calm. I barged into the pantry, which was more of a closet and barely big enough for both of us. "What do you think you're doing?"

Dave spoke matter-of-factly. "After brunch, I received the results from Dale's autopsy."

"On Christmas?"

"Not everyone is off, you know. It was probably issued yesterday afternoon, but I received it today. Dale was stabbed six times with a narrow knife of some kind. We think the blade is about ten inches long and an inch wide. We're searching for it."

"But . . . but why look here?"

"Holly, who do you think most likely sliced the Grinch?"

I knew what he was after. He expected me to say I thought it was Aunt Birdie. It could have been, but in that instant nothing in the entire world would have moved me to admit that possibility. "It was never solved. You abandoned the whole thing after Rupert asked you to."

"Deftly avoided, Ms. Miller. I believe we both know the real answer to that question."

"We do not! Do you have any witnesses? Anything tying Aunt Birdie to the stabbing of the Grinch?"

"I'm sorry, Holly. One of the neighbors saw Dale go into her house the night he was murdered."

"Are you kidding me? That doesn't mean anything. Someone saw you walk into the inn this morning. That wouldn't mean you were responsible for something that happened at The Blue Boar."

"You didn't notice the Grinch, did you?"

"What? Stop talking in riddles."

"On your way over here you obviously didn't notice that the Grinch was gone. I deflated it and took another look at the *wounds*, as it were."

"And you're so brilliant that you can tell Aunt Birdie made those slits?"

"No. I'm not."

"Aha!"

"But there are pros in Snowball who were able to confirm that the same size knife that made those holes also probably stabbed Dale. We have a search warrant."

"Didn't anyone in Snowball celebrate the holiday this morning?"

"Don't be sassy. These are people who work hard twenty-four hours a day to keep us safe."

"From Aunt Birdie? You have to be kidding me."

Dave faced me, his eyebrows tilted with annoyance. "I appreciate your desire to defend your aunt, but being related to you does not mean she's incapable of killing her lover. I have to look at facts, Holly. In all likelihood, she is the one who stabbed the Grinch. It's a fact that she had an affair with Dale. It's a fact that the knife that stabbed the Grinch was the same size as the one that stabbed Dale. It's a fact that she is the last person who was seen with Dale. And it's a fact that she had a motive."

"What was her motive?"

"Jealousy. The oldest motive of all. She was the other woman."

"Look, Dave, I know Aunt Birdie is a crank, but if she were going to kill someone, it wouldn't have been Dale, of whom she was very fond. She would have murdered Vivienne to get rid of her. This makes no sense."

"Murder never makes sense. Something drives people over the brink, and they lose their ability to be rational."

Dave's radio crackled. He stared at me while he listened. "Stay right here," he said, then made a quick call. When he was through with the very brief conversation, he asked, "Did you know that Vivienne is missing?"

"I wouldn't have called it missing. Her family thought she didn't come to brunch because she and Dale weren't giving big gifts this year. I checked her room. It appeared that she probably didn't sleep in her bed last night."

"Anyone else missing?"

"Not that I know of." I frowned at him. "She could be shacked up with some guy, you know. I saw her coming out of the Wagtail Springs Hotel in the middle of the night."

"What were you doing out at that hour?"

"Being an elf."

"Why didn't you tell me she was gone?"

"Her own family wasn't worried. Maybe it was her habit to go off by herself." I shrugged. "Or maybe they knew about her nighttime excursions and didn't want to admit to them. They didn't seem concerned, and they know her much better than I do."

"They're such a caring family," he said sarcastically. "Well, she's officially missing now. You better hope Birdie didn't have anything to do with that."

"You should take yourself off this case. You're so biased! There's not a reason in the world to think Aunt Birdie had anything to do with Vivienne's bizarre behavior."

Dave remained placid. "The whole town is talking about

the confrontation between them at the party last night. It's not every day that ladies throw booze at each other."

"That's not fair. Vivienne was the aggressor and Birdie was the victim!"

"Revenge, Holly."

Ugh. He was stuck on Birdie as a murderess. "So you'll be wrapping up here?" I was hopeful that the news about Vivienne would distract him.

Dave placed a hand on my shoulder. "I'm sorry, Holly. I truly am. But thanks for the tip about Vivienne and the Wagtail Springs Hotel."

I walked out to the porch where Aunt Birdie still waited to be allowed inside her home. "I have valuable antiques! I'll sue them if they've removed or damaged anything. I will!"

"Maybe you should come back to the inn and relax for a while. A cup of coffee to warm you up and maybe a piece of Fluffy Cake?"

I had never seen her so angry. "Have you lost your mind? My *home* has been invaded. They will have to carry me away, because I'm not budging from this property. This is no time for a tea party."

A couple of officers walked out, followed by Dave. He stopped in front of us and, looking straight at Aunt Birdie, said, "I'm sorry about this, Miss Dupuy. I will be in touch."

"I'll see you in jail for malfeasance and conduct unbecoming an officer," she shouted as he left.

"I think that's for military," I whispered to her.

"I don't care. Where's Ben? I need a lawyer."

I doubted she would find one working on Christmas Day. While I wasn't interested in Ben romantically, he had been helpful when Wagtailites needed legal advice. "Ben is with his parents in New Jersey."

"Aargh," she snarled. Holding her head high, she strode into her house and slammed the door. I heard the bolt clank when she locked it.

She was still wearing my coat. I shivered and knocked on her door. "Aunt Birdie? May I have my coat back?"

Apparently not. I didn't wait long before taking off for the inn as fast as I could walk. I couldn't blame Aunt Birdie for being outraged. It must feel like a terrible violation to have strangers rummage through your things. I would hate it.

Trixie and I wound through the neighborhood as fast as I could go. But it wasn't fast enough to avoid Dave.

He ran up beside me and threw his official police jacket over my shoulders. "They're calling for more snow. You're going to freeze."

"Thanks," I grumbled, angry that he had the nerve to be nice to me. Nevertheless, I jammed my arms through the sleeves and zipped it closed. "I think I'm already frozen. Aunt Birdie locked her door, and I have a feeling she's not planning to leave the premises for a very long time."

Dave exhaled so hard that a puff of condensation formed in the air. "If someone had come to me and asked for a list of Wagtail residents most likely to commit a felony, Aunt Birdie would not have been on the list. She wouldn't have even made the top hundred. But so far, everything is pointing right at her. I can't ignore that."

"That's the trouble with living alone or sleeping alone. I've been through it and it's really not fair. If you're home alone you have no alibi, no one who can confirm where you were. Did that nosy person who watched Dale enter Aunt Birdie's house hang around to see what time he exited?"

"Obviously not. In that case, he would be the last person to see Dale alive, and I would have found it very odd and suspicious that he was spying on Birdie or Dale."

"Would Rupert have made your top hundred list?" I asked tentatively.

Dave shot me a look. "I'm not going to start maligning the citizens of Wagtail. Some people can be ornery, but that doesn't make them likely to murder."

"Aunt Birdie, for instance," I said.

"She has no idea how lucky she is to have you on her side."

We walked up the stairs of the inn and entered the lobby. Most of Vivienne's family clustered in the Dogwood Room.

Tim jumped to his feet when he saw us. "Did you find her?"

It was wishful thinking of course, because she wasn't with us. Still, I thought it nice that he was concerned about his mother, especially in light of the fact that most of the other family members made no effort to hide their contempt for her.

"Not yet." Dave warmed his hands by the fire. "Who saw her last?"

Mouthing *thank you*, I raised his coat to get his attention and draped it across the back of a chair.

The Kedrowski family was exchanging glances.

Tim raised his palms. "Don't look at me. I left the party early last night."

Tiffany's eyes narrowed with anxiety. "I remember seeing her at the party, right before we all walked over to the church. She was sitting next to Great-Grandma Doris. Maybe she stayed over with Holmes's parents?"

"Yes, that sounds just like something she would do," Linda said dryly.

While they speculated, I bustled over to the phone to call Holmes's parents and ask if Vivienne had spent the night. It was a long shot, but Vivienne was peculiar at best.

Holmes's mom was completely taken aback by my question. "No, honey. No one stayed with us last night." Speaking to someone else, she relayed my question.

"Especially not her," grumbled Holmes's dad in the background.

"Is there anything we can do?" she asked. "Do you need help searching?"

I promised to keep her apprised. When I returned to the

Dogwood Room, Dave was saying, "So no one saw her back here at the inn after the party?"

In spite of their dislike of Vivienne, they looked at one another with worry in their eyes.

All except for Blake, who chortled when he said, "Not after she had that old-lady fight. That was hysterical!"

Dave's gaze zeroed in on Blake.

Twenty-six

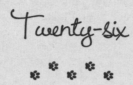

I cringed. I knew what was coming, but that didn't prevent me from hoping Vivi had had a fight with someone else that I didn't know about.

"This was the incident with Birdie Dupuy?" asked Dave.

"Sure. No fists involved." Blake smirked. "I didn't know Vivi had it in her. She took a glass of the bourbon punch, which was surprisingly good, and threw it in the face of some other old lady. It was hilarious!" Blake slapped the arm of the chair in which he sat.

His mother didn't find it funny at all. "Blake! Have you no respect?"

"Oh, Mom!" Blake cried. "It was the single best moment of this entire trip."

That was odd. I thought Blake ran out of the party after the dogs barked at his attire. He must have returned.

Tim puffed up his chest. "She had the nerve to come here for brunch today. Birdie somebody. Apparently she was having an affair with Dale."

Dave didn't move, but his gaze slid from Tim over to me.

Doris spoke up. "When everyone left the party to go to the church, Vivienne finished her drink and left, too."

I ran upstairs as fast as I could go to retrieve a jacket. If Dave wasn't going to the Wagtail Springs Hotel, I was! I grabbed one for me and one for Trixie, who was excited that I was on the run.

When I made it back down to the lobby, Dave was standing beside the front door like he was waiting for me.

In a very quiet voice he asked, "Would you mind if I took Trixie for a walk?"

I stared at him for a minute. He had never asked that before. And then it dawned on me. If something had happened to Vivienne on her way back from the party, she could be dead and lying out in the snow. Trixie might pick up her scent. A chill ran through me.

"Let's not make a big deal out of this, okay? I don't want everyone outside distracting her," he said.

I nodded. Pulling on my jacket, I very calmly stepped out with him. "Can you hold up a minute while I dress Trixie?"

He paused and watched. I pulled a red sweater with a white zigzag pattern that she had received for Christmas from Oma over her head and inserted each of her front paws through armholes. We set off, letting Trixie lead the way.

"I never had a dog who wore clothes."

"She's small and mostly white. In these low temperatures, she starts to shiver."

We turned off the green and walked into the west side of Wagtail.

"So how does this work?" asked Dave. "Do you put her on a leash?"

"No. Usually, we're just walking along, and she takes off. Then I have to follow the sound of her barks."

Trixie stayed relatively close to us, but she stopped to sniff gateposts and bushes.

"I doubt that she will lead us to Birdie's," I said.

"You're right about that."

"But you have to try anyway?"

"We're not going to Birdie's. We're going to the Richardsons'. If Vivienne walked home by herself, she might have fallen. I'm hoping Trixie might pick up her scent."

I hated that thought. She would have been out in the cold all night. Even Vivienne didn't deserve that. We walked in silence, watching Trixie. She followed her nose and ignored the people coming out of restaurants and walking off their lunches.

She ran up to the Richardsons' front door as though she knew where we were going.

Notes of "White Christmas" filtered out to us. Holmes's dad opened the door. "Dave! Did you find that woman?" He reached out and gave me a hug.

Trixie ran inside before he could pet her.

"Gosh, I'm sorry to interrupt. Looks like you're having another party," said Dave.

"Come on in and join the fun. Some of Holmes's friends dropped by. We didn't plan on this, but they keep showing up."

Friends? It appeared to me that every single woman in Wagtail between the ages of twenty-five and forty had come to visit. News of his broken engagement must have traveled fast.

"I'd like to speak with you and your wife if I might." Dave gestured toward the kitchen.

I followed them, but I didn't miss the scowl Sugar McLaughlin sent my way.

Dave closed the kitchen door. "I'm very sorry to disturb you—"

The door opened and Holmes peeked in. "Is this a private conference or may I attend?"

Dave motioned him in. The combination kitchen and

family room was blissfully peaceful. Holmes perched on the edge of a chair, and I slid Trixie's sweater off her so she wouldn't overheat.

"I'm looking for Vivienne Thackleberry. Apparently she attended your party last night?"

Holmes's mom nodded. "I hope she's okay."

"Oh boy. Here we go again." Holmes's father massaged his forehead. "Son, I don't care how much that Norma Jeanne girl cries, do not get involved. She showed everyone her true character last night. You stay away from her."

• Holmes just smiled.

In a very low voice, Dave asked, "Any of you notice if Vivienne hooked up with some guy?"

Holmes's mother twisted her hands in her lap. "The last I remember is her sitting with Doris and knocking back several glasses of the bourbon punch."

"So she might have been intoxicated when she left?" asked Dave.

Holmes's father said, "For sure. That punch is strong."

"There are a million ways to walk from their house to the inn," I said, thinking of a search.

"Honey," said Holmes's mom, "most of Wagtail turned out for the carols and the ringing of the bells last night. Don't you think someone would have noticed her on the way home if she had fallen . . . or something?"

It was a good point. But then, where was she?

"You all went to the church?" Dave gazed around at us. "Any of you remember seeing her there?"

No one did.

"I assume you saw the altercation between Vivienne and Birdie?"

Holmes's father snorted. "Altercation might be a bit strong. It was more like a little catfight. Holmes and Holly separated them."

I didn't care for the glance that Dave shot my way.

"What happened afterward?" he asked.

Holmes spoke first. "Vivienne's glass was empty after she threw the punch on Birdie. She went straight to the punch bowl for another drink."

They all looked to me. Dave's face didn't show any reaction. But I feared I knew what he was thinking, because I would be drawing the same conclusion. What if Aunt Birdie had returned to confront Vivienne? What was I thinking? Birdie was opinionated and obstinate, but she wasn't violent. Besides, it had been Vivienne who'd thrown punch on Aunt Birdie, not the other way around.

"Thanks for your help," Dave said, pulling on his coat.

I took his cue and did the same.

"Won't you stay and have a cup of eggnog?" Holmes's mom smiled at him. "I made it myself."

"I'm sure it's delicious. Maybe some other time."

"Are you mounting a search?" Holmes asked. "I'd be happy to help."

"Thanks. I have a couple of leads to follow up before I get everyone out there looking for her. But it's beginning to look like that might be what we'll have to do."

"He wanted to let Trixie sniff around," I said.

"Mercy!" cried Holmes's mom. "Trixie, I hope you haven't found her anywhere in our house."

Trixie, never one to miss an opportunity for a treat, ran to her, danced in a circle, and let out one yelp.

"I think she just gave you the all clear," I joked.

She was rewarded with a treat and lots of petting. I dressed her in her sweater again.

We walked through the living room, where an inordinate number of women still gathered. Several of them clearly had eyes for Dave. I was beginning to think we might never get out of there when Holmes swung a jacket on and escorted us out the door.

"I'm coming along if that's okay. You might need a hand."

"And what am I?" I asked.

"Trixie's assistant." Holmes winked at me. I knew he was being silly but couldn't help wondering if part of him wanted to escape the madness at his parents' house. "Where are we going?"

"The Wagtail Springs Hotel," said Dave.

Holmes's eyes widened. "That's right! What mischief could Vivi have been up to in the middle of the night?"

We kept to the sidewalks, where most of the ice and snow had melted thanks to dog-safe ice melt. Trixie ambled in a zigzag, sniffing tree trunks and mailbox posts.

Dave watched Trixie scamper along. "This isn't very productive."

"Maybe Vivienne isn't dead," observed Holmes.

"Thank heaven! Everyone would be so relieved," I said. We walked up to the Wagtail Springs Hotel, which anchored the north end of the green. After years of neglect, it had been nicely restored. When Dave opened the door, Trixie trotted inside as though she were a regular there.

"Hi, Ricky." Dave sauntered up to the front desk. He pulled out his cell phone and showed Ricky a picture of Tiffany and Vivienne.

"Where'd you get that?" I asked.

Dave grinned. "Tiffany is into documenting everything with photographs on her cell phone. She e-mailed it to me while I was talking with her at the inn." He focused on Ricky. "I hear the older woman in the picture has been visiting the hotel."

Ricky peered at the photo. "She looks vaguely like my grandmother."

"You sure about that?" Dave prodded him.

I tugged at Dave's jacket sleeve. "Wrong shift."

"Huh?"

"We saw her after midnight. Ricky probably works three to eleven?"

"Yeah, right. I just came on duty today. I might have seen her sometime, but a lot of people come in for a drink or to have dinner. I don't pay much attention." Ricky appeared relieved. "Yeah, you'd have to talk to Percy. He works nights."

"Did you work yesterday until eleven at night?" There was a slight edge in Dave's tone.

"Yeah. And Percy took over at eleven."

"But you did not see this woman enter the hotel before eleven?" Dave sounded very official.

Ricky licked his lips and glanced to the left. "I did not see her."

I exchanged a look with Holmes. There was something fishy about his denials. Had someone paid him off? I was wondering how Dave might coax it out of him when Trixie ran to the front door and started her odd bark. The one that sent shivers down my spine. She scratched at the door desperately, frantic to get out.

Twenty-seven

When I opened the door, Trixie leaped over the porch steps and took off flying across the snow.

"Dave!" I didn't wait for him. I ran after her.

Her nose to the ground, she sped to the green. I raced behind her. Even though I had a head start, Holmes and Dave passed me.

Intent on a scent, Trixie circled back when suddenly, I heard the sound of a crash and cries of distress behind me.

I turned to see people flocking to two small figures sprawled on the ground. Lights of some kind flashed near them.

Dave and Holmes rushed by me, going in the other direction.

I started to follow them but turned to look for Trixie. "Trixie! Trixie, come!"

The two largest Christkindl booths had not yet been dismantled like the others. A large sign in front of them advertised the Christmas Night celebration, when they would be open for refreshments.

Trixie ignored the commotion. She lowered her nose to one of the Christkindl booths and methodically sniffed the base.

I figured she would come looking for me in a minute, and I ran to help Dave and Holmes.

People clustered around two young boys, one of whom I recognized as Rupert's son. The boys cried, and far too many adults asked what had happened. From the grotesque angle of Rupert's son's leg, I assumed it was broken.

"Have you called Rupert?" I asked Dave.

"911 is on the way. Is this his kid?"

I tried to dial Rupert's number, but we were in the middle of an annoying dead zone. I walked back toward the Christkindl hut until I was able to call Rupert to tell him he needed to come quick.

I returned to the boys, who were getting plenty of attention from reassuring adults. "What happened?" I asked Holmes.

"They were racing each other on hover boards. One kid was in the lead, but his hover board hit a shoe and went flying. Rupert's kid was right behind him, crashed into the other hover board, and he flew off, too."

Breathing heavily, Rupert jogged toward his son, who cried even louder when he saw his dad.

The siren of an ambulance blared in the distance. They would be in capable hands soon.

Unfortunately, as the siren drew closer, Trixie began the desperate bark that I had come to dread.

"She found something." Fear welled up inside me.

Holmes turned to look at her. "She's just barking because of the siren."

There was no question in *my* mind. I knew that bark all too well. She faced the Christkindl hut and barked at it.

Ignoring Holmes, I dashed toward her. She danced away from me. I followed her all the way around the chalet-style Christkindl hut. She still yowled at it. A door on the west side of it had a latch with a padlock on it. The wood around the latch was splintered. I pushed gently on the door, which swung open easily.

Vivienne lay on the floor.

Twenty-eight

❊ ❊ ❊ ❊

I knelt beside her. "Vivi? Vivienne?"

She was cold as ice. Her face and lips were unnaturally pale. Nevertheless, I reached for her neck to check for a pulse. It was cold and stiff.

Vivi's eyes were closed. She looked peaceful, not tense and angry as she usually appeared. But where was her coat? Why wasn't she wearing it? And she only wore one shoe. A wine suede strappy open-toed shoe appropriate for a party, but not for walking around in winter weather.

I felt terrible. She had been unfriendly and horrible to everyone, including her own family, but no one deserved this kind of end. Had she somehow stumbled into the hut and passed out from drinking?

I heard someone behind me and looked over my shoulder.

"Is she alive?" asked Holmes.

"I don't think so."

He turned and shouted to Dave.

"No sign of blood," Holmes observed.

"Maybe she was stabbed in the back like her husband," I said.

"You'd think there would be blood on the floor then." Holmes backed up and examined the splintered door frame.

Dave jogged over to us. He stepped inside and knelt by Vivienne's body. I watched his shoulders sag as he realized she was dead. He stood up. "Trixie found her?"

I nodded.

"Did you do this?" Holmes pointed at the latch holes on the door.

"I don't think so. The wood was already splintered. I guess I could have, but if I did, those screws weren't in there tight. I barely pushed the door and it gave way."

Dave motioned to us while he called it in on his radio. When he was through speaking to the dispatcher, he said, "Let's try to keep this clean. It could be a crime scene."

We stood outside of the Christkindl chalet, where a crowd was beginning to gather to see what was going on.

"We didn't see any evidence of bleeding," said Holmes.

"She's only wearing one shoe," I added. "Have you got the shoe that tripped up the kids on their hover boards?"

Dave held up a wine red strappy suede shoe. "You think she was running from someone? It's kind of odd to lose a shoe and keep going."

"Especially in this weather." Dave examined the shoe. "Definitely not made for sprinting."

"Would she have had the strength to bust open the door on the Christkindl chalet?" Holmes asked.

"Hard to tell. People can do surprising things when adrenaline kicks in." Dave glanced at me. "Or Holly might have done it."

"I really don't think I did," I protested.

"It's pine," said Holmes, "which is a soft wood. It even dents easily."

I'd forgotten that Holmes was into woodworking.

"Her family said she had a heart problem. Maybe the door was open and she died of a heart attack caused by fear of something. Or someone," I suggested.

"Could have been the same person who hid Dale's body in the Grinch."

When Holmes said that, Dave's eyes met mine.

"Do not go blaming this on Aunt Birdie."

"Seems like someone told me just a few hours ago that if Birdie was going to murder someone, it would have been Vivienne." Dave watched my reaction.

In spite of the cold, I could feel the heat rise in my face, and knew I was turning red. "Instead of Dale." I said it as calmly as I could, even though I wanted to scream it. I struggled to sound reasonable. "And anyway, we don't know that she didn't die of natural causes yet."

Holmes nodded. "She got in there somehow. Think she was there all night?"

Dave shrugged. "Hard to tell. I don't know if she's stiff from rigor mortis or from the temperature. But I'd guess she's been here a good number of hours at any rate."

We waited with him for the ambulance. When they placed her in a bag, Holmes remarked, "Still no sign of blood."

"So she wasn't stabbed." I was very relieved about that. "She probably died of a heart attack, or she bashed in the door and couldn't call for help. She might have died of exposure."

The ambulance doors closed and it drove away.

Dave took a deep breath. "Now for the hard part. I hate having to inform relatives that their loved one is deceased. It's the worst feeling in the world."

We were somber as we walked back to the inn. Even Trixie didn't run with joy anymore.

The entire Thackleberry family sat in the Dogwood Room by the fire.

Tiffany held the white kitten on her lap. Twinkletoes sat at Tiffany's feet, mesmerized by the newcomer.

Tim stood up when he saw Dave. In a fearful voice, he stated, "You found her."

Momentarily forgetting Holmes's connection to the family, I tugged at his sleeve. I thought it best for us to retreat and leave the family to their grief.

But Holmes obviously felt a tie to the family. He walked to EmmyLou and wrapped an arm around her shoulders.

I, on the other hand, did not belong. I hustled to the kitchen, thinking about all the ugly things Vivi's family had said about her. I guessed they were true. Would any of them remember her warmly? Maybe her son, Tim.

Oma, Rose, and Mr. Huckle sat by the fire in the dining area, drinking hot chocolate.

Oma perked up when she saw me. "What happened? Where have you been?"

I told them about Trixie finding Vivi.

"You think someone killed her?" Oma asked.

"I don't know. She lost a shoe near the big Christkindl chalets. I don't know if that means she was running from someone or was drunk. It's a little odd that she wouldn't have retrieved it and put it on when it was so cold out. She didn't show any signs of injury, though. No blood or gashes or anything."

"I bet the same person murdered both Mr. and Mrs. Thackleberry," said Mr. Huckle.

"A family member most likely," added Rose.

"For money," said Oma.

She poured a mug of hot chocolate for me and plunked mini-marshmallows on top. "This certainly narrows down the field of suspects."

I sat on the fireplace hearth with Trixie at my feet. "How so, Oma? They all hated her. What an awful Christmas for their family. To lose two family members in a matter of days? I don't know how they can hold it together." I sipped the hot chocolate and slurped out a mini-marshmallow.

Rose's eyes narrowed. "Where is Holmes?"

"With the Thackleberrys in the Dogwood Room."

"Nooooo," she hissed. "That girl will entangle him again. You just watch. He will forgive Norma Jeanne."

She was right. He probably would do exactly that.

Dave pushed open the door and poked his head in. "I presume Holly has filled you in, Liesel. Do you mind if I use your office? I'd like to speak to the family members individually."

"Of course," said Oma. "Hot chocolate?"

Dave looked at it longingly. "Sure. It doesn't have booze in it, does it?"

Oma smiled. "Just milk."

Dave rubbed his hands together in front of the fire. "Thanks, Liesel. It was cold outside." He accepted the mug and left.

The crackling fire and soft strains of "The Christmas Song" only made me more melancholy. It was cozy and warm, and I was surrounded by friends and family. I couldn't imagine how traumatized the Thackleberry family members must feel.

"There should be a rule," I said. "No dying over the holidays. It's twice as depressing."

"There are laws against murder," Mr. Huckle pointed out. "Yet someone did them in. Neither one of them would be dead if someone hadn't killed them."

"Vivienne could have died of natural causes," I pointed out.

"Fat chance! Can you even imagine being a Thackleberry right now? They must all be looking at one another with suspicion," said Rose. "What a nightmare to imagine that one of your family members is a murderer."

Oma scowled. "Perhaps the three of us should watch over Doris so she is not alone."

"That might be a very good idea," I said.

"If Vivienne was murdered, then it changes the picture, no?" said Oma. "Someone wished to rid himself of both of them."

Rose, who was seldom catty, snarled, "For money. I bet anything they were murdered for money."

"Are you worried about Aunt Birdie?" Mr. Huckle gazed at me.

"No!" I tried to maintain a level voice. "Not a bit. Aunt Birdie can be very cranky, cantankerous even, but I suspect she thinks murder would violate the rules of social etiquette, if nothing else."

Rose snorted when she laughed. "But it didn't bother her to sleep with a married man? She must have very different etiquette rules than the rest of society."

"Surely you do not believe that Birdie murdered them," said Oma. "Birdie is, how do they say, nutty as the fruitcake, but even *I* don't think she would kill anyone."

"Why are we talking about my relative when it's so much more likely that one of the Thackleberry clan did them in?" Mr. Huckle stretched. "My money would have been on the bitterly indignant Vivienne. Had I been her husband, I believe I would have feared closing my eyes at night to sleep."

Rose cocked her head. "Well! What can a husband expect if he's sleeping around with other women? I would be furious. No wonder she was angry with him."

"But you would have divorced him," Oma argued. "There was no need to murder him. Who else had a motive?"

"The whole family wanted to clobber Vivienne!" Rose lowered her voice to a whisper. "Didn't you hear them carrying on this morning when they looked in their stockings? I thought Blake was going to blow his top."

"What happened?" asked Oma. "I was busy with the brunch. I must have missed that."

Rose continued in a hushed tone. "Apparently they get an expensive gift every year from Dale and Vivienne. Not this year. They got something worse than a lump of coal—a letter telling them they were officially cut off. No more money! They have to live on their own."

Mr. Huckle chuckled. "It's a bit difficult to be empathetic about that. Most of us have to earn our own way in life. It was probably long overdue for some of them."

"But you can see why they were so angry with Vivienne," whispered Rose.

I debated whether to tell them what I knew and decided there was no harm in it. After all, Dale and Vivienne were dead. "Vivienne probably never came back to the inn last night, so she couldn't have put the envelopes in the stockings."

"That's right!" Oma's eyes widened. "But then who—"

"Me," I said. "Before he died, Dale asked me to stuff the stockings with the envelopes. I had no idea what was in them, of course."

Mr. Huckle frowned. "This is most intriguing. It all fits in with Doris's concerns about the younger Thackleberrys being too spoiled. One has to wonder who else knew about this. Could it be that he told one of them and that led to his death?"

"Blake." Rose clearly disliked the Thackleberrys, and at the moment her nostrils flared like she had smelled a skunk. It was a good thing the engagement had been called off.

"Dressing peculiarly is hardly a hallmark of murderers," Mr. Huckle said.

"I don't care what he wears, although I do think he has a strange wardrobe, and I still think it's wrong for a man to wear a dress of rags, much less to a holiday party. But that's not what worries me. It's his attitude. He acts like we're all beneath him. Seriously, he snapped his fingers at me like I was his servant. I've never seen anything so rude in my life. I'm telling you, something isn't right with that young man."

"Speaking of which, I had better go check on them. By now they probably would like something to nosh on." Oma stretched and stood up.

"You stay here, Oma. I'll go." I rinsed my mug and headed for the Dogwood Room.

Tim was slumped in an armchair. "Mom's biggest fear was to be broke again."

The others gazed at him. I saw a few making faces.

"You don't know what it was like. My dad ran off before I was born. Her parents wanted nothing to do with her or her baby because she wasn't married. It was just the two of us. It wasn't like this family where someone would have stepped in and been kind. She had to drop out of high school. To support me, she worked nights cleaning offices so she could take me with her. When I went to school, she took an assortment of day jobs, the kind that don't offer benefits or possibility for advancement. I never had a bicycle, let alone a car like you kids did. She actually darned my socks because new ones weren't in our budget." He looked around the room. "How many of you ever had to fix holes in your socks? You throw them out like they're worthless. I worked from the time I was old enough to deliver newspapers. But then one day, she was driving a limousine for a Mr. Dale Thackleberry and everything changed. For both of us."

"I'm sorry, Tim," EmmyLou murmured. "I knew she had a difficult life, but Dad never told me the details."

"She didn't want people to know. She thought it made her look weak."

Linda stared at her husband. "Oh, Tim!" There was no mistaking the pain in her tone. "You should have told us. We might have been kinder to her instead of treating her like a thorn in our shoes."

Tim sniffled. "I never thought I would lose her." He rose and walked outside.

Linda followed him.

"Could I bring you anything?" I asked.

EmmyLou rose and took Doris's arm. "Not for us, thanks. I think Doris could use a nap."

No one else responded.

I hustled to the housekeeping closet to retrieve a large garbage bag. Trying not to be too intrusive, I quickly gathered the discarded papers, bags, ribbons, and bows. Twinkletoes amused everyone by chasing each item as I picked it up. She finally nabbed a piece of paper before I reached for it. Holding her head high, she proudly marched off with it in her mouth.

I tossed the bag into the garbage bin and returned to the kitchen, with Holmes right behind me.

A look flashed between Oma, Rose, and Mr. Huckle. Suddenly, with assorted excuses, each of them had to be somewhere else. They vacated the kitchen in short order.

They couldn't have been more obvious. A flush rose up my face. I tried to act nonchalant. "Hot chocolate?"

Holmes looked at his watch. "Sure. If you'll go to the sledding contest with me afterward."

"Deal. That sounds like fun."

I poured the hot chocolate into two red mugs and added marshmallows and whipped cream. A total indulgence, but what day was better for that than Christmas?

We settled in the cushy armchairs before the fire.

I had kicked off my shoes and propped my feet on the warm hearth when Holmes asked, "Who do you think murdered Dale and Vivienne?"

I hadn't expected the conversation to turn in that direction, but it had to be uppermost on all our minds. "You think the same person murdered both of them?"

"Most likely. Unless you have reason to think otherwise. It's unlikely that Vivienne was so loaded that she stumbled into that Christkindl chalet and perished."

"A lot of them seem to have financial motives." I couldn't suggest that Norma Jeanne might have killed Dale in the hope that her mother would inherit the money to fund her glamorous wedding.

"You mean like Blake?"

"Exactly. And Vivienne. She claims she would have gotten more money if he were alive, but I'm not certain of that."

"No kidding. She told plenty of lies, even to her family," said Holmes. "I can't imagine having a relative like that."

"Do you know anything about Tim and Linda?"

He shrugged. "Not much. They've been nice to me."

"I suppose it's vaguely possible that someone unrelated to the family murdered Dale. But the little felt wool Jack Russell that Trixie found was probably brought back to the inn by Dale's killer. It could have been dropped by a visitor who isn't staying here, but the odds of that seem much slimmer to me."

Holmes studied his hot chocolate. "They say to follow the money. That leads straight to EmmyLou but she's the least likely to have killed him. I can't see her murdering her own dad."

"If Vivienne was killed, it surely wasn't for money," I said.

"So something else must be going on."

Suddenly, harsh voices rose in the lobby. Holmes and I leaped to our feet and rushed out to see what had happened.

Twenty-nine

❀ ❀ ❀

"Why are you blaming me?" Tiffany asked. "Why are you always so hateful to me? You're the perfect one. The boy that everyone doted on. I didn't make you drop out of med school. You did that all by yourself. Apparently, you're not the genius our parents always thought. How does it feel to be the one who screwed up?"

"Whoa!" Blake put his hands up in the air. "Don't take out your anger on me. I'm not the one whose lover slept with our cousin."

Austin looked like he wished he had never come to Wagtail.

Norma Jeanne shook her head and backed away. "Do not bring me into this. How was I supposed to know that Tiffany would invite the man I love to our family Christmas?"

Holmes blinked. "Excuse me?"

"Stay out of this, Holmes," Norma Jeanne barked. She turned back to her step-cousins. "Look what a mess we're in. We're all stuck in this forsaken place, our grandparents are dead, and now our source of income is about to bite the dust."

"Don't yell at us." Tiffany's eyes reduced to slits as she stared her cousin down. "We don't work in fabrication. You're the bozo who ordered the cheap material that's sending us in a downward spiral. It's your fault!"

"I did no such thing. I don't know what's wrong with those stupid dogs and cats."

"Stupid? They paid for your condo and the pearls around your neck and everything you have." Tiffany threw her hands wide. "How can you be so callous? These sweet, innocent animals are suffering because of you."

"Like I care. I hate my job. I spend all day drawing sketches for stupid outfits only to have them come back from my boss with snide comments like *Where does the tail go?* and *You do know that cats have ears?* I don't care. I don't like dogs, and cats are like having *you* around all the time. So annoying. As far as I'm concerned, I hope Thackleberry closes for good so I won't have to be bothered with it anymore." Norma Jeanne crossed her arms over her chest.

"I can tell you this, Norma Jeanne," spat Tiffany. "I would never have betrayed my own cousin, or a friend for that matter, the way you did. You and Blake are exactly the same. It's all about you. You get everything you want and you don't care who's in your way. You trample right over them. No wonder Grampy cut you off. You don't deserve a penny of his hard-earned money."

"Gramps?" Blake's eyes widened. "It wasn't Vivi? How do you know that?"

"He told me. And you know why? Because he trusted me."

Norma Jeanne laughed unpleasantly. "Don't flatter yourself, Tiffany. You think he couldn't see through your fake attentions to him? He knew you were scum who would rat on your own relatives."

"That's not true. You're just jealous. And you're the one

who turned on us. None of this would have happened if it wasn't for you. We wouldn't even be here if it wasn't for you and your engagement. You're the one who would sell us for a dime."

Norma Jeanne gasped and marched to the grand staircase so fast I felt a breeze. "Holmes!" she whined.

He looked at her but didn't say anything.

"Aren't you coming?"

Were I in his shoes, I would have used some choice words to put her in her place. But Holmes said, "Your family is about to lose the Thackleberry company. Instead of fighting and being petty, I think it's time for you three to put your heads together and save Thackleberry."

Norma Jeanne shot him an angry look and ran up to the second floor. A door slammed upstairs.

Blake grabbed a jacket and stalked out the front door, slamming it behind him.

Crying, Tiffany picked up her kitten and hurried to her room in the cat wing. A third door slammed.

Which left Austin, Holmes, and me in the lobby. I forced a smile. "Quarreling is how all the best families spend Christmas."

Fortunately, both of them smiled.

Holmes looked at his watch. "What do you say we take Trixie and Gingersnap over to the sledding contest?"

Austin bashfully said, "I guess I'll go call the airline again."

Holmes's jaw twitched as he regarded Austin. "You know they're not going to tell you anything different. Come with Holly and me."

"Are you sure?" Austin walked toward Holmes and held out his hand.

Holmes shook it. "We're okay. I owe you one. You gave me a chance to walk away from this mess without smelling like a skunk."

Holmes had to go to his parents' house to fetch a sled but promised to catch up to us. We scattered to don coats, gloves, and boots. I traded my skirt for jeans, dressed Trixie in her red sweater, and Gingersnap in a Santa hat and red scarf. Austin and I met in the lobby and set out for the best sledding hill in Wagtail.

Darkness was falling while we walked and Austin spilled his woes. "I want to apologize to you. This weekend hasn't been at all typical of me. I'm sure that's hard for you to believe. The sad thing is that I really like Tiffany. We have a great time together. But when I saw Norma Jeanne, all those old feelings reappeared. They had been locked away for a long time. It's not every day that your first love turns up again."

"You didn't know they were related?" I asked.

"How would I? They have different last names. And they're not actually related by blood anyway. They're nothing alike. *Nothing!*" He rubbed his face. "All the good memories of Norma Jeanne came back initially, but it took a day and a half for the reasons we split years ago to resurface. And the sad thing is that I've lost any chance I ever had with Tiffany."

I stopped walking when I spotted Tim talking with the bald man who had told me about the itching problem with Thackleberry garments.

"Is something wrong?" asked Austin.

"No. Not at all." I smiled at him, but I couldn't help thinking if he had truly been in love with Tiffany, he wouldn't have fallen for Norma Jeanne again.

When Holmes caught up to us, pulling a sleigh, the scent of a bonfire wafted by on a breeze. Voices and laughter rang through the air. Unfortunately, Sugar McLaughlin and another woman had tagged along. They clearly had eyes for Holmes. We walked another block and arrived at the contest.

The hill had been used for sledding since I was a kid. It was much more modern now, with light posts surrounded by safety buffers in case someone slammed into one. Little wonder that Holmes hadn't wanted to miss out on the fun. The atmosphere was delightful. Children squealed with excitement. Brand-new Christmas sleighs with the bows still on them were being tried out. Hot cider was being served, and marshmallows were in a bowl next to twigs for roasting.

The sledding contest was somewhat informal, with special categories for children under three, from four to six, from seven to nine, ten to twelve, and thirteen to eighteen. There were additional special categories for grandparents, dogs, and cats. But most of the contests were open to everyone. There were even designated people who dragged sleds up the hill for dogs and cats to ride down.

I had trouble imagining that any cats would want to go sledding though.

Buck was there with the green sleigh Dale had hired so he could play Santa Claus. It made me melancholy to see it, but the kids going for free sleigh rides in it were thrilled.

The veterinarian who had treated Trixie was there, cheering as her three-year-old slid down the hill.

Gingersnap, eager to ride, loped up the hill and stole a sled. She rode down all by herself, the wind blowing her fur.

"I wish Maggie could do that." I turned to find EmmyLou with her German shepherd on a leash. Maggie was well behaved but whined as though she were eager to run off leash again.

"You think it's too dangerous for her?" I asked.

"There's the vet. Think she would give me the okay?"

As if in answer to her question, the vet joined us with her Great Pyrenees. "I'm so glad to see you here. Is Maggie getting tired of being on a leash?"

"She's restless," said EmmyLou. "I don't know if that's a good sign or not."

"I have good news. Merry Christmas, Maggie!" The vet rubbed Maggie's ear with affection. "It's safe to let her run."

The second EmmyLou unlatched the leash, Maggie soared up the hill with Gingersnap and Trixie, where they romped with the other dogs.

She didn't look like a dying dog to me. It was heartbreaking to know she was ill and soon wouldn't be bounding around.

The vet smiled as she watched Maggie. "I never thought I would give this diagnosis and say it was good news, but in light of what we expected, it's terrific. The issue with her kidney is blastomycosis. It usually shows in the lungs because it's a fungal disease that dogs get from sniffing and inhaling the fungus in dirt. But we have cells that are indisputable. Come by tomorrow morning, and we'll give you meds for it."

"Is it curable?" EmmyLou seemed to be holding her breath.

"She'll be fine. The problem with the liver turned out to be Cushing's disease. Maggie will be on meds the rest of her life for that. There are a few side effects, like thirst and having to go out more often to urinate, but overall, she'll be okay. Your vet at home can monitor her to make sure she's getting the right dosage. I'll explain in detail tomorrow when you come in."

"Maggie isn't dying?" EmmyLou sounded incredulous.

The vet grinned. "Nope!"

At that moment, the vet's little girl called, "Mommy! Watch me!"

The vet yelled encouragement before saying, "Merry Christmas!" and jogging away.

Tears rolled down EmmyLou's cheeks. She covered her eyes with her hands. "After all the terrible things that have happened, this is like a Christmas miracle. If only I could roll back time and change things so Dad would still be here."

I wrapped an arm around her. "I wish we could do that, too."

"He would be thrilled to see Maggie prancing around with your dogs. He loved her so much."

"You love dogs. How is it that Norma Jeanne doesn't like them?" I asked.

EmmyLou groaned. "It started when she was a baby. She didn't like being licked or touching their fur. She's just fussy about that sort of thing. Her father and I never understood it. But she's our baby and we love her warts and all."

Maggie jumped on the back of a sled that Trixie rode and sat there like a pro. At the bottom, she ran to EmmyLou, panting and grinning like a silly dog.

EmmyLou bent over her and sobbed. When she stood up, she said, "I'm sorry. I think all the tension and horror of the last few days has gotten the best of me. I'm not usually such a basket case."

She wiped her eyes. "Do you think your Aunt Birdie would mind if I paid her a visit? I'd like to meet her. I was hoping to chat at the brunch today, but she left in such a hurry that I didn't get a chance."

"I think it might be good for both of you. She was very fond of your father."

"I wish that Vivienne had felt as kindly toward him. If she hadn't had that heart condition, he would have left her long ago. He sacrificed his own happiness for her health. And now look what happened. It was the cruelest fate of all that she murdered him. But justice was swift. I think her heart couldn't take what she had done. Maybe there was just a tiny bit of guilt and compassion in her after all."

"So she definitely died of natural causes?"

"I haven't heard anything official. But how could she live with herself after murdering my dad? She did a great job of playing the wronged wife. If Dad hadn't been such a softy, he would have left her long ago and would still be alive today. She caused her own death, I'm sure. Even her evil heart couldn't take her savageness."

I couldn't blame EmmyLou for being hateful toward Vivienne, but the anger in her tone was exceptionally harsh. Had she caused Vivienne's death? Was it possible to scare someone so severely that her heart problem killed her? The death would appear to be from natural causes. I couldn't help wondering where EmmyLou had been after the party. Had she gone to see the children sing? Had Oma given her a ride home? I didn't think I had given her a ride back.

I was reconsidering her motive in wanting to see Aunt Birdie. What if she really suspected Birdie of murdering her father and was only pretending to be nice? Holmes and I had seen her sneaking back to the inn in the wee hours of the morning. Where had she been? That was the night her father was killed. Could seemingly sweet EmmyLou have had a reason to murder her own father?

I wasn't quite sure how to approach that possibility. "It's a real shame that Thackleberry is struggling."

"That's a kind way to put it. More like hanging by a thread. I still can't believe that Dad knew about this and never mentioned a word to me, his own daughter." Her brow wrinkled. "Why would he discuss the details with Tiffany, of all people? Makes a person wonder."

"Are you implying that Tiffany might have murdered your dad?"

"No!" She appeared horrified by the mere thought. She took a deep breath. "But one of us did. It would be folly to exclude her from possible suspects, especially since she seems to have insider information. And it is interesting that her boyfriend is an accountant."

"You think he's in on it, too?" I looked over at Austin, who was dragging a sled uphill.

"Probably not. He wouldn't have slept with Norma Jeanne if Tiffany could blackmail him."

That made sense. "What does your husband think?"

EmmyLou sighed. "He's worried, of course, but he has his own problems."

"Oh? He seems so content."

She shook her head. "It's all an act for Norma Jeanne. She'll find out soon enough, though." She watched Holmes coach a little boy who kept falling off his sled. "I really wanted Holmes as a son-in-law. He would be so good for Norma Jeanne. He would ground her, you know? I haven't given up hope yet, but they're both going to be looking for jobs."

"But Holmes doesn't work for Thackleberry—" The second I uttered Thackleberry, I wanted to take it back. Holmes worked for her husband's architecture firm. My eyes met EmmyLou's.

Thirty

She gasped. "I shouldn't have said that. It just slipped out. Holmes doesn't know yet. Please don't say anything to him."

"What's going on?"

"I've said too much." She called Maggie and turned to leave.

I gently placed my hand on her arm and looked her in the eyes.

She buried her face in one hand and said, "A building collapsed, and lawsuits are coming in every which way. Chances are pretty good that the firm will close, of course."

"Don't businesses have insurance for things like that?" I asked.

EmmyLou sucked in a deep breath. "Of course. But would you ever hire a company with that kind of reputation? He won't get any more contracts. And who would insure him after this? We were a little cocky, I guess, and put a lot of our own money into that building. I took comfort in knowing that my job would be safe. But if Thackleberry collapses too, we'll be sunk."

Maggie came running, panting and happy.

"Please don't say anything to Holmes," she begged.

I didn't want to make promises. Besides, I had to tell Dave. If her husband was losing his business, they might have been in a position to want to inherit from Dale.

"I'll try not to." It wasn't much and most certainly wasn't the assurance she wanted.

She left in a hurry.

Holmes rushed up to me, breathless. His jeans were dusted with snow. "I thought that looked like Maggie, but she was romping around like a dog who is well."

"She's going to be okay. She has two conditions, both of which are treatable."

"Maggie isn't dying? That's great!" Lowering his voice, he said, "Could you do me a huge favor and team up with me for the contests? Sugar McLaughlin has been attached to me like a tick."

I snickered. "I would be delighted."

"Come on, then!" He led me to the sled, and we raced uphill to lose Sugar, who followed more slowly, calling Holmes's name.

I was out of breath at the top. "You know this is kind of mean to Sugar."

"Sugar is a sweet kid but way too young for me. I don't want to encourage her."

"You should be flattered by her attention, you old geezer."

Holmes made a face at me. "Get on the sled and hold on tight."

Across the way, the man with dimples I had seen at the Christkindl Market nodded to me. A woman about my age demanded his attention. He bent over to show her how to steer.

Holmes took the front position to steer, and I hopped on

behind him and held him close, which I didn't mind at all. The starter gun went off, and Trixie jumped on behind me.

Austin and Sugar came precariously close to us on another sled. So close that Trixie barked at them. Holmes steered away so sharply that I feared the sled would topple, throwing us all into the snow. No wonder his jeans had been snow covered.

But Holmes's maneuvering was successful. Even Trixie managed to stay on the sled. We slid in a hair ahead of Austin and Sugar, coming to stop at Dave's feet.

Holmes and I were laughing when we piled off the sled. He high-fived me. "That was the most fun I've had this holiday! Dave, want to take a turn?"

Dave was not amused. Without even a glimmer of a smile, he said, "Vivienne died from an overdose of sleeping pills combined with alcohol."

"Oh no! Wouldn't she know better than to take sleeping pills and drink?" asked Holmes.

"One would think so." Dave rubbed his chin. "Holly, can you let me into her room?"

"Of course." I called Trixie and Gingersnap.

Holmes loaned his sled to Ethan, who had been fighting with his sister about whose turn it was.

The three of us walked back to the inn. Our gay mood ratcheted down with the grim reminder of the deaths in Wagtail.

We entered the inn through the registration lobby, where I grabbed a key to Vivienne's room. We walked up the stairs, and I unlocked the door.

Dave paused for a moment upon entering. He took in the details of the room, the array of clothing draped on chairs, the welcome basket from the inn. It intrigued me because the goodies were gone, and it was now loaded with sugar packets from various restaurants around town, as well as napkins full of breads and after-dinner mints. Next to the basket were other freebies from stores.

But that didn't draw Dave's interest. He marched to the bathroom, slid gloves onto his hands, and looked in her various toiletry bags. He opened jars of creams and assorted bottles. "Don't touch anything, but do you guys see any pills out there?"

"They could be in her purse," I suggested.

"They could be, but they weren't in the purse she had with her." Dave opened the closet door. "Did she think she was staying for a month?"

She had brought at least a dozen pairs of shoes, and the closet was packed with clothes. I recognized some of the designer labels.

He pulled out her suitcases and pawed through the contents. "Still no pills. I haven't even found an aspirin."

"Would she hide them?" I asked Holmes. "Maybe from Tim and Linda?"

He shrugged. "Not that I know of. Vivienne always seemed a little *me against the world*, though. I never knew quite what to expect from her."

I watched Dave as he looked through pockets of clothes hanging in the closet. "How did you get this information so fast on Christmas Day?" I checked my watch. "She's probably not even at the medical examiner's office yet."

"A buddy of mine at the hospital took a blood sample. Didn't take long to get results."

Dave heaved a big sigh and surveyed the room. "What am I overlooking? Do you see anything out of the norm, Holly?"

"Only the items she took from restaurants. Where's that big bag that she stuffed everything into?"

"Is that it on the chair?" asked Holmes.

Dave emptied the contents on the bed. More bread fell out along with wrapped chocolates and candies, and two champagne glasses from The Blue Boar!

"No pills at all." Dave groaned. "Don't people with heart problems carry nitroglycerin with them?"

"Doesn't look like she did," I said. "Though she helped herself to everything that wasn't chained down. Did you ask her family members about her heart?"

"I can answer that," said Holmes. "Everyone in her family was aware of her heart issue. EmmyLou told me that Vivienne could just collapse and die at any time. She had to avoid anything strenuous, and they made efforts not to upset her."

"So Dale's death could have triggered it. Or struggling through the snow after the party?" I looked at Dave.

"Could have. But I'm told there's no way someone could take that many sleeping pills by accident."

Holmes said softly, "She murdered Dale out of jealousy and then couldn't live with herself?"

"I would believe that about someone else, but not about Vivienne," I said. "Didn't you hear how her own family talked about her? They hated her!"

Something was wrong with this scenario. I gasped when I realized it. "Dave, that doesn't make sense. Nobody takes sleeping pills *before* they go somewhere. You take them when you're ready for bed. Not before a party."

Dave eyed me as he slid off the gloves. "Unless she wanted to be the center of attention when she collapsed."

"Then why did she leave the party?"

"That's what I'm trying to figure out. But I don't see anything helpful here."

"Holly? Is that you?" EmmyLou rapped on the door. "I've been calling your Aunt Birdie, but she's not answering her phone. Does she have a cell number? I'd very much like to pay her a visit tomorrow."

"Aunt Birdie is a holdout on cell phones. She refuses to use one. She's probably not answering the phone because the cops searched her house and removed some of her belongings earlier today. She's quite upset about it. They took all her kitchen knives."

EmmyLou gasped. "I knew she was a suspect but had no idea they were that serious about her. I can't believe it. I don't even know the woman, but I can't imagine her killing my dad. He always said such nice things about her."

That was a surprise. Although when I thought about it, Vivienne made Birdie seem like a sweetheart.

Dave began to ask EmmyLou questions about Vivienne's health.

But I started worrying about Aunt Birdie. It was Christmas, and she was all alone, holed up in her house. The least I could do was go over and get her to come to dinner with the rest of us.

I left them to discuss Vivienne's health and hustled to my apartment. I grabbed the spare key to Aunt Birdie's house in case she was being stubborn and wouldn't open the door.

But on my way out, I was waylaid by Tiffany, who called to me from the library.

Tiffany sat on the window seat and pulled a tiny tassel along the cushion. Her white kitten trembled with excitement and pounced on it.

Tiffany smiled and repeated the trick for the cute little ball of fur.

I joined her on the window seat and admired the kitty. "She's so cute. Have you given her a name yet?"

Trixie watched the kitten as though she wanted to play. She behaved though and only smelled her.

Tiffany looked up at me. "I like Snowy or Snowflake, but maybe that's just too obvious? Dad couldn't have given her to me at a better time. I'm emotionally hollow. Does that make sense? I'm just drifting around in a state of shock. Losing Grampy is the worst thing that has ever happened to me."

I knew how I'd felt when I thought Oma might be ill a

couple of years before. Losing her was unimaginable. "I'm so sorry."

"You know what else is awful? Wondering which one of your relatives could have stabbed him. It had to be one of us. I'm sure of it. But I don't know which one."

They couldn't trust one another anymore. We all relied on family to get us through the dark times, but that had been torn from them, too.

Tiffany dangled the tassel for the kitten. "And I couldn't be more embarrassed about what happened with Austin. All my life I've listened to them say Norma Jeanne is the pretty one and Blake is the smart one. Tiffany was just there, blending in with the woodwork. My mother has been after me for years to bring home a boyfriend. She even set me up with some horrible dates. They were guys *she* liked, but not my type at all. I was so psyched about Austin joining us for Christmas. Especially since Norma Jeanne was engaged and planning her wedding. My mom was drooling over the idea of a wedding. It was perfect timing to keep her off my back. How was I supposed to know that Austin had dated Norma Jeanne? Huh? In the future, do I have to quiz every man I meet? Excuse me, do you like cats and have you ever met my femme fatale cousin Norma Jeanne?"

Her words came fast and thick in anger and frustration. "At least Holmes and I know the truth about them." Her eyes widened, and she tore her attention away from the kitten. "Can you imagine if that hadn't happened until the wedding?"

There wasn't really much I could say except, "I think you're right. It's best that everyone knows now."

"Holly, am I a terrible person for not grieving about Vivi? I feel so guilty. Dale wasn't really related to me, but his death hit me like a sledgehammer. Vivi was my father's mother, my flesh-and-blood grandmother. You'd think her death would be more devastating. To tell you the truth, I think everyone, especially my mother, is breathing a huge sigh of relief that the days of Vivi's torment are over."

"I think you just answered your own question," I said. "It's harder to grieve for someone who was cruel."

"My dad is very upset. I have never seen him like this. At least he loved her and is genuinely grieving for her."

I rose to leave. There wasn't much I could say. Vivienne had probably lost their love long ago. She had brought that on herself.

"Hey, Holly? I got Austin some Christmas presents. I don't really want to give him anything, but it's Christmas and he's not with his own family, so I feel kind of guilty and think maybe I should give them to him after all. Not out of love or anything, just to make his Christmas a little brighter. Assuming he's not in bed with Norma Jeanne again."

I understood her feelings, because I would be thinking the same thing. "What would Dale do?"

Tiffany jumped from her seat and hugged me. When she let go, tears were running down her cheeks. She wiped her eyes and sniffled. "You couldn't have said anything more perfect. If I follow his lead, Grampy will always be with me, especially in the tough times."

I was feeling a little teary myself when I left. Bundled up against the cold, Trixie and I set out for Aunt Birdie's house.

The lights on Birdie's house still sparkled and looked welcoming. I didn't expect her to be feeling quite as festive as her house looked.

I walked up the front porch steps and knocked on the door. "Aunt Birdie! It's me, Holly!"

There was no response. I tried again, knocking as loud as I could. "Aunt Birdie! Please open the door."

Still nothing.

I took a deep breath. She was a stubborn old coot. I slid the key into the lock and turned it.

The house lay silent. I didn't hear a television or any

music. She had drawn the drapes, leaving the house dark. I switched on lights as I went, calling, "Aunt Birdie! It's Holly. Aunt Birdie, where are you?"

I walked through the first floor, then ventured upstairs. There wasn't a single sign of Aunt Birdie.

I wished she had a cell phone. Even with the spotty reception in Wagtail, I would feel better if I could at least do something to try to find her.

I phoned Oma, but Aunt Birdie hadn't shown up at the inn. Standing in her foyer, I wondered where she would go. To church? To the cemetery, maybe, to honor our ancestors? Birdie was very fond of talking to their gravestones. Maybe she felt alone and would find it comforting? A little odd, but not implausible.

Was this how the Thackleberrys had felt waiting for Vivienne? Two people had been murdered. Could Aunt Birdie be next?

My heart pounding, I stepped out onto her porch and locked the door. I walked to the church, noting the happy family celebrations going on inside brightly lighted homes. Families arrived laden with gifts, and notes of Christmas carols floated out when front doors opened. I thought I even caught a whiff of ham baking.

The church was empty. The graveyard was covered in snow. In the dark, a few Christmas arrangements adorning graves took sinister forms.

It felt desolate and lonely. I hurried back to the decorated streets where people gathered. Maybe the bustling streets had made Aunt Birdie feel left out. She had us, but at the moment, visiting with us also meant seeing Dale's family.

There was one other possibility. One that I had put out of my mind and refused to accept. What if Dave was right about Aunt Birdie? Could she have flipped out and murdered Dale and Vivienne?

Thirty-one

I closed my eyes in pain. How could I even think that? Of course, it *would* explain Birdie's disappearance.

I was trudging back to the inn, trying to banish that gloomy thought, when I ran into Dave.

"Percy's at the Wagtail Springs Hotel."

I checked the time. Dinner was at eight o'clock. I still had a little time before I had to change clothes. "Can I come?"

Dave gazed at me for a long second. "Sure."

We walked over to the hotel. Percy waited at the front desk.

He shook Dave's hand. "The police have never called me for questioning before."

"I hope you keep it that way," said Dave. "Thanks for coming in at my request." He showed Percy the photograph of Vivienne. "Did you see this woman last night?"

Percy's eyes grew large.

He knew something! I watched Dave, who remained calm and appeared to wait for Percy to speak.

Percy chewed his upper lip. "Look, I want to cooperate,

but I can't afford to lose my job. I didn't commit any crimes or anything. Can you promise not to tell my boss?"

Dave's head tilted a tiny bit. "No."

Percy looked away. He wiped his eye. "She's been coming to the hotel to see Mr. Oathaut."

It seemed like I had heard that name recently. But where? I struggled to remember.

"Did she visit him last night?"

Percy took a deep breath and winced. "I don't know for sure. I left the front desk and ran down to the church to see my kid sing. I saw her coming in this direction, though. She was kind of staggering, like she'd had too much to drink."

"Thanks. Which room is Mr. Oathaut staying in?"

"Room five. That's him right there, coming in the door now."

Dave and I whipped around. The bald man who had told me about the problem with Thackleberry fabric strolled into the lobby.

I saw fear in his eyes when Dave said, "Mr. Oathaut?"

To his credit, he strode toward us, held out his hand to Dave, and said, "Steve Oathaut."

"Could we speak privately in your room?" asked Dave.

There was a quiver in Steve's voice when he said, "Sure."

We followed him to a modern guest room. The lines of the furniture were simple and clean. He appeared to be a neat man. No clothes lay on the bed. Nothing cluttered the dresser.

Dave asked him some preliminary questions. Steve was from Michigan. He owned a company that manufactured pet beds.

"What brings you to Wagtail?" asked Dave.

"I do a lot of business here. Thought it would be a nice place to spend the holiday." He reached out and scratched Trixie behind the ears.

I wished I could slide Dave a note about the fact that

Steve had told me about a problem at Thackleberry. I thought I'd better just shut up and see what happened.

Dave showed him the photo of Vivienne. "Do you know this woman?"

"Vivienne Thackleberry. Sure. I know of her. We're in the same business."

"Have you seen her recently?"

Steve glanced around the room. "Yeah. I'm sure Percy told you that she paid me a visit."

"More than once?"

"Yes. We were, um, talking business."

"In the wee hours of the morning?" I asked.

"Okay, look. We had a little fling is all. It wasn't the right thing to do. I knew she was married, but that's what happened. Nothing illegal about that, right?"

I guessed not, but he had to be ten or fifteen years younger than Vivi.

"Did she pay you a visit last night?" asked Dave.

Steve wriggled uncomfortably. "Yeah. She was very drunk. She came by, but I told her to go back to the inn where she was staying, and she left."

"By herself?"

"Yes."

Dave stood there gazing at Steve.

Why did his name seem familiar? I stifled a gasp. Doris had called him *Stevie Oathaut*. What had she said? That he would buy Thackleberry over her dead body? Something like that.

"Did you have business with Tim Kedrowski?" I asked.

Dave shot me a look of surprise.

"With Dale and Vivienne gone, Tim wanted to discuss the possibility of my company buying Thackleberry."

Steve Oathaut rubbed me the wrong way. His blue eyes were cold and wary.

"Mind if I look around?" asked Dave.

Steve shuddered just the tiniest bit. "Go ahead. What's this about?"

Dave didn't respond. I waited quietly while Dave checked out the bathroom and closet. I noted, though, that Steve glanced at the window several times. Was he planning to make a break for it?

Just to prevent that, I wandered over to the window. It brought back memories of the night I'd played a ghost in the old hotel during a Halloween ghost tour of Wagtail. The backyard had improved dramatically and now appeared to be a lovely garden covered by winter snow.

When I turned around, Steve was watching me carefully.

Dave pulled up a chair and sat down in it across from Steve, who sat on the edge of the bed. "I think you know why we're here. It would be better for you to come clean."

"Look, I didn't kill her. I swear!"

Dave recited the Miranda rights. "Did she take medicine while she was here?"

"No! Nothing like that. She had a drink is all."

I opened the window and frigid air blew inside. On a stupid hunch, I said, "She went out the window, didn't she?"

Steve panicked. "My family has wanted to buy Thackleberry for as long as I can remember. Vivienne met with me about selling the company a year ago. We started having an affair. The plan was for me to come to Wagtail when she was here with Dale. She would get him to agree to sell the company, and then Vivienne would come to work with me as the president of Thackleberry. But he refused and then she killed him."

Thirty-two

"I didn't want to be part of anything like that. It was never part of the deal. I tried to get a flight out of here, but everything was booked, and then the airports closed, so I was stuck."

"She told you she killed Dale?" asked Dave.

"No. She denied it, but the timing was too coincidental. I figured they fought over selling Thackleberry and she flipped out and stabbed him."

"Or maybe you did," said Dave.

Steve raised his hands in protest. "I had nothing to do with that. I've never killed anyone. Honest."

"Why did you tell me about the Thackleberry fabric?" I asked.

"See? Now I am guilty of that. I wanted to drive down the value of Thackleberry so I wouldn't have to pay so much for it. I thought it would make Dale more eager to sell if he thought the business was failing."

"So it wasn't true?" I asked.

"No. And I admit my guilt about that. It was harmless business strategy. But I did not murder either of them."

"What happened last night?" asked Dave.

"She showed up drunk. It was late and she was acting weird. Like she was disoriented. She had a drink, and I thought she'd probably just sleep it off, you know? The next thing I knew, she was dead. I swear I didn't kill her. She just died."

"And you threw her out the window?" I asked.

"She was already dead. I couldn't exactly roll her out through the lobby on a bellman's cart, could I?"

"If you were innocent, why didn't you call 911?"

"I knew if our plan came out everyone would think I murdered Dale and Vivienne. It just looked bad, even though I didn't do anything. So I slid her out the window, but when I went outside, throngs of people were coming back from the church. I waited until three in the morning, when everything was quiet, and dragged her to that Christkindl booth."

Dave arrested him on the spot. He clicked handcuffs on Steve, who continued to protest and insist he was innocent.

People stared as they walked through the lobby.

I left, relieved that it was over. I had seen him around town so many times but never suspected that he could be the murderer. Still, his protests rang in my head, leaving me with a smidgen of doubt.

I raced home, thinking I was running late, but when I walked into the inn, I found Oma, Mr. Huckle, and Doris having cocktails in the Dogwood Room with EmmyLou, Barry, and Maggie.

I sat down and told them what had happened with Steve Oathaut. The Thackleberrys were stunned.

"I knew that Stevie Oathaut was trouble." Doris shook her finger. "It is in his eyes. Snake eyes!"

"I can't believe that Vivienne planned everything." EmmyLou seemed at a loss. "I was so stupid. I played right into her hands suggesting we come here for Christmas. She must have been secretly pleased that everything was working out for her. I hate to say it, but she planned her own demise. She got what she deserved."

"Did you say Tim offered to sell Thackleberry to Steve?" asked Barry.

"Apparently so."

Doris scowled. "We have to watch him. He has no power to do that. I didn't sign anything. Did you, EmmyLou?"

"No. I would never sell the business."

"Did you find Birdie?" asked Oma.

My heart fell. "I was hoping she might be here. Where could she have gone?"

Barry said wryly, "I would be in a bar. Are there any bars open on Christmas Night? I might join her."

"Barry!" EmmyLou scolded him. "Maybe she went to a place that was special to her and Dad. Someplace where she could remember him? I took Maggie for a walk down to the lake. It was so peaceful with Canadian geese swimming around. I felt like Dad was there with me."

"Perhaps she will meet us at The Blue Boar," said Oma. "You'd better get dressed, Holly."

I knew Oma was right, but I felt restless. Aunt Birdie was stubborn and obnoxious, but she was still family. *My* family. I followed Oma's advice and walked up to my apartment to change clothes. The Blue Boar was the fanciest restaurant in town. Oma had made reservations far in advance for this Christmas dinner.

I should have gone for something festive, but I reached for the black dress that I called my Audrey Hepburn dress. The sleeveless top was fitted, and the skirt flared with one big inverted pleat in the front. A necklace of rhinestones provided a bit of fun bling. I added a chunky black-and-white bracelet and gold earrings, and slid my feet into open-toed black shoes that made me think of Vivienne. Just like her, I would be walking in the cold in dressy shoes that wouldn't keep my feet warm.

I tried to pull myself out of my funk. Aunt Birdie would be fine. Actually, I was a little surprised that I cared so much. Even though she was a pill and had pulled some stunts on me that I didn't appreciate one bit, she had grown on me.

Trixie whimpered as though she understood that something wasn't quite right. I slid a black velvet holiday collar over her head, and she pranced in circles until I laughed.

We joined the others, and the first thing I noticed in the lobby was Norma Jeanne staring wistfully at Holmes. I guess that was to be expected. The holiday that should have been one of her best ever had turned sour in every way possible. But she was talking with Tiffany and Blake!

Aunt Birdie was still a no-show.

I probably shouldn't have stared so hard at Norma Jeanne and her cousins. I tried to appear to mingle and sidled toward them, ostensibly in search of something in the desk near the front door. I opened a drawer but positioned myself to hear them better.

"I still think it's that Birdie woman," said Tiffany. "It's just a matter of time before they find the knife that killed Grampy and match her DNA to it."

"I'd like to think you're right, Tiffie, but I'm not sure that we can count on Deputy Dufus." For once Blake wasn't insulting his sister. "We're out in the boonies! Don't you think they overlook the crimes of locals? They're liable to hide the evidence or lose it accidentally-on-purpose to protect their friends."

I recognized Tiffany's voice. "I hope it was that horrible Steve Oathaut. We need to put this behind us and band together so we can go home and start fixing the problems with Thackleberry. I can't believe he started that rumor about our fabric. It doesn't get lower than that!"

"What if it was Holmes's Grandma Rose?" asked Norma Jeanne.

I had to stifle my gasp.

"That old lady? Face it, Norma Jeanne. It's over with Holmes, and you brought it all on yourself." Blake sounded matter-of-fact. "We need to save what we can and move forward."

"That's right," added Tiffany. "And there's no evidence pointing toward Holmes's grandmother."

"What if she was having an affair with Gramps, too?" asked Norma Jeanne.

One of them snorted and laughed. Blake?

Holmes sidled up to me and grinned. Evidently he hadn't overheard their discussion about Rose.

I was painfully aware that the tables had turned and they were probably listening to the two of us now. Before he could bring up the murders, I hastily said, "Hungry? I'm looking forward to dinner."

We mingled with the others, but I couldn't help noticing that Norma Jeanne kept a close eye on Holmes.

Leaving the inn in the capable hands of Casey, who had celebrated the holiday earlier with his family, we walked the short distance to The Blue Boar, located next door to the inn.

When we arrived and took seats, I wound up sitting next to Holmes. I looked around for Aunt Birdie, but she wasn't there. Oma was seated nearby. I walked over to her and asked in a low voice, "No word from Aunt Birdie yet?"

Oma took my hand into hers. "I wish Birdie could see how concerned you are. Maybe she will still come."

Rose leaned toward me. "Norma Jeanne, Tim, and Blake are too depressed to join us tonight. Maybe Birdie is feeling the impact of Dale's death and wants to be alone. This has been a tragic holiday for all of them."

I returned to my seat. Rose was right, of course. If I had

lost a loved one, I probably wouldn't be up to celebrating, either.

But plenty of their family members were sociable. Tiffany sat between Linda and Doris, chattering as though she were feeling upbeat.

EmmyLou seemed pensive. She held her hands as if in prayer but slid her fingers against one another somewhat nervously while gazing out the window.

Maggie, Gingersnap, Muffy, and Trixie roamed the room, visiting with one another and getting attention from everyone.

All things considered, spirits were high as we devoured a rich shrimp bisque. If I hadn't known other dishes were coming, I would have wanted more.

Holmes nudged me and hissed, "You were there. Do you think it was this Steve Oathaut fellow?"

My eyes met his. "He's a crook, but I don't know if he killed them. I'd feel better if we had some DNA or the murder weapon or something."

"They're probably checking his room for a sleeping pill bottle."

"Doris takes prescription sleeping pills," I whispered.

"One of the Thackleberrys could have swiped some. I can't imagine it was Doris. Really, can you see her jabbing her own son with a knife?"

"Can she stand without her cane?"

He shook his head. "I don't think so."

I was gazing at the sweet old lady at the exact moment that Trixie sneaked close to the hiking stick that was propped by her chair. To my complete horror, Trixie sniffed the bottom of it and pawed at it, knocking it to the ground.

Muffy barked and jumped off Doris's lap. She growled and seized the wrist loop attached to the stick. Trixie gripped the bottom of the stick in her teeth and pulled ferociously.

Trixie weighed more than little Muffy, which gave her the
upper hand.

A waiter happened by with a tray, didn't see the dogs,
tripped over the stick, and went flying. Dishes crashed to
the floor. Shards and food flew everywhere.

I jumped up as Gingersnap and Maggie rushed to join
the excitement. The dogs were going to step on shards if we
didn't stop them.

Holmes was right behind me when I picked up Trixie,
who refused to relinquish her grip on the hiking stick. He
nabbed Muffy, who continued to growl. But as we lifted
them, the walking stick suddenly opened.

Thirty-three

We all watched as a knife blade appeared at the end of the hiking stick.

Trixie still held the cover in her mouth.

I heard people gasping at the blade, which gleamed as it caught the light.

Muffy still growled, but Holmes held her fast.

Oma stood up. "No one touch it." She pulled out her cell phone and dialed.

I didn't have to ask whom she was calling. I was fairly sure we were looking at the blade that had killed Dale. Steve Oathaut might be innocent after all!

Either Doris was in shock or she did a great job of pretending. "I had no idea. Who would have suspected there was a knife in the hiking stick?"

Everyone stared at her as she reached for it.

"Don't touch it, Doris," said Oma. "I fear it may be the murder weapon."

"Nonsense." Doris flicked her hand. "It was a gift from Dale."

"Do you know that for sure?" asked Rose.

"Well, it wasn't from anyone else. It must have been Dale who gave it to me."

Holmes's eyes met mine. I hated to imagine that Doris was trying to cover up the murder of her own child. Could that be possible? Had she wrapped it herself and pretended it was a gift? That would have been diabolical.

"I still think it's better that no one touch it until Dave examines it," said Oma.

"May we clear the broken dishes?" asked the headwaiter.

They were sweeping up the shards when my phone buzzed, alerting me to a message. Casey had texted, *Received phone call about problem with your Aunt Birdie at Rupert's house.*

Still carrying Trixie, I walked over to Holmes, who was returning Muffy to Doris. "Get a doggie bag for Trixie and me?"

"What's going on? Can I help?"

"Aunt Birdie is up to her old tricks. Hopefully, I'll be back before the turkey arrives."

I stopped by Oma's table to let her know what was going on, then hurried to the inn to change into boots. I would break my leg or my neck if I tried to rush in my high-heeled dress shoes. Trixie and I left the inn at a run. As it turned out, snow boots weren't very good for running, either. I slowed to a fast walk after a couple of blocks. I wasn't a runner, but I blamed the stiff soles of my boots.

As we neared Rupert's house, I saw a small crowd outside again. My heart sank. What craziness was Aunt Birdie up to now?

Trixie sped ahead of me. I broke through the crowd.

Aunt Birdie stood in Rupert's doorway, illuminated from behind. She wielded something in her hand like a sword.

Another one? How many other women in Wagtail had hiking staffs loaded with a knife?

"Birdie!" I screamed. I ran toward her. She held a hiking stick from which a knife protruded at the end. "Put that thing down."

"Holly! Don't tell me you finally noticed my absence at Christmas dinner."

"You could have called," I muttered, while very slowly reaching for the hiking staff.

She whipped it away from me.

"You related to her?" called a man. In the darkness I couldn't make him out too well. Medium height, with a local accent.

"She's my aunt."

"Tell her I want my kids."

"They're not your children, and you'll have to kill me to get to them. Now go on your way."

"Aunt Birdie," I whispered, "what's going on?"

"I'll tell you what's going on," the man yelled. "I'm here to pick up the kids, but she won't let me have them."

"Rupert's children?" I asked.

"Those children have been left in *my* custody, and I have no authorization to turn them over to the likes of you!" Aunt Birdie stood erect and pointed the knife at him.

A cheer went up behind me in the house. I turned around and found three children smiling, one of whom was dancing with Trixie. "Who is that man?"

One of Rupert's daughters said, "He's our mom's boyfriend." She wrinkled her nose and stuck out her tongue.

"We don't like him," said the one who played with Trixie.

"Where's your dad?"

"He's at the hospital with our big brother."

Aha. That explained a lot. If he had broken his leg in the hover board accident, they might be there all night, especially if it required surgery to set it. "Rupert asked you to sit with his children?" I asked Aunt Birdie.

"He didn't ask," said the older girl. "Aunt Birdie told him to get on over to the hospital because Howie needed him. Daddy gave her a big ole sloppy kiss on her cheek and called her an angel from heaven."

That was a Christmas miracle if ever I heard one.

"Aunt Birdie, would you lower that blade for a moment?" I asked.

"I will not!"

Trusting that she wouldn't intentionally stab me with it, I walked over to the man in the dark. "Hi. I'm Holly Miller." I had barely finished saying my name when my eyes focused and I recognized him from the photos posted in stores around town so clerks would be on the lookout for him.

"Jed Kaine. Their mother sent me to collect the children."

I flushed in spite of the cold. The last thing I expected was to be confronting the infamous thief, Jed Kaine. I tried to hide my discomfort. "Jed, do you have an obstinate elderly aunt?"

"What?"

"Don't you have some older relatives who are stubborn?"

His eyes squinched up, and he gazed at me like I had lost my mind. "My grandma Bethany. Don't nobody cross her."

"My Aunt Birdie is like your grandmother. You can camp out here in the freezing cold all night, but you're not getting those children. I can guarantee you that. What do you say we both leave them with Birdie and let their parents fight over the children tomorrow?" A brilliant thought came to mind. "Otherwise, we'll have to get the law involved."

Jed's eyes widened, and he focused on me intently. "That would, um, be a bad thing. It is Christmas after all."

"It is. Merry Christmas, Jed."

"Yeah. To you, too." Jed turned and walked to the street. The children cheered again.

I returned to Aunt Birdie and hustled her into the house.

When the door was closed behind me, I turned the lock and leaned against the door.

"Their mom is at the hospital, too?" I asked Aunt Birdie.

She took on a snooty attitude. "I presume so. Such darling children. It's a pity she took up with the likes of Jed Kaine."

The children played with Trixie under the glittering lights Rupert had draped along the ceiling. A fire blazed, and I spied cups of cocoa. It was a cozy scene. I had never suspected that Aunt Birdie would be good with children. "Have you eaten?"

Aunt Birdie appeared taken aback, as though I had insulted her. "We had some of Rupert's cookies in the afternoon."

I went to Rupert's landline and phoned The Blue Boar. When I explained the situation, the owner agreed to pack up some Christmas dinners for them if I would transport them.

That taken care of, one thing still worried me—Aunt Birdie's weapon. Unless I missed my guess, the blade on one of the hiking staffs was going to match the holes in the Grinch. And even worse, the holes in Dale's back.

Thirty-four

While Aunt Birdie jabbered with the kids, I took a minute to examine the hiking staff, gingerly holding it with paper napkins. Made of oak, the bottom was hollow with a cover for the retractable knife. "Where did you get this?"

Aunt Birdie spoke as casually as if I had asked what was for lunch. "Those foolish cops. They were so intent on my kitchen knives. Do you know I had to spread butter with a spoon? I can't eat any meat now. How would I cut it?"

"They missed this?"

She turned the most innocent face toward me. "Never underestimate a woman, Holly."

"I hope you don't say things like that to Dave."

I took a closer look at the knife blade. She could have cleaned it with bleach. Any thinking killer would have done that. In any event, I didn't see any sign of blood.

I promised Aunt Birdie that I would return with dinner

and left, waiting to be sure I heard the latch lock behind me before I ambled toward the street with Trixie.

I paused a moment and looked around for Jed in case he was up to something.

We walked back slowly. I wished the stores were open, because I wanted to know how common those hiking staffs were. In my head, I knew I had to tell Dave about Aunt Birdie's staff. But in my heart I was reluctant. Given what they already thought about Birdie, they might really haul her off to jail. Would it be wrong not to say anything about it until they had ruled out Doris's hiking staff?

At The Blue Boar, Dave and Holmes were talking in front of the host stand. Dave held the staff in a gloved hand.

My heart beat so hard that I was afraid Dave would hear it and know I was holding back information about Aunt Birdie owning the same kind of hiking staff.

Holmes glanced at me. "I hear you were present when Doris opened this gift."

I nodded. "It was wrapped. I understand why Doris thinks it was from Dale. But that makes no sense. One of them brought it downstairs to the Dogwood Room. Unless one of the Thackleberrys found it in Dale's room and carried it down . . ."

"Holmes told me about Doris's sleeping pills. How mobile is Doris? Could she have stabbed Dale?"

"She wouldn't have," I said. "She was so proud of him. She loved her son."

"That wasn't what I asked." Dave eyed me with suspicion. Or was that my own guilt putting ideas into my head for not coming clean about Birdie's hiking staff?

"She walks well with a cane. I do have a little trouble imagining that she would walk all the way over to Rupert's house, though. I don't think she knows him. Why would she take a midnight stroll over to the Grinch?"

"Curiosity?" suggested Dave.

Why was I defending her? I truly could not imagine her killing Dale, but the more I argued against it, the more guilty it made Aunt Birdie seem. "It had to be another family member. *If* this hiking staff was the murder weapon, then it was very clever to pass it along to someone else who used it without knowledge of what it really was."

"That's true," said Holmes. "I've seen them before, but the knife is so well hidden that it's hard to know which ones are loaded with a knife. If Trixie hadn't been persistent about it, we might not have known until Doris got caught with it at the airport."

Dave looked down at Trixie. "That little girl has some nose. I bet she can smell the blood that we can't see."

"I bet you're right." I had never heard sweeter words. Trixie had been with me at Rupert's house, but she hadn't made the same kind of fuss about Aunt Birdie's hiking staff.

"Does this mean Steve Oathaut is off the hook?" I asked.

Dave frowned. "Not for Vivienne's murder. He dumped her out a window!"

Holmes reached into his pocket. "All of a sudden I'm getting a bunch of texts." He frowned as he read them.

"Everything okay?" I asked.

"Probably." He stuck his phone into his pocket. "I'd better go. See you later, Holly?"

"Sure." I watched as Dave took the staff and left, and Holmes set off for who-knew-where.

While I waited for the meals for Aunt Birdie and the children, I peeked into the dining room. Oma and most of the Thackleberry crew were finishing their main course.

My mouth watered at the scent of the traditional German meal of goose with potato dumplings. But I'd have enjoyed the roast turkey with mashed potatoes every bit as much. I hoped someone would remember to bring a doggie bag home for Trixie and me.

The dinners were ready, neatly packaged in two bags to make them easy to carry. Trixie and I left in a rush so they wouldn't be too cold by the time we delivered them to Rupert's house.

Notes of Christmas music tinkled in the distance, and I realized that the Christmas night event was under way on the green.

Even before I knocked on Rupert's door, I could tell Aunt Birdie and the kids were having a great time. High voices sang "Jingle Bells."

The music stopped at the sound of my knock. Aunt Birdie opened the door a crack and peered out at me. I held up the bags. "Oh, lovely, Holly! Thank you so much. Angels! Dinner is here!"

The children clustered behind her, the smallest girl clinging to Aunt Birdie's dress.

She handed the bags to the two older children. Aunt Birdie embraced me and pecked me on the cheek. "Merry Christmas, Holly."

She closed the door and turned the lock. I was fairly sure that Oma and Rose would be through with their dinners at The Blue Boar. No point in going back there.

I strolled toward the green and heard the notes of "I Saw Mommy Kissing Santa Claus." Hundreds of people mingled in front of the huge Christmas tree. In the gazebo where Holmes had posed as Santa Paws, a band played, and a group of carolers coaxed people to join in. A few dogs added to the fun by howling.

I was considering buying myself a nice hot Glühwein, the German version of mulled wine, when Trixie began sniffing around the Christkindl chalet that was draped with yellow police tape. I joined the line of people waiting to buy a hot drink. Snowflakes were beginning to drift down.

"Trixie!" I called her name repeatedly, but no amount of

calling did a bit of good. She planted herself by the empty booth, stared at it, and cocked her head to the side.

I gave up my place in line and walked over to her. "Trixie? What's up?"

She whined. The barest little hum of a whine. It was hard to hear with the loud music. But when I listened very carefully, I thought I heard something moving inside the chalet.

Thirty-five

I crept around to the door. The line of tape crossed the entrance. There was no way anyone would miss it. But it wouldn't have been difficult to duck underneath it. The door itself was about three inches ajar.

"Hello?" Using my knuckles in the hope I wouldn't mess up any fingerprints, I shoved the door open wider. In the dim glow of the festive lights, I could make out a figure inside on the floor. "No!" I hissed. *Not again!*

I lifted the police tape and darted inside. Enough light filtered in for me to make out Norma Jeanne lying on the floor, as beautiful as if she had been posed. Her hair cascaded over her left shoulder. Her face was peaceful, her lips ruby. Her skirt had been hiked up just enough to show the knee and part of the thigh of her left leg. There was no sign of blood or bruising.

Outside I could hear Trixie barking. Not her corpse bark, though.

I grabbed Norma Jeanne's shoulder and shook it gently. "Norma Jeanne! Norma Jeanne!"

"Go away," she murmured.

"Are you okay? Let me help you sit up." I slid an arm around her back to help her.

"Stop that! You'll ruin everything!" She swung her elbow back, landing it squarely on my nose.

I howled in pain.

The door creaked as it opened fully. "Norma Jeanne? What's going on?" I recognized Holmes's voice.

"Holmes!" she cried. "Thank heaven you're here!"

Holding my hands over my nose, I blinked, trying to see through watering eyes.

"She threw me in this place. I was unconscious!" said Norma Jeanne. She held out her arms to Holmes.

Huh?

Holmes reached past her and helped me up. "What happened?"

"She hit me with her elbow." I sounded congested.

"To get away from her!" Norma Jeanne cried.

Holmes placed an arm around my shoulders. "It's over, Norma Jeanne." We started to walk away, but she grabbed Holmes's jacket.

"You don't understand. I'm the victim here! Holmes, please! I made a mistake with Austin. It was the stress of Gramps's murder and of having to cook!"

Holmes's expression was so sweet and sad that I wanted to hug him.

"NJ, I have friends all over this town. You took me on a wild-goose chase, but I know you were alone. Looking for a likely place to hide, I guess. I'm—" he paused, and I could feel his fingers tense on my arm "—really surprised that you would pull something like this. I never expected it of you. I wonder now if I ever really knew you at all."

He gently propelled me forward.

Unfortunately, a bunch of his pals stood just outside hooting and high-fiving.

Norma Jeanne caught up to us. "Holmes, don't you see? You're reacting the way I knew you would, but toward the wrong girl. Austin doesn't mean anything to me. It's always been you, Holmes."

One of his friends said, "Are you kidding? You thought if you pretended to be hurt that Holmes would come to the rescue and all would be well again?"

Norma Jeanne shot him an angry look. "Not exactly. I thought we would be able to spend some time together. Just the two of us, without everyone else butting in. And Holmes would realize that we were meant to be together."

Holmes's buddies snickered. I bit my upper lip and was a little bit ashamed that Holmes's friends and I were so obvious. But at that moment, I was more concerned about my nose than about Norma Jeanne's humiliation.

Very gently, in a kind tone, Holmes said, "I'm sorry, Norma Jeanne. There's no going back. I never should have let the relationship go on as long as it did. You'll find someone who loves you the way you are."

He steered me to the lights of the other Christkindl chalet where goodies were being sold. "Do you think it's broken?"

It hurt like it was broken. I pressed on it gently. Nothing was out of place.

Holmes made a joke of peeling my hands away from my nose. His expression grew grim. "Maybe you should have it looked at."

"It's that bad?"

He made a face like he'd eaten something sour. "Maybe you should go see the new doctor."

"It feels fine." I ran my fingers along my aching nose. "If it's not better in the morning, I'll have him check it out."

Two of Holmes's friends escorted a man our way. "Look who we found!"

The man bent his head to look at me. "I'm Dr. Engelknecht. Oof. What happened?"

The lighting wasn't great, but there was no mistaking the man with the dimples whom I had seen around town.

I held out my hand. "Holly Miller. Welcome to Wagtail. My grandmother is the mayor. She told me you had arrived in town."

"The lovely Liesel?"

"The very same."

"So what happened to you?"

"I took an elbow to the nose."

"May I?" He raised his hands toward my face and gently palpated my nose. "You'll be fine. You might take a nonsteroidal anti-inflammatory tonight for pain if you can't sleep. And wear sunglasses for the next few days." He smiled at me. "Unless you're eager for some pity."

"Hi. Holmes Richardson." Holmes reached out to shake the doctor's hand. "Should she sleep sitting up?"

"Ah. Holmes. I've heard of you and your crazy girlfriend."

Holmes's buddies laughed. Holmes didn't find it as funny as the rest of us.

Dr. Engelknecht stared at me quizzically. "I hope I haven't stepped in it. You're not . . . ?"

One of Holmes's buddies snorted. "Nope. The crazy girlfriend was the owner of the elbow."

Dr. Engelknecht's eyebrows rose. "If I were you, Holly, I think I'd steer clear of her."

"I plan to."

"Maybe I should walk you back to the inn," said Holmes.

It could have been my imagination or wishful thinking, but I was slightly amused that the tables had turned and Holmes might have been feeling a bit of jealousy. Truth be told, though, I had had about enough for one night. My nose throbbed like crazy, and more than anything, I wanted to curl up by the fire and finally indulge in a slice of Fluffy Cake.

Even Trixie seemed worn-out as we strolled through the green on the way back to the inn.

"I'm sorry, Holly. I never imagined that Norma Jeanne would pretend to be injured just to get attention, much less that she would hit you."

"It's not your fault. I was stupid to assume she had been hurt. I'm not completely convinced that she elbowed me on purpose. At least I don't think she meant to slam me in the nose. She must have been very desperate to go to such lengths."

"It's *all* my fault. I never should have brought her here. None of this would have happened. No one would have died. It's been the worst Christmas ever."

"Holmes, if Dale and Vivienne were murdered by a member of their own family, or by Steve Oathaut, it probably would have happened no matter where they were. One of them must have had a pressing reason to get rid of Dale and Vivienne."

We walked up the stairs to the porch and entered the inn. A number of the Thackleberry clan were in the Dogwood Room. Without saying a word, Holmes and I walked through the lobby and to the private kitchen.

I put on the kettle for spiced tea with cinnamon and cloves, and held my breath when I opened the refrigerator. My beloved Fluffy Cake was inside. But would it be as good as I remembered?

I cut a slice for each of us. Ruby red cranberries glistened in between the layers. I couldn't resist picking up a bit of the icing that had fallen onto the cake plate. It was ridiculously sweet and yummy.

But when I passed the stainless steel toaster, I caught a warped glimpse of myself and sucked in a sharp breath. "You didn't tell me I had black eyes! Both of them!"

I pawed in a drawer for a mirror. I was a mess. My nose was swollen and red, and each of my eyes had a dark circle underneath. No wonder the doctor had told me to wear sunglasses.

I dashed up the hidden stairs to my apartment, donned sunglasses, and returned, feeling a little less hideous.

Holmes had poured the tea and brought the slices of cake to a tiny table between the big armchairs in front of the fire. He grinned at me. "Now you're as sophisticated as Blake," he teased.

I settled into the chair and took a bite of Fluffy Cake.

"Barry is in trouble."

It was a simple statement, but I knew what Holmes was getting at.

"I've worked for him a long time, and I know him very well. I just can't imagine him committing a murder. Even if he does need money."

I treaded carefully. "Have they told Norma Jeanne about the trouble with his business yet?"

When Holmes looked at me in surprise, I was glad to be wearing the sunglasses. He obviously picked up on my implication that Norma Jeanne would flip out when she learned her side of the family was broke, too.

"She won't take it well."

"She did gloat a little bit about her mother being the beneficiary of Dale's estate. At least before they knew he had invested everything in the business to keep it afloat."

"She's used to having money, there's no doubt about that." Holmes shook his head.

"For the purposes of discussion only, let's say Norma Jeanne had a motive. But did she have the opportunity? She would have had to follow Dale when he left the inn, I guess?"

"She has the strength to have stabbed him. And no one would have thought a thing of it if she had been in Doris's room to steal some sleeping pills to poison Vivienne. But why do that? If her mother was going to inherit Dale's estate, then why kill Vivi?"

I must not have hidden my smirk.

"Everyone hated Vivienne," he conceded. "But with Dale gone, I don't see the motive for anyone on Norma Jeanne's side of the family to murder her. I think it may have been Steve."

"Unless she knew something about one of them and was blackmailing them."

"On the other side of the family, Blake, Tim, Linda, and maybe even Tiffany thought Vivienne would inherit Dale's estate," Holmes said. "We know Blake wanted more money. And he might have knocked off Dale when his tuition funds were cut off."

"Do you believe that guy? Who makes it into med school and then blows away that kind of opportunity?" I asked. "I like Tiffany a lot, but I wonder if she really knew all that stuff about the firm and her Grampy. How do we know she's not making it up?"

"How would it have benefitted her to do that? Unless they get back to Chicago and it turns out that Vivienne inherited Dale's estate after all."

"I'd say that's unlikely. Even Aunt Birdie knew about Vivienne's prenuptial agreement."

"So can we narrow it down to Tim, Linda, Blake, and Tiffany?" Holmes asked.

"Blake is so obvious that it seems unlikely." I licked the last morsel of cake crumb and creamy frosting off my fork, noting that he hadn't mentioned Norma Jeanne.

"We're working on the assumption that it involved money. Maybe it was something else. A slight or a secret that someone needed to hide?"

"In other words, we've got nothing. Not even a decent lead, except for Steve Oathaut. We have to look at facts. What do we know for sure? Vivienne, Barry, and Blake need money. The person who murdered Dale took the contents of his wallet. That same person must have a heart of coal, because he or she had the nerve to wrap up the murder weapon and give it to Dale's mother as a gift."

Holmes shivered. "Killing him was brutal enough, but that was horrible."

"And we know pretty much for certain that the same person took the little wool felt Jack Russell from Dale and brought it back here."

Holmes sucked in a deep breath. "So we know for sure that his killer is staying here and that it's one of the Thackleberry clan."

"Blake, Vivienne, and Norma Jeanne wanted to leave immediately after Dale's murder," I pointed out.

"Showing their eagerness to get away and possible guilt? I guess we now know why Norma Jeanne was anxious to leave. Once Austin entered the picture, I was out." Holmes raised his eyebrows and shook his head. "I still think that that might have been a lucky break for me."

"So then, by process of elimination, does that point to Blake as Dale's killer?" I asked.

"It doesn't make sense that he would have killed Vivienne. He knew by then that she didn't have much money. Not the kind they were used to anyway."

"Unless he didn't believe her. But that could have been Steve."

For a few minutes, we sat quietly by the crackling fire, enjoying the cozy tranquility in spite of the cruel murders.

"I have a little something for you, but I haven't had a minute to give it to you yet," said Holmes.

"Me, too!" I had jumped out of my chair to fetch it when the door swung open a bit and Dave peeked in the kitchen.

"Just who I was looking for," he said. "Is the fire too bright for your eyes?"

"I got smacked in the nose. A Christmas gift from Norma Jeanne."

Dave lifted his eyebrows. "Are you okay?"

"Sure. Could I interest you in some tea and Fluffy Cake?" I asked.

"Absolutely. It's freezing outside." He shed his coat and hung it on the back of a chair. "I have some news."

Thirty-six

"I didn't think I would hear anything for a week or so. But it's quiet over at the police lab. It takes weeks to get a DNA confirmation, but one of the guys was smart enough to disengage the knife on the end of the hiking stick. Our murderer cleaned the blade very nicely, but I guess he didn't realize that blood got up inside of the stick."

"So it *is* the murder weapon!" I screeched.

"Don't go getting too excited. We don't have a DNA match yet, but the blood inside is Dale's blood type." Dave smiled at me. "Pretty good deduction, Holly."

I should have been thrilled, but I felt just a hair guilty for not telling him Aunt Birdie had the same kind of hiking stick. I told myself it didn't matter anymore unless the DNA didn't match.

"How about the blade? Did it match the holes in the Grinch?" asked Holmes.

"It did. Now if we could just lift a fingerprint off the stick." Dave accepted the plate with cake and dug in like he was starving. "Umm. Haven't eaten since I was here for brunch earlier today. What a bizarre Christmas."

"Holly?" Someone knocked on the door and pushed it open. "Thank goodness, I found you. I've lost Snowflake."

Tiffany might have been looking for me, but her eyes locked on Dave. "Oh, hi! I didn't know you were here."

Holmes and I gazed at each other and tried to stifle grins. Tiffany appeared to have an interest in Officer Dave.

"We'll help you look. I wouldn't be too worried," I said. "Cats like to curl up in oddball spots. I'll just run upstairs to my apartment and make sure that Twinkletoes didn't take the kitten there again."

"Tiffany! Tiffany!"

"That sounds like my mom." Tiffany called out, "We're all right here."

"There you are!" Linda walked in and looked around. "What a wonderful kitchen. I love the turquoise island. It gives the room so much character. Tiffie, honey, could I borrow your phone? I'd like to call my side of the family to wish them a Merry Christmas. They're probably finishing dinner right about now. But my phone quit working. And so did Daddy's and Blake's."

"There's only one carrier that works in Wagtail," Dave explained.

"I've heard that." Linda smiled at him. "Very odd. But all our phones worked a few days ago, so we must have the right carrier."

"Sure, Mom." Tiffany pulled her phone out of her pocket and handed it to her mom. "We're looking for Snowflake. Have you seen her?"

"Goodness, I hope she didn't get out. It's snowing like crazy, and with her white fur we'd never see her in the snow."

Tiffany's eyes grew large. "No! She better be inside somewhere."

"I'll check my apartment." I dashed up the back stairs with Trixie. "Look for kitties, Trixie. Where's Twinkletoes?"

Unfortunately, they weren't curled up in Twinkletoes's favorite chair like I had hoped. That would have been too easy. I was about to search my bedroom when Trixie barked. I hurried into my bedroom, expecting to find the kitten with Twinkletoes. They weren't on the bed or in the closet that I could see.

"What was that barking about?"

She wagged her tail, her eyes bright and excited.

"Silly doggy." I checked the guest room, but they weren't there, either.

Trixie ran to the door. There was a charming, cushy bench on the landing near my door. Maybe they had settled there. I swung the door open and realized immediately that the light bulb in the hallway had gone out. I still wore my sunglasses though and couldn't make out who punched me in the side of my face.

Thirty-seven

I could hear Trixie barking in the distance as I came to. Woozy, I tried to sit up. The world looked very dark until I remembered the sunglasses and ripped them off. I must have been unconscious for only a minute or so.

I struggled to my feet. "Trixie? Trixie?"

I didn't see her anywhere. The barking had ceased.

Stumbling, I made my way to the second-floor landing, just in time to see Twinkletoes fly down the hallway toward the reception lobby.

I followed her and watched as she jumped up on the railing. She looked down, intent on something. Probably the kitten.

I rushed to the railing to grab her, but she jumped a split second before I could wrap my arms around her.

"Noooooo!" I howled.

She flew through the air and landed on someone's back. Aside from the shock of having a cat jump on him, I assumed his screams might have stemmed from her claws sinking into him.

He twisted and turned, frantic. I got a good look at his face. It was Tim.

He dropped the pillowcase he carried and staggered around the reception lobby like a maniac, trying without success to dislodge Twinkletoes from his back.

The pillowcase wriggled, and I could hear something inside whining. "Trixie?"

I ran down the stairs yelling, "Dave! Holmes!"

Tim glanced at me and made a mad rush for the sliding glass door with Twinkletoes still riding his back.

I flew behind the counter and pressed the locking button so the doors wouldn't open. Twinkletoes sprang away and ran to the curiously active bag.

Tim smashed into the glass door like a locomotive full steam ahead. It shattered into tiny bits of safety glass and rained down on him as he fell into the snow.

I relaxed a little. Even if Tim ran, Officer Dave could follow his footprints in the snow. I hurried to the pillowcase and untied it. Trixie bounded out, apparently none the worse for her horrid experience.

In the bottom of the bag were three credit cards, all in the name of Dale Thackleberry. Each one had been chewed.

Holmes, Dave, and Tiffany rushed down the hallway and into the reception lobby. They stopped dead, probably trying to figure out what had happened.

Trixie stood in the middle of the room, barking like crazy at Tim. Twinkletoes sat on the counter, nonchalantly washing her paws.

Tiffany and Officer Dave walked over the glass shards to Tim and were helping him up when Linda arrived and screamed.

Tiny rivulets of blood ran down his face. "I thought it would open," he muttered.

Linda plucked bits of glass off her husband. Tears streamed down her face.

I could hear Dave calling it in over his radio.

Tiffany watched her parents in horror. "I knew you were drinking too much. I told Mom we should stage an intervention."

They clearly didn't realize what had happened. Or maybe they didn't want to. "He slugged me."

"Tim? He would never do that." Linda looked at the credit cards that Dave held up for her to see. "There must be some kind of explanation. It's a mistake. Just a big mistake."

Tiffany backed away. "No, Mom. We've all been in denial. I thought Dad's behavior was from his drinking, but I think he was drinking heavily because of something else."

"Is that true, Tim?" asked Linda.

"Tiffie caught me. She didn't know it was me, I don't think." He gazed at his daughter.

I heard gasps above and looked up. EmmyLou, Barry, and Norma Jeanne listened to him from the balcony.

Blake and Austin had drifted in and watched, followed by Oma, Rose, Doris, and Mr. Huckle.

"But when Tiffie went to Dale, he figured it out."

Tiffany appeared to be in shock. "You're the one who was stealing from Thackleberry? My own father?" She wobbled, but Dave caught her before she fell backward.

"Why, Tim? Why?" whispered his wife.

"It was never enough. We always needed more money. More, and more, and more. It was so easy to just reimburse myself a little more here and there, and then the checks got bigger, and I had to have them made out to fake suppliers. I thought no one was onto me, but when we arrived in Wagtail, Dale lowered the boom. I didn't want to kill him. But there was no way out. I had no choice. We would have lost everything. No one would ever have hired me. He left me no choice."

Linda had turned as green as the Grinch. I thought she might be sick.

"You should have told us, Daddy." Tears rolled down Tiffany's face. "Grampy would have tried to help. I know he would have."

"He said—" Tim smirked "—that it was time we all learned to live within our means. I hated him for that. He never had to. He had everything handed to him on a platter. He didn't know what he was talking about."

"Please tell me you didn't kill Vivienne, too?" begged Linda.

The peculiar thing was that Tim hadn't looked one bit remorseful when he was talking about Dale. But at the mention of Vivienne's name, he turned into a blubbering fool.

"It was a mistake. A horrible mistake." He gazed around the room. "I meant to kill you!"

He pointed at Doris. He was at least fifteen feet away from her, but she recoiled anyway.

"Once I knew the business was heading down the tubes, I figured we had to sell it. It was my only chance of hiding what I had done. But with Dale's death, Doris held the power, and I knew she would never agree."

"I don't get it." Linda's brow furrowed. "Then how did Vivienne die?"

"I put mashed sleeping pills in bourbon punch and brought it to Doris. Mom must have drunk it."

Doris raised her head high. "Evil begat evil. It went full circle when you murdered your own mother." She turned abruptly and headed away, her cane tapping as she walked along the hallway.

She was right about that. He had wrapped the weapon with which he had killed her son and given it to her as a gift. Only a person with a truly dark heart could have done that.

"Why did you slug me, and why did you put Trixie in a pillowcase?"

Tim didn't seem ashamed. "I was going to dispose of her."

I gasped and clasped Trixie to me too tightly. She didn't complain.

"She and your cat are a clever team. They kept sneaking into our room. They stole that little dog ornament and chewed up Dale's credit cards. I saw the dog running off with Dale's cash in her mouth. Every time I opened my door, either your cat or your dog was there being a pest. I was going to get rid of her once and for all. I think she must have hidden the cash in your apartment. I can't find it anywhere. If your dog hadn't found Dale and my mom, I would have been out of here by now. Of course, I was counting on the private jet being at my disposal."

Tim sounded delusional to me. Even though it was cold, Dale's and Vivienne's corpses would have been found rather quickly. Had he grown overconfident about his ability to commit crime?

"You were planning to break into Holly's apartment?" cried Linda.

"I needed cash. I was going to pick the lock, but she opened the door and the stupid dog wouldn't stop barking."

Stupid dog, indeed. I planted a big smooch on Trixie's forehead.

Under the lights outside the glass doors, two police officers walked up and surveyed the damage.

Over the next hour, Mr. Huckle, Holmes, and I cleaned the floor of the reception lobby, while Dave prepared to transport Tim to the jail in Snowball via police snowmobile.

We had just finished when Tiffany ran into the lobby. "I forgot all about Snowflake!"

I was so weary I could barely keep my eyes open. "I'll take the first floor. Mr. Huckle, would you look in the basement? And Holmes, how about you search the second floor?"

Tiffany accompanied me on the first floor. Mr. Huckle and Holmes joined us when they were through. There was simply no sign of the little kitten. "We can call Zelda and see if she can communicate with Snowflake," I suggested. "The inn offers so many places for a cat to nestle."

"I don't believe in animal communicators, but I'm willing to give it a try."

I headed for the lobby phone, and when I picked it up, I spied something moving in the Christmas village. I hung up, placed a finger over my lips in a signal to be quiet, and sneaked up on the village that Linda had set up.

Nestled in a semicircle of houses, Twinkletoes was curled in the shape of a *C*, with tiny Snowflake hidden in the white fur of Twinkletoes's tummy. They were fast asleep.

"That's so adorable!" Tiffany immediately photographed it and posted the picture on Instagram.

I dragged myself into the private kitchen, planning to take the secret stairs up to my quarters, but encountered Oma, Rose, and Mr. Huckle, who made a huge fuss over my black eyes and the growing bruise on my cheek. I had taken a good battering, and bed was beginning to be very appealing. I begged off and promised to tell all the next day.

I had never looked worse than I did in the morning. Makeup was useless. I showered and pulled on a ribbed white turtleneck, a navy blue plaid skirt, and brown boots. I let my hair hang loose, in the hope it would help cover my face, and donned the biggest sunglasses I owned.

Shelley was back to waiting tables, and Zelda should have been at the registration desk, but I found her having breakfast with Oma, Rose, and Dave.

Fortunately, Dave was filling them in on the details of what had happened.

Shelley didn't bother taking our order. She rushed over to the table with Trixie's favorite—steak and home fries. "I hear Twinkletoes is a heroine. I hope it's okay that I fed her people tuna this morning."

"She deserves it. If she hadn't jumped Tim, he would have left the inn and none of us would have known what he was up to. Heaven only knows what he might have done to poor Trixie."

Shelley handed me a cupcake with a tiny dog bone on top. "Holiday Hound Cake for Trixie when she finishes her breakfast. And this is for you. Cook knows how you love French toast with fresh berries."

"Thanks, Shelley."

"It's crazy," said Dave, "but even though Tim admitted to murdering Dave, and accidentally killing his own mom, he absolutely will not admit that he stabbed the Grinch to hide Dave's body."

Suddenly, I felt a chill run through me. "Um, is there a way to match a particular blade to the tear in the plastic?"

"We already did. The size of the blade is a match to the holes that were made."

"I meant do the blades leave characteristics, so you'd know which blade made the hole out of, say, five that were exactly alike?" I asked, trying to pretend that my heart wasn't beating like mad.

"Not that I know of. I just think it's curious that he copped to the big crimes but insists he didn't make those holes."

I breathed easier. I was pretty sure I knew who actually tried to kill the Grinch. But I didn't see the point in getting Aunt Birdie into trouble again. After Dale left her house she must have sneaked through the yards in the dark of night to kill the Grinch, not knowing that Dale was dead inside of it. I smiled sweetly at Dave, thinking this was one sleeping dog I should let lie.

While I was eating, Rupert showed up.

"I got me a passel of kids!" Rupert grinned with delight.

"I want to thank you, Officer Dave." Rupert extended his hand. "Aw. Gimme a hug!" The two of them embraced.

"It wouldn't have happened without you giving me a good recommendation. I wasn't sure after the fuss about the Grinch," said Rupert.

"You got custody of your children?" I guessed.

"You betcha! Four of my own and two more make an even half a dozen."

"Two more?"

"I'm adopting Ethan and Ava Schroeder. Their momma was a distant cousin of mine."

"Six children!" He had decorated his bungalow so beautifully for Christmas, but it wasn't very big. Where would they all sleep? "Is your house large enough?"

"I'm buyin' a mansion with eleven bedrooms. It's on the east side of town, but's that's okay. Been empty for nearly two years, so I got it for a steal. There's room for all of us and my mama, too."

"Birdie will be sorry to see you move. She loves your kids."

"That woman has a heart of gold. I best get back. She's sitting with them right now. Merry Christmas, y'all!"

Rupert ambled out, happier than anyone had a right to be.

I leaned in and whispered, "How can he afford a mansion?"

Dave laughed at me. "You really don't know? Have you heard of RG Backhoe and Excavation?"

I gave him an annoyed look. "No."

"It's the biggest company of its kind around here. He excavates and does crane work, too. Has a small fortune invested in huge machines, and he has three crews that work for him."

"I had no idea."

He nodded. "Rupert dropped out of school in the eighth grade when his dad died. He went to work to help support his brothers and sisters. He started with nothing and worked like a dog. Now he's the boss."

"Sort of like Doris. Speaking of which, how are the Thackleberrys this morning?"

"Linda is busy lining up lawyers for Tim," said Oma. "I think the rest of them are booked on flights home later today."

While I ate, they drifted away and went back to work. I needed to do that too, but I couldn't help thinking what a close call it had been for Trixie. I had a lot to be thankful for.

When we finished eating, I headed for the office, but stopped when I spied Blake, Tiffany, and Norma Jeanne in the Dogwood Room. They had coffee mugs and breakfast breads and sat together around a coffee table.

Tiffany called me over. At her feet Snowflake played kitty games with Twinkletoes.

"Holly, we're probably leaving around lunchtime. I want to thank you and to apologize. None of us ever imagined that anything like this would happen. I'm so sorry that Dad punched you."

"I think he needs help. He obviously lost his way. But I'm happy to see the three of you have reconciled."

"It wasn't until we realized that we were losing Thackleberry that we understood how special it is to have a family company," said Norma Jeanne.

"I thought you hated your job."

"I do! But it's a big company. If we can save it, I'll find another division that I'll like better, I'm sure."

"Are you going back to med school, Blake?" I asked.

"I don't think that would be possible. I sort of messed that up for myself. For a year or two, I'm going to concentrate on Thackleberry. After all, I'm pretty good at promotion. If I still want to go to med school after that, I'll consider it."

"I'm glad Thackleberry will survive. We love your products!"

EmmyLou was walking by with Maggie and overheard

me. She stopped and gazed at the three of them. "Who would have ever thought a nightmare like this would be the thing that brought us back together? I'm so proud of you three."

She strolled down the hallway toward the elevator with me.

"EmmyLou, if you don't mind my asking, there's one thing I was wondering about. The night Dale died, you came back to the inn very late, looking around like you were afraid someone might see you."

She laughed aloud. "And someone did. You!" She lowered her voice to almost a whisper. "You are one of the few people who would understand this. I was sneaking out to be with Maggie." We both looked down at Maggie, who barked. "I was so afraid these were her final days, and I couldn't bear the thought of her dying alone at the animal hospital. I know there were all kinds of people there looking out for her, but I had to be close to her. They kicked me out! Can you believe that? I didn't want anyone else to know. Not everyone in the family would have understood why I did that."

"I understand completely."

"I wanted to tell you that Aunt Birdie invited me to tea at her home this morning. Just the two of us." EmmyLou's eyes welled up with tears. "We cried and cried together. Dad always spoke fondly of her. I couldn't leave without meeting her and thanking her for being so kind to Dad."

"I'm glad you could meet her. Did she have any knives?" I asked.

EmmyLou laughed uproariously. "Not a one! She's still angry about that. She had to borrow a neighbor's knife to cut the cucumbers for the sandwiches."

She stepped into the elevator, and I went to work.

It was evening before I saw Holmes. He loped into the inn like his old self.

"Shh. Get a warm jacket."

What was he up to now? He followed me upstairs to my

apartment. I donned a warm coat and grabbed the Christmas present that I hadn't had a chance to give to him.

We left through the hidden staircase that led to the private kitchen and exited through the back door. We walked through the snow to the reception entrance, which was still blocked off.

A green horse-drawn sleigh awaited us. Trixie sat on the seat in her red sweater next to Twinkletoes, who wore a red scarf around her neck.

We climbed on and tucked a blanket over our legs. It turned out that Holmes, who never ceased to amaze me, knew how to drive the sleigh!

We pulled out, just in time to hear Sugar McLaughlin calling, "Holmes! Holmes! Wait for me."

"I haven't been able to get away from Sugar all day long."

"The price of being popular."

He drove to a lighted tree in the middle of nowhere, where I had stopped when Trixie was in the hospital. We were high enough to see the lights of Wagtail glittering in the night.

Holmes pulled out a thermos of spiked hot chocolate, which hit the spot.

I handed him his Christmas gift. He tore the wrapping open and lifted the top of the box. "It's the leather jacket!" He laughed aloud. "I was so disappointed when it didn't turn up under my parents' tree. I was thinking about buying it for myself. This is great! Thanks, Holly."

He pulled a box out from under the seat and gave it to me.

I opened it gingerly and withdrew a figurine of hand-carved wood about eight inches tall. He had captured Trixie and Twinkletoes perfectly. Trixie wore her red sweater and sat on the seat of a sleigh, her head bent to Twinkletoes, who wore a red scarf and lifted her front paws to lean into Trixie. "You carved this yourself!"

"Do you like it?" he asked.

"I love it. It's the most wonderful gift I've ever received."

Holmes wrapped his arms around me and kissed me just the way I had dreamed.

In spite of everything that had happened, it was a pretty good Christmas after all.

Recipes

One of my dogs suffered from severe food allergies that did not allow him to eat commercial dog food. Consequently, I learned to cook for my dogs and have done so for many years. Consult your veterinarian if you want to switch your dog over to home-cooked food. It's not as difficult as one might think. Keep in mind that, like children, dogs need a balanced diet, not just a hamburger. Any changes to your dog's diet should be made gradually so your dog's stomach can adjust.

Chocolate, alcohol, caffeine, fatty foods, grapes, raisins, macadamia nuts, avocados, onions and garlic, salt, xylitol, and unbaked dough can be toxic to dogs. For more information about foods your dog should not eat, consult the Pet Poison Helpline at petpoisonhelpline.com/pet-owners/.

Krista's Modern Christmas Stollen

For people only

Christmas Stollen is a German bread traditionally baked for the holiday. Krista has updated this bread with dried fruit in place of the typical candied fruit. She bakes it for the holidays every year.

1½ cups dried apricots
1¼ cups dried cherries
½ cup rum
¼ cup lukewarm water
2 packs of fast-rising instant yeast
¾ cup sugar + pinch of sugar
5½ cups all-purpose flour
1 cup milk
½ teaspoon salt
2 eggs (room temperature)
1 cup unsalted butter, softened and cut
    into ¼-inch pieces
6–8 tablespoons melted unsalted butter
confectioners' sugar

Chop the apricots and cherries with a knife (do not use a food processor) and place in a bowl. Pour the rum over them and let sit for 1 hour.

Pour the lukewarm water in a 2-cup or larger bowl. Sprinkle with the yeast and a pinch of sugar. Stir to help dissolve. Set aside (Krista puts it in a cold oven) for 10–15 minutes. It should have doubled in size.

Pour the rum from the fruit into a bowl and set aside. Lay paper towels out, and spread with the fruit. Dab with additional paper towels to dry. Pour the fruit into a dry bowl and sprinkle with 2 tablespoons of flour. Turn several times to coat. Set aside.

Combine milk, ½ cup sugar, and salt in a heavy-bottomed pot and heat until the sugar dissolves and a thermometer registers 110°F. Remove from heat. Stir in the rum and the yeast mixture.

Fit dough hook into mixer. (This may be made by hand, but a heavy-duty mixer like a KitchenAid is a big help.) Measure 4 cups of flour into a mixing bowl. With the mixer on low speed, slowly add the milk mixture. Whisk the 2 eggs well, then add to the dough, and continue mixing. Slowly add as much of the remaining 1½ cups flour as needed. Mix in the softened 1 cup butter. The dough should begin to shape into a ball.

Dust your hands and kneading area with flour. Remove the dough from the bowl and knead 10–15 minutes until the dough is smooth and pliable. Incorporate the fruit by pressing it into the dough a bit at a time. Flour your hands as necessary and continue to add the fruit and turn the dough.

Grease a deep bowl with butter, place the dough in the bowl, flip it once to coat with butter, cover with a kitchen towel, and place in a warm area away from any drafts for 2 hours or until doubled in size. (A cool oven will work.)

Punch the dough down and divide into 2 pieces. Allow to rest for 10 minutes. Working with one at a time, roll each ball of dough out into a rectangle roughly 12 inches long and 8 inches wide. Brush each with 1 tablespoon of melted butter and sprinkle with 1 tablespoon of sugar.

Fold one side (of the 8-inch width) over about ⅔ of the way. Fold the other side over so that it overlaps the top of the first side by about 1 inch. Press the top seam gently. Shape it into an oval with floured hands as necessary, patting it so that it is approximately 4 inches across.

Prepare a very large cookie sheet or lipped baking pan by covering with parchment paper. Transfer the dough to the parchment paper, leaving at least 3–4 inches between the two loaves. Brush each with 1 tablespoon of melted butter. Place in a warm location away from drafts and allow to rise for 1 hour or until doubled in size.

Preheat oven to 375°F. Slide the baking sheet into the oven and bake 25–30 minutes or until they are golden brown and crusty.

When cool and before serving, dust generously with confectioners' sugar.

Cranberry Breakfast Rolls

Dough

   1 cup milk
   ⅔ cup sugar
   1½ tablespoons active dry yeast
   1 stick unsalted butter, softened (plus extra for
      greasing)
   2 large eggs
   1 teaspoon vanilla
   ½ teaspoon salt
   1 teaspoon cardamom
   4¼ cups all-purpose flour (plus more for dusting)

Filling

   1 10-ounce package frozen cranberries, not
      thawed

¼ cup plus 2 tablespoons sugar
1 teaspoon cornstarch

Glaze

¾ cup confectioners' sugar
3 tablespoons unsalted butter, melted
1½ tablespoons heavy cream

Heat one cup of milk to 95°F. Pour into a mixing bowl.
Stir in the sugar and yeast. Let stand 5–10 minutes until foamy. If it's very cold in your kitchen, let stand in
an unheated oven or other warm spot.

Add the butter, eggs, vanilla, and salt. Stir together.
Mix the cardamom with the flour and add to the
dough, mixing on low for 3 minutes. Turn the speed
up to medium-high and mix for 10 minutes. Turn the
dough (scrape the sides, too) out onto a flour-dusted
board. Knead two to three times and shape into a ball.
Grease a bowl with butter, add the dough, cover with
plastic wrap, and let rise for 1 hour or until it has
doubled in size.

Line a 9-by-13-inch baking dish with parchment
paper and allow the ends of the paper to stick out.
Butter the parchment paper. Mix the cranberries with
the sugar and cornstarch. Cut the dough in half and
make two 10-by-12-inch rectangles. Scatter the cranberries over the dough and roll into a tight log. Cut the
log in half and slice the halves into 4 pieces. Place them
in the baking dish. There's not a specific way to line
them up, and there will be extra room because they
need to rise again.

Cover with a clean, dry kitchen towel and let rise for
2 hours. At this point, you can cover with aluminum
foil, refrigerate, and bake the next day.

Preheat oven to 425°F. Bake about 25 minutes. The tops should be golden. Cool on a rack for 30 minutes.

Meanwhile, mix the glaze in a small bowl. You don't need a mixer for this. Just whisk the ingredients together. Lift the rolls out of the pan using the ends of the parchment paper as handles.

Using a spoon, dot the tops with the glaze, then spread it over the rolls.

Cranberry Scones

For people only

2 cups flour
⅓ cup sugar
1 tablespoon baking powder
½ teaspoon salt
¾ teaspoon cinnamon
¼ teaspoon nutmeg
pinch of cloves
5 tablespoons cold butter
1 cup heavy cream
1 cup fresh or frozen cranberries

Preheat oven to 400°F. Place a sheet of parchment paper on a baking sheet. Place flour, sugar, baking powder, salt, cinnamon, nutmeg, and cloves in a food processor. Pulse 12 times to combine. Cut the butter into small pieces and scatter over the flour. Pulse 12 times to combine. Place the flour mixture into a bowl. Pour the cream and the cranberries over the top of it. Fold to combine about 15 times. Pour out and knead about 12 times until it forms a loose ball. Place in a 9-inch cake pan and gently spread and press into place. Flip onto the parchment paper. Cut in half with a long knife by pressing down. (Do not use a sawing motion.) Separate the halves slightly. Cut each half into 4 pieces, again pressing the knife into the dough to cut it. Separate the pieces slightly. Bake 15–18 minutes, or until lightly golden on the top. Serve with sweetened cream, jam, or clotted cream, or use one or both of the sugar drizzles below over the top of the scones.

Sugar Drizzle (optional)

1 cup powdered sugar
2 tablespoons milk or cream

Whisk to combine, adding milk gradually until it's smooth and just past spreading consistency. Spread over the tops of the cooled scones.

Spiced Sugar Drizzle (optional)

1 cup powdered sugar
¼ teaspoon cinnamon
⅛ teaspoon nutmeg
pinch of cloves
¼ teaspoon vanilla
3–4 teaspoons milk or cream

Whisk the dry ingredients to combine. Slowly add the vanilla and part of the milk, and mix, adding milk until it reaches drizzle consistency. Use mini-whisk, fork, or squeeze bottle to drizzle over the scones.

Fluffy Cake

For people only

Like its name, Fluffy Cake is light and fluffy in texture. If part of a layer should break when transferring it during assembly, just piece it together. It's very forgiving. No one will know.

1½ cups milk (Krista uses 2%)
1 tablespoon vinegar
3¾ cups flour
1 tablespoon baking powder
¾ teaspoon baking soda
¾ teaspoon salt
1½ sticks butter (12 tablespoons, room temperature)
2 cups sugar
1 cup vegetable oil (canola or sunflower/coconut)
6 eggs (room temperature)
2 teaspoons vanilla

Preheat oven to 350°F. Grease and flour three 9-inch cake pans. Use parchment paper cut to fit the bottoms. Mix the milk with the vinegar and set aside. Mix together the flour, baking powder, baking soda, and salt in a bowl and set aside. Cream the butter with the sugar and the vegetable oil. Add the eggs and beat at least 2 minutes. On a slow speed, alternate adding the flour mixture and the milk mixture. Add the vanilla and beat at least 3–4 minutes. Pour into the pans and bake 25–30 minutes or until a cake tester comes out clean. Cool on racks.

Cranberry Filling

> 12 ounces frozen or fresh cranberries
> ¾ cup sugar
> ¾ cup water
> ¼ cup cornstarch
> ¼ cup water

Mix the cranberries, sugar, and ¾ cup water in a heavy-bottomed pot. Bring to a boil, lower heat, and cook about 5 minutes. Whisk the cornstarch into the ¼ cup water until completely dissolved. Add to the cooking cranberries and stir well. Cook another 1–2 minutes. It should be thick. Cool. You can speed up cooling by placing it in the refrigerator or freezer very briefly.

Cream Cheese and Marshmallow Buttercream

> 1 stick of butter (8 tablespoons, room
>   temperature)
> 6 tablespoons cream cheese (room temperature)
> 1 cup marshmallow fluff
> 1 teaspoon vanilla
> 2 cups powdered sugar

Place the butter, cream cheese, and marshmallow fluff in the mix and beat well. Add the vanilla and beat. Add 1 cup of powdered sugar at a time, and mix on low, raising the speed as it is incorporated. Beat on high for 5 minutes.

Assembly

> Seedless raspberry preserves or jam

Using a long serrated knife, slice each layer into two layers. Place the bottom layer on a cake plate and dab jam on it by the teaspoonful. Lightly smooth together. Place the next layer of cake on top. Pipe a plain border of buttercream around the edge to contain the cranberry filling. Spoon the cranberry filling in the middle and spread to the buttercream line. Repeat with the next layers. Frost the sides and top in festive swirls. Leave plain or decorate as you like.

Gingerbread Pancakes

For people. Your dog may have a bite.

2 cups milk
2 tablespoons vinegar
2 cups flour
2 teaspoons sugar
1 teaspoon baking powder
1 teaspoon baking soda
½ teaspoon salt
1 teaspoon cinnamon
1 teaspoon ginger
¼ teaspoon nutmeg
pinch of cloves
2 eggs
4 tablespoons molasses
½ cup melted butter
vegetable oil

Mix the vinegar with the milk and let stand. In a large bowl, mix together the flour, sugar, baking powder, baking soda, salt, cinnamon, ginger, nutmeg, and cloves.

Set aside. Whisk the eggs in a large bowl. Add the milk mixture, the molasses, and the melted butter. Whisk. Pour into the flour mixture and stir until just combined. It's okay if there are some lumps. It will appear somewhat thin. Pour enough vegetable oil into a pan to coat it and heat at medium-high. Ladle in pancake batter. When the edges are firm and bubbles break through the center, flip the pancakes and cook the other side. Cook about 2–3 minutes on each side. Serve with powdered sugar, a pat of butter, and your favorite syrup.

Bourbon Cranberry Punch

For people only

water
2 cups cranberries
1 freezer-safe Bundt pan
3 cups cranberry juice
3 cups orange juice
⅓ cup fresh lemon juice
2 cups bourbon
1½ cups pink champagne (or ginger ale for a
    sweeter, less potent version)

Pour ½ inch to 1 inch of water in the bottom of the Bundt pan. Freeze. When frozen, add the cranberries and enough water to cover them. Freeze again until ready to use.

Pour cranberry juice, orange juice, lemon juice, and bourbon into a punch bowl. Mix well. Add pink champagne. Run warm water over bottom of Bundt pan briefly to unmold and place ring in punch.

Peppermint Bark Martini

For people only

1 candy cane
1 ounce peppermint schnapps
1 ounce vanilla vodka
2 ounces chocolate liqueur
½ ounce cream

Crush the candy cane into very small bits. Wet the rim of the martini glass and dip in the peppermint. Pour the schnapps, vodka, liqueur, and cream into the glass and stir well.

Happy Howliday Feast

For dogs, though people may enjoy it, too. The turkey, sweet potatoes, rice, and peas may be served to people in the traditional fashion, not mixed.

Makes about 4 Gingersnap-sized portions
plus 2 Trixie-sized portions.

Refrigerate leftovers and reheat the next day.

> *2 small sweet potatoes, no larger than 2 inches*
>   *in diameter*
> *2 turkey breast tenderloins (use white meat*
>   *only, do not substitute legs or thighs)*
> *vegetable oil (like canola or sunflower)*
> *½ cup water*
> *10–20 cranberries (fresh or frozen)*
> *2 cups uncooked white rice*
> *1 bag frozen peas*

Preheat oven to 400°F. Wash sweet potatoes and place in a roasting pan with the peels on. Roast for 30–45 minutes depending on thickness. Lightly brush the turkey tenderloins with vegetable oil. Add to bottom of same pan. Pour in ½ cup of water and scatter the cranberries on the bottom of the pan. Roast for 30–40 minutes, until the turkey is 170°F. The amount of roasting time will vary depending on the size of the tenderloins.

Meanwhile cook rice according to directions on bag. When done, add the frozen peas on top of the rice, cover, and allow to steam for at least 10 minutes, then stir the peas into the hot rice.

When the tenderloins are done, remove them from the oven and let stand for 10 minutes. Peel the sweet potatoes and cut into bite-sized pieces. They may be very mushy, which is fine. Slice the tenderloins lengthwise, and cut each of the 4 pieces into bite-sized cubes. If you have a very picky eater, cut the pieces as small as possible. Pour the juices and cranberries from the pan over the rice. Toss the rice with the tenderloin bits and sweet potato bits.

Holiday Hound Cakes

For dogs

¾ cup flour
½ teaspoon baking powder
½ teaspoon baking soda
½ teaspoon salt
½ teaspoon cinnamon
¼ teaspoon nutmeg
pinch of cloves
½ stick (4 tablespoons) butter (room
    temperature)
½ cup honey
1 large egg (room temperature)
½ cup applesauce

Frosting

plain Greek yogurt
tiny dog bone–shaped cookies

Preheat oven to 350°F and place cupcake papers in pan.
Use a fork to mix together the flour, baking powder, baking soda, salt, cinnamon, nutmeg, and cloves in a bowl.
Set aside. Cream the butter with the honey. Add the egg
and beat. Add the applesauce and beat. Beat in the flour
mixture until smooth. Fill cupcake papers a little over
halfway full. Bake 15 minutes or until a cake tester
comes out clean. When cool, add a teaspoon of Greek
yogurt on top and garnish with a tiny dog bone–shaped
cookie.

Spaghetti and Meatballs

For dogs. People will find they need salt.

Note: If your dog snarfs food and does not chew, you should cut the meatballs in half or quarters depending on the size of your dog.

½ pound very low-fat ground beef (preferably
   8% or less fat)
½ slice bread toasted dry and crumbled
2 teaspoons milk
2 teaspoons Parmesan cheese
⅛ teaspoon turmeric (optional)

Preheat oven to 350°F. Place all ingredients in a bowl and mix together. Make small meatballs about the size of a quarter in diameter. Bake 25–30 minutes.

This makes a nice appetizer for dogs, a treat at a party, or may be served as a meal over cut-up spaghetti and steamed green beans.

Ready to find
your next great read?

Let us help.

Visit prh.com/nextread

Penguin
Random
House